"What's so bad about me?"

"Beau, you've been married three times. You're a slick-talking, woman-loving son of a gun with a voice that'd melt stone. I've seen your kind before. Shoot, I've married your kind before. You're safe with me."

"The husband whose, um, grave you wanted to dance on? I remind you of him?"

"You could have given Eric lessons. At least you were smart enough to divorce one wife before you married another. Or am I assuming too much?"

Beau didn't know whether to be fascinated or insulted by Nancy's disclosure. "Your husband was a bigamist? Really?"

"Yes, really."

No wonder she didn't want another man in her life. It was a damn good thing he had no intention of acting on his attraction to her, because he wouldn't stand a snowball's chance in hell with a woman like her.

Extending his hand, he said, "We should be safe as buddies, then. Deal?"

They shook. "Deal."

He couldn't help but chuckle at the absurdity of their situation. This would be a first for him since puberty. A woman as a friend. Who'd have thought?

Dear Reader,

While writing *The Secret Wife* (Harlequin Superromance, May 2005) I was intrigued when my critique partners voiced very different reactions to Maggie and Nancy McGuire—two women who, through no fault of their own, were married to the same man. At the same time.

So I mulled over the idea and came to the conclusion that, like authors, readers have a voice they bring to each book— a voice shaped by their perceptions and life experiences. In other words, every time the book is read, there's a unique interaction between author and reader that might never be duplicated. How very cool!

My perception of both Maggie and Nancy was positive from day one, despite their difficult, frequently opposing circumstances. In *The Secret Wife,* I thoroughly enjoyed facilitating as Maggie overcame a disastrous relationship and achieved her happily-ever-after. Oh, and helped solve a murder, too.

But what about Nancy? *Home for Christmas* is her story. In it, she adopts a daughter from Russia, moves to upstate New York and works through the fallout from her past. Of course, I couldn't make it too easy for her. I added Beau Stanton to the mix—a thrice-married, smooth-talking salesman who appears to be the worst man on earth for Nancy. But Christmas is a time for miracles and appearances can be deceiving....

I hope reading *Home for Christmas* is a joyous experience, a precious collaboration between author and reader.

Happy holidays!

Carrie Weaver
www.SuperAuthors.com

P.S. I love to hear from readers. I can be reached by e-mail at CarrieAuthor@aol.com or by snail mail at P.O. Box 6045, Chandler, AZ, 85246-6045.

HOME FOR CHRISTMAS
Carrie Weaver

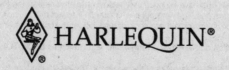

TORONTO • NEW YORK • LONDON
AMSTERDAM • PARIS • SYDNEY • HAMBURG
STOCKHOLM • ATHENS • TOKYO • MILAN • MADRID
PRAGUE • WARSAW • BUDAPEST • AUCKLAND

ISBN 0-373-71311-8

HOME FOR CHRISTMAS

www.eHarlequin.com

Printed in U.S.A.

Books by Carrie Weaver

HARLEQUIN SUPERROMANCE

1173–THE ROAD TO ECHO POINT
1222–THE SECOND SISTER
1274–THE SECRET WIFE

Dedicated to the Smith family:
Debbie, Paul, Melissa, Kristi, Liz and Sergei.

PROLOGUE

NANCY MCGUIRE ALLOWED the strange sound of Russian to flow over her as the house mother and the translator conversed.

Glancing around, she noted the house mother's office was neat and tidy, but sparse. The translator had indicated the budget was stretched to the breaking point.

Her gaze strayed to a collage on the wall. Hundreds of photos of children, some candid, some posed, most smiling broadly, attested to the orphanage's success in finding adoptive homes in the U.S.

Nancy shifted, crossing her legs. Her foot bounced as if she were some sort of marionette. How ironic that her husband's death should have jump-started her decision to adopt a child. Even more ironic that the sale of their house had financed her endeavor.

In some small way, it took away the sting of Eric's betrayal. And allowed her to heal.

Leaning forward, she doubted her excitement could be contained another second. She'd been waiting for this moment her whole adult life and now that it was here, she could scarcely breathe.

A knock sounded at the door and the house mother rose. Opening the door, she stepped aside as an assistant carried in a toddler.

The assistant placed the child on Nancy's lap and said something in Russian.

Nancy's eyes blurred as she cradled the little girl as naturally as if she'd held her every day for the past fourteen months. Her breasts tingled as if responding to memories of breastfeeding this child. Nancy stared into the baby's solemn brown eyes and time seemed to stand still. There was an instant connection, a peace she'd never known before. It was the overwhelming certainty of being in exactly the right place at exactly the right time. She'd waited all these years for this moment, this girl. Her daughter.

Brushing a silky brown lock of hair from the toddler's forehead, she stumbled over the Russian greeting, "*Zdravstvujte,* Tatiana."

Tatiana smiled shyly, then patted Nancy's face. "Mama?" The word was heavily accented and probably coached, but it still brought a lump to Nancy's throat. She'd nearly lost hope of ever hearing a child call her that.

"Yes, Mama's here, baby. Everything's going to be all right."

CHAPTER ONE

TATIANA WAS mid-temper-tantrum when the new guy entered the Parents Flying Solo meeting. Nancy McGuire didn't pay much attention. Kneeling by her daughter, she was too busy trying to catch a flailing fist before it connected with her nose.

"Shh, Ana," she whispered. The plea sounded ragged and desperate, even to her.

Two large, tanned hands grasped Ana beneath her arms and lifted her in the air. "Hey, there, little sweet pea, what's the problem?"

Ana stilled, probably from the shock of a tall stranger holding her above his head.

Nancy paused, too. The man's slow drawl brought a longing for home so intense she almost doubled over. And an idiotic longing for a man she couldn't have. Ever.

Rising, she said, "Please put down my daughter. Now."

The stranger set Ana on her feet. Tantrum apparently forgotten, Ana zipped off in search of playmates.

Frowning, Nancy wondered if Emily's son, Jason,

would keep as close an eye on the two-year-old as he'd promised.

"Little spitfire, isn't she?"

"Ana has a mind of her own. I try to encourage her to be her own person." So she wouldn't grow up trying to please a man and lose herself in the process.

Tipping his head, he said, "Then you've succeeded."

Nancy wasn't sure whether his comment was tongue-in-cheek, so she decided to simply take it at face value. "Good. Because children, girls especially, should be encouraged to seek, explore, achieve."

"I agree with you." He looped his arm over the shoulder of the thin teenage girl beside him. "I'm Beau and this is my daughter, Rachel."

The girl stiffened, crossing her arms over her chest, glaring at him until he released her.

Nancy murmured an acknowledgment as she scanned the room for Ana. She exhaled in relief when she saw Jason helping Ana select a cookie from the refreshment table.

"I agree with you, but I want Rachel to be independent *and* use good manners."

Nancy bristled. He was probably another one of those parents who thought she should be able to control her own child. That Nancy wasn't doing her job properly if Ana didn't mind her one hundred percent of the time.

Okay, maybe Nancy secretly wondered if she *was* doing her job properly. She'd be the first to admit to a certain feeling of ineptitude when Ana pitched a public fit. But she was not about to confide in some know-it-all redneck.

Her voice was icy when she said, "She is a normal twenty-one-month-old child, testing limits. I'd appreciate it if you would keep your opinions to yourself."

"Whoa, lady, I didn't mean to offend you. I was just being friendly, tryin' to make it to the refreshments without getting nailed in the family jewels. I remember when my daughter was about that height." He shuddered, his eyes twinkling as he nudged Rachel.

"Daaad," she whined, and slouched away, slipping into a crowd of kids.

The man's smile was probably intended to charm, but it merely put Nancy on her guard. Surveying his lanky frame from the tips of his Roper boots to his mussed dark brown hair, she doubted his sincerity. "I think you might want to watch your knees instead. I, for one, am not interested in your family jewels and my daughter isn't nearly tall enough to damage that area." Otherwise, she'd be tempted to offer Ana a cookie if she'd make the cocky cowboy sing soprano.

The man shrugged, as if to say there were plenty of women who were downright fascinated by his anatomy. Then he turned and headed toward the refreshment table.

Emily Patterson came up to Nancy and whispered, "He's a looker, isn't he?"

"I guess."

"You weren't very friendly."

"I'm here to network with other parents, not to pick up some lonesome cowboy."

"Oh, I guarantee that one's not lonesome. Maybe you need your eyes checked."

"And maybe you need your head checked." Nancy smiled to soften her words. "You've got four kids to feed already and he looks like he has wild oats to spare."

Emily winked, her round face and dewy complexion giving the impression she was no more than a teen. A few strands of silver through her brown ponytail were the only signs she was approaching forty. "Well, he can sow those oats at my house any day."

Nancy chuckled in spite of herself. "You're an original, you know it?"

"Yes. And I know you need more fun in your life."

Fun? The concept seemed foreign. Her life revolved around Ana and seeing that her every need was met. "Fun is highly overrated."

"Just because you've been burned once doesn't mean you have to give up on men completely."

"I wasn't just burned, I was roasted, toasted and annihilated."

"Hmm. Are you sure that's not just an excuse?"

Nancy shifted. "You sound like my mother. So what if it is an excuse? There are worse things than being single. At least this way I know there are no surprises."

"Oh, but surprises can be wonderful. Two of my children were surprises."

Nancy raised an eyebrow. "My point exactly."

No, Nancy had lost her taste for surprises the day she'd found out there was another woman who claimed

to be Eric McGuire's wife. The same day, coinciden-
tally, that Eric had turned up dead.

RACHEL NIBBLED on a cookie, watching her dad work the
room. The meeting was lame. The people were lame.
And Rachel would rather have been anywhere else.

But since her dad didn't trust her, she was stuck here
with the little kids. Like that two-year-old drama queen
who watched her with big, dark eyes.

Rachel turned her back on the kid.

Why couldn't her dad have believed in her enough
to let her stay home?

Home. Whatever that meant.

There had been a time when she'd felt like she'd had
a home. Not like some kids had—a mom, a dad, brothers and sisters. Meals, picnics, movies, vacations together.

For as long as she could remember, it had just been
her and Mom. Every once in a while Dad would blow
into town. Laughing, fun Dad. He'd taken her to great
places, stuffed her full of junk food, bought her a bunch
of things, and then, poof, he was gone. She'd stare at
his picture to convince herself that he was real—not just
a fabulous dream.

And then two months ago, her mom had sat her
down for one of those serious talks. The don't-do-drugs
or don't-have-sex-till-you're-thirty kind. But her mom's
ultra serious tone should've warned her it was way
worse than the don't-do-drugs talk.

This conversation had started out with her mom telling Rachel how much she loved her. Nothing too scary

there. Until she said Rachel's dad wanted her to go live with him. And Mom thought it was a good idea. Total shocker, but kinda nice to know Dad wanted her. Still, her friends were in Texas, and all she'd ever known was Texas. She'd asked her mom to tell her dad, "thanks but no thanks."

Mom had made it clear refusal wasn't an option. A week later Rachel stood in front of a motel-room door, waiting for her dad to answer. And when he did, he'd gone completely pale, as if he'd seen an alien.

Well, it hadn't taken a brain surgeon, or even an honor student, to figure out Dad hadn't had a clue she was coming. For the first time since the Easter Bunny, Mom had lied. Lied. And that could only mean one thing—Mom didn't want her anymore. Nearly as bad, Dad didn't want her, either.

Rachel was distracted from her moping by a small hand patting her knee.

The little girl with the big, brown eyes murmured, "Sad."

Rachel's eyes filled with tears. She wiped them away with her sleeve. "Yeah. Sad."

BEAU KNOCKED on the bathroom door, trying not to lose patience. "Come on, sweet pea, you're gonna be late for school."

"I look like a geek. Uniforms are stupid."

Sighing, he figured he'd have to endure another replay of Rachel's fashion woes. "You look fine."

"No, I don't. I look like some kind of preppy loser."

"Then you'll blend in with the rest of the preppy losers."

"Daaad."

"If you want a ride, you better get out here in five minutes. Otherwise, you take the bus."

The bus. A fate worse than death to a high school freshman. Beau didn't know much about raising a teenage girl, but he had a pretty good idea only the losers, preppy or otherwise, rode the bus.

Sure enough, Rachel was waiting by the front door, backpack slung over her shoulder, expression sullen, when he was ready to leave.

He complied with her request and dropped her off a block from school so he wouldn't embarrass her. Beau hoped it was just the fact that she was a teen and he was a parent and not that she was ashamed of him. He might be a redneck son of a bitch at times, but he loved his daughter like crazy and would rather cut off his left arm than hurt her.

When ex-wife number one, Laurie, had dumped Rachel and her suitcases three months ago, he hadn't seriously noted his ex's muttered threats about sacrifice. The only thing that really stood out in the whole surreal conversation was one sentence. "I raised her the past fourteen years, you can raise her the next four."

And that's how he'd become a full-time father and certified lunatic.

NANCY PACED outside the dealership and glanced at her watch. Their ad said they opened at 8:00 a.m. It was now ten after eight. She pulled on the door handle one more time to make sure it was locked, despite the low lighting inside and lack of activity.

"Sorry, I'm late, ma'am. I had to get my daughter to school."

She stifled a groan. The cowboy from Parents Flying Solo trotted in her direction, his boots replaced with athletic shoes.

"You're late."

"Are you always this observant?"

Nancy opened her mouth to blister his thick hide, but noticed the twinkle in his eyes. That and his crooked smile defused her anger. "No, usually I require coffee first."

"Good thing I make a killer cup of coffee." He stuck out his hand. "Beau Stanton, I believe we met at the Parents Flying Solo meeting?"

She accepted his handshake. "Nancy McGuire." For some reason, he didn't seem quite as annoying today.

"Nice to meet you." He fished a large key ring out of his pocket and opened the glass door. "Let me turn off the alarm and then you can come on in. You can tell me what kind of car you're looking for while I make coffee."

Following him into the showroom, she admired a convertible BMW, red of course. It looked like fun.

There was that word again. She needed safety and stability for Ana, if not herself. Lord knew Eric had been fun. Faithful would have been nicer.

Shaking her head, she wandered toward a minivan.

"I never figured you for a minivan kind of woman."

Turning, she raised an eyebrow. "Oh. And what kind of woman do you think I am?" Damn, it came out almost flirtatious when that was the last thing she intended.

He looked her up and down, much as she'd done to him the night before at the meeting.

Nancy's cheeks warmed. She was accustomed to male attention, even after she'd traded low-cut T-shirts and jeans for tailored pantsuits. Her conservative look was more consistent with her new life as a successful real-estate broker than aging prom queen trying to hold on to her husband.

Why did this man bring out the extremes in her? Last night, his cocky attitude had made her mad enough to spit nails. Today, she was experiencing the forbidden thrill of the chase. She did *not* want male attention. She did not need male attention. And if she repeated the mantra to herself enough times, maybe she would believe it.

Beau let out a low whistle under his breath while he absorbed the woman's sultry question, "What kind of woman do you think I am?" It was a loaded question, a little like, "Do I look fat in this dress?" No matter which way he answered, he was toast. "Darlin', I tell my daughter women can be anything they want to be. President, rocket scientist or the best damn mom on earth. It's just a matter of wanting it bad enough. I'm betting you're a success at whatever you do."

Mentally congratulating himself on his smooth escape, Beau poured two cups of coffee and handed one to her.

She crossed her arms. "Why couldn't I be president *and* the best damn mom on earth? The two aren't mutually exclusive."

Uh-oh, they were back in dangerous territory. He was supposed to sell her a car at a hefty profit, not debate women's rights. "Darlin', let's go look at that minivan."

Two hours later, Beau was sweating bullets and crunching numbers like crazy. "Lady, there's no way I can sell the minivan to you for that price. We'd lose money."

"No, you won't." She pulled a sheaf of papers from her cavernous purse and showed him the reasons he *could* sell her a minivan at that price.

Running a hand through his hair, he did some quick mental calculations. His commission would be practically nonexistent, but it was nearing the end of the month and one more sale would pretty much clinch Salesman of the Month. The prize, a big-screen TV, would more than make up for the lost commission.

"You drive a hard bargain. But you've got a deal."

She smiled. Not the tight, polite smile she'd given earlier, but a joyous, triumphant smile that lit up her face like a Christmas angel.

Beau sucked in a breath. If she'd smiled like that in the beginning, the minivan would have been hers in half the time. And that was a very, very bad sign.

Beau reminded himself of his responsibilities. There

was only one female in the whole wide world he could allow himself to obsess over these days, even if his body told him otherwise.

CHAPTER TWO

BEAU SIDLED into the Parents Flying Solo meeting almost a week later and scanned the room. He exhaled with relief. Nancy McGuire wasn't there.

He'd have been able to spot her halo of long, blond hair anywhere. Or her smile. Or her extremely lovely body.

Beau shook his head. He had a young, impressionable daughter to raise. His playing days had to be firmly in the past. But Nancy made him respond physically whether he wanted to or not. Worse, she challenged every brain cell he had. Contrary to his rough exterior, he read voraciously and could carry on a conversation about world politics or great philosophers as well as the next guy. He just chose not to let on most of the time.

No, it was better if he didn't run into Nancy. A man had only so much self-control, and he, it seemed, had less than most. He had three ex-wives to prove it.

Beau absently fingered the business cards in the breast pocket of his western shirt. His reason for joining Parents Flying Solo was to network, plain and simple. If he wanted to hang on to the job that allowed him to stay in town with his daughter, he needed to keep generating more sales than the owner's cousin.

So Beau concentrated on his personal three Ms: mix, mingle, make eye contact. "Hey, how's it going?" He greeted a man he'd met the week prior. Chip? Trey?

They chatted for a few moments when the group leader, a balding, middle-age man, signaled for quiet. "I attended a Parents Flying Solo summit last weekend and gleaned a few tips on increasing participation. It's been brought to my attention that some of the members are too shy to utilize the group phone list. This is an important resource during those times when you need to talk to another adult or you think you'll lose your mind." The leader chuckled and so did Chip or Trey or whatever his name was.

Beau found himself nodding. He sure could have used another adult to talk to when he'd first found himself the sole parental unit responsible for a teenage daughter.

"A few other groups in the region have had success with the buddy system. Each member is assigned a buddy to help him or her through the rough spots." He picked up a basket and held it aloft. "Here are names of all our members. Pairs will be assigned randomly. I'm asking you to leave personal likes and dislikes at the door and make the buddy system a success. Each and every member has the potential for learning *and* teaching."

Glancing around the room, Beau was relieved Nancy still hadn't appeared. And a little disappointed, too. But that was the old Beau. The new Beau was all business.

Yeah, right.

The group leader pulled names from the basket. Some announcements were met with dead silence, as if Snidely Whiplash had been paired with Dudley Do-Right or worse, the lovely, innocent Nell. But nobody protested aloud.

"Beau Stanton."

Beau glanced around and mentally catalogued the people still available. Emily Patterson hadn't been paired yet and seemed relatively safe. Maybe he'd get her. He liked her cheerful, down-to-earth attitude. And there was an underlying layer of steel that might be helpful when dealing with Rachel. Somehow, he knew Emily could whip Rachel into shape in five minutes flat.

Shoving his hands into his pockets, he rocked back on his heels while he waited for the other slip of paper to be drawn.

"*Two* cookies," a child screeched from the direction of the ladies' restroom.

Beau was pretty sure he recognized the voice.

An adult female admonished the girl to be quiet as they exited the restroom.

He would have known that honeyed accent anywhere.

"Nancy McGuire," the leader read from a slip of paper. "You're buddies with our newest member, Beau Stanton."

Beau cleared his throat. "Um, are you sure that's right?"

The hostile glances sent in his direction would have

wilted a lesser man. But Beau was a three-time loser fighting for his life. "I mean, um, my daughter's fourteen. It might be more beneficial if I was paired with another parent of a teen."

He could feel the crowd turning on him. They'd stoically accepted their fate, why couldn't he accept his?

"Certainly not. Again, all members have the ability to teach and learn. Our next name is…."

The roaring in his ears drowned out most of the rest. He was aware of Nancy handing him her business card, as if he didn't already have access to her phone number from her loan documents. As if he hadn't copied it to his desk calendar, toying with the idea of asking her out.

He automatically withdrew a card from his pocket and handed it to her. She mouthed something about calling him later and pulled Ana, kicking and screaming, toward the door.

He was a dead man.

Beau had a vision of God somewhere above, laughing his ass off.

NANCY HELD Ana's warm, little frame close to her chest and inhaled the scent of baby shampoo and freshly scrubbed little girl. Her heart did a flip-flop of joy. These were the times to be treasured.

Easing into the antique bentwood rocker, she sighed at the pure luxury of sitting. She pushed gently with her foot.

Ana snuggled close and murmured, "Mama."

"Yes, sunshine, Mama's here."

She continued rocking long after Ana's eyes had fluttered closed and her breathing slowed. Having a child was a miracle Nancy had given up on long ago.

Sighing, she rolled her neck to work out the kinks. The power struggles and tantrums would ease in a few months. Tatiana would grow out of them, she was sure. Nancy just wished she was half as sure she'd survive her first year of motherhood. Nobody had told her how all-consuming it was. And rewarding. And frustrating. And how she wouldn't change a minute of it.

She'd joined Parents Flying Solo at the urging of Ana's pediatrician. After two sleepless nights for both mother and daughter, and one ruptured eardrum for Ana due to an infection, Nancy had surrendered to her doubts. Would she ever get it right?

The kindly doctor had told her there were no right or wrong answers with parenting. Children, even children who weren't adopted from a foreign country, didn't come with instruction manuals. With the initial cultural and language barriers and the fact that Nancy was single and had no one to help pick up the slack, she had been severely in danger of burnout. And what would have happened to Tatiana then?

That's how he'd convinced her to join the support group for single parents. For Ana, not for herself.

But then she'd met Emily and a few other parents and she'd enjoyed talking with people who understood what she was going through. No one seemed to look down on her because she, a single woman, had chosen to adopt a child and now was experiencing the trials that went with it.

It was a much different scenario from some of the people back home in McGuireville, Arkansas. Many of those had made veiled comments about her suitability as a parent. As if having a man in the house would guarantee a bright, normal, carefree childhood for Ana. She'd be willing to bet those narrow-minded folks would feel she deserved to struggle in her new role as a mother.

So how to handle her new parenting buddy? Her concentration had been so focused on getting Ana outside before a full-blown tantrum, she'd barely heard her name and the fact she'd been paired with Beau Stanton. She'd only had time to fling her business card in Beau's direction, accept his card and leave.

As she placed Ana in her crib, the phone rang.

It was Beau.

His accent brought memories of another man, another place. And a sense of loss so intense she sucked in a breath. No, she couldn't allow memories of Eric to somehow get tangled up with Beau, urging her to rewrite history by trying to get another restless man to change.

Beau's words seeped through her distraction. "I'm quitting."

"You're dropping out of the group?" Her voice was shrill.

"I've given it some thought. I, um, joined the group

under false pretenses and it wouldn't be fair for me to be a buddy to anyone."

Just as she'd suspected. Beau was a lying, cheating charmer, just like Eric. Her voice was cool when she said, "Oh, and what false pretenses would those be?" *A wife at home?*

"Um, well, I figured it would be a good way to meet people."

"There are bars and singles groups for that."

"No, not that way. Lord, no." His voice held a convincing note of horror. "It seemed like a good way for the new guy in town to drum up business leads."

Nancy couldn't help but chuckle. "If that's the case, I joined under false pretenses, too. I only went because Ana's pediatrician suggested it. I did it for Ana, not me. And I have to admit, I always make sure I have plenty of business cards in my purse before I leave for the meeting. Hey, it's a reality of sales."

"But you see why it's not a good idea for us to be buddies?"

The man was giving her an out. So why didn't she pounce on it? Because she was afraid her unofficial buddy, Emily, might not have as much time for her now that Emily had an official buddy. And that made her feel terribly alone. "I appreciate you being honest with me. The brochure says honesty and trust are the key components to a successful buddy friendship."

"But it doesn't say how often we have to talk." He hesitated. "Maybe we could ease into this whole thing?"

Nancy smiled. She'd had several impressions of Beau and easing into things wasn't one of them. The man jumped into life without worrying about consequences. "Yes, we can ease into it. We don't even have to see each other face-to-face except for meetings."

She could hear the relief in his tone, when he said, "Yeah, that's right. We just call each other once in a while, no big deal."

"No big deal."

Nancy was still smiling after he ended the call. Beau Stanton was afraid of her. The thought lifted her most pressing doubt about him. He wasn't about to try to seduce her. As a matter of fact, he seemed to prefer not to be anywhere near her.

Shaking her head, she realized her analysis of him remained sound—Beau would definitely be bad news in the romance department. But since she seemed to scare the heck out of the man, it wasn't a problem.

NANCY LED Ana by the hand. "You'll get to play with the other kids. It'll be fun."

They entered the Parents Flying Solo meeting and Ana made a beeline for the toys. As usual, children were everywhere. It was one of the things she liked about the group. Children were always welcome at the meetings. Otherwise, she might have hesitated to take the time away from Ana.

The group was small enough, though, that she could keep an eye on her daughter as she joined some little friends.

"There you are," Emily said. "I've been waiting for you."

Curiosity shone in her friend's eyes. "So dish. How's your buddy?"

"Beau is fine. We've decided to be phone friends."

"Oh." Emily sounded disappointed.

"What did you expect? Wedding bells? Fireworks?"

"I was hoping you'd had great sex. Since I don't get any, I figured I could live vicariously through you."

"I'm not sure I'll ever trust enough for that kind of intimacy again, so you'd better live vicariously through someone else."

Emily patted Nancy's arm. "I have confidence in you. I took a vow of celibacy after Jason was born." She winked. "And you see how well that worked."

Jason was Emily's oldest, followed a year later by Jeremy, with a gap of several years before two little ones stair-stepped behind him.

Nancy frowned. "*I* mean it though."

"Ah, yes, the widow in mourning. I know you too well, Nancy McGuire. I know for a fact there's a part of you that would dance on your husband's grave."

Fanning herself with a napkin, Nancy deepened her accent to *Gone With the Wind* proportions. "Ah'm shocked. Genteel Southern ladies do not dance on their husbands' graves." Nancy chuckled. "At least not while anyone's looking."

"I'll second that."

Nancy turned to see Beau approach. He looked amazing. His smile was wide and infectious, his hair slightly damp from a shower. She inhaled. And he smelled absolutely wonderful. Some sort of subtle aftershave with a hint of danger.

Emily nudged her with her elbow.

Yikes! She'd been caught staring. Emily would never let her hear the end of it. There was absolutely no reason she couldn't have a good-looking male friend, Nancy reasoned. Shoot, she could pretend he was gay.

Except for the testosterone that seemed to ooze out every pore.

He said, "Family legend has it that my great-aunt Charlene poisoned her husband, and every full moon she tiptoed out to the family cemetery and waltzed on his grave. Or did the Lindy or whatever dance they did."

Nancy pursed her lips. "And your point is?"

"Great-Aunt Charlene would have been drummed out of polite society if she'd danced on his grave during daylight hours. But at night, well, that was a different matter. My grandpa always said what went on after dark was nobody's business."

"Hmm, I'm pretty sure I married into the same family. Your grandfather's name wasn't McGuire, was it?"

"Nope. He was a Stanton."

Nancy waited for the overwhelming sense of betrayal she normally felt when recalling her late husband. When it didn't come, she murmured, "That's the first time I've been able to laugh about Eric. I do believe you two helped me reach a milestone today." Raising her plastic cup of soda, she toasted, "To friends."

Emily smiled. She knew the whole story and undoubtedly realized what an important step this was for Nancy. She raised her cup and touched it to Nancy's. "To friends."

They both turned to Beau and waited. He looked like he didn't feel well. "To friends," he added weakly. Then he turned and strode from the meeting room.

Emily shrugged. "Must've needed some air."

"Must have." Nancy thought of following him, but decided against it. When he hadn't returned ten minutes later, she knew she had to do something. What if he was ill?

After making sure Ana was with Jason, Nancy worked her way to the door. She hoped Emily wouldn't notice; her vivid imagination would be off and running.

Crisp air and a hint of snow tickled her nose as she went out to the garden. She didn't see Beau anywhere. But as her eyes adjusted to the dusk, she located him seated on a bench in the butterfly garden.

His shoulders hunched, he was staring off into the forest beyond the property.

Stepping close, she tentatively touched his shoulder. "Hey, is everything okay?"

"Um, yeah." His voice was husky.

Nancy missed his ready smile. This new, somber Beau was an enigma. "The meeting's started."

"I'll be there in a minute." Yet he appeared welded to the bench.

Nancy sat next to him. It was a small bench, so she clung to the edge.

"Did I say something to offend you?" she asked.

"Offend me?" He glanced up. "No, why'd you get that idea?"

"Because you left so suddenly. I know some people don't always appreciate my humor."

"No, I enjoy talking to you. Your sense of humor is a little screwy, but I can handle that."

"What, then? Something happened. Is it Rachel? Is she in trouble again?"

He sighed heavily. "It seems like Rachel's always grounded, but this time it had nothing to do with her. All of sudden, I could visualize each of my three ex-wives dancing on my grave."

Nancy felt her jaw drop open. *"Three."*

"Uh-huh." He nodded glumly. "I saw myself through their eyes and it wasn't pretty."

Shaking her head to clear it, she contemplated the number of failed marriages Beau had put behind him. Three. In her book, that made him nearly as bad as a bigamist.

Nancy swallowed hard. She'd been there, done that and bought the T-shirt. There was no way in Hades she'd ever get on that merry-go-round again.

CHAPTER THREE

NANCY'S STUNNED EXPRESSION did nothing to alleviate Beau's misery. She might as well have made an *L* with her thumb and forefinger and pressed it to her forehead in the international sign for *Loser.*

He liked Nancy. He didn't want her to think he was some kind of sleazy guy with an inability to commit. Okay, so he *had* been a sleazy guy with an inability to commit. But that was in the past. "I've changed."

The disbelief in her eyes told him she'd heard that line before.

"Really. I turned over a new leaf when Rachel came to live with me."

Nancy raised her chin. "It's none of my business."

"Yes, it is your business. You're supposed to be helping me hang on to my sanity while raising Rachel. The buddy brochure says trust is essential. I need you to trust me."

"I'm the wrong woman for the job, Beau. I'm not nearly as trusting as I used to be."

Beau's heart sank at the bitterness in her voice. Someone had hurt her badly. Maybe the way he'd hurt his ex-wives? He rebelled at the idea. Sure, divorce had been difficult each and every time. Well, except for ex-wife number three. They'd gladly parted ways once they'd sobered up enough to realize what they'd done.

But certainly Laurie and Vivian, ex-wives number one and number two, respectively, hadn't been scarred for life. Had they?

Nancy stood. "Beau, this isn't going to work."

Panic propelled him to his feet. "Look, I know I didn't think this buddy thing would work, but, um, I have to admit you've been a lot of help. You understand teenage girls."

"*Nobody* understands teenage girls."

"Yeah, well, you do a hell of a lot better than I do. All the buddies have already been assigned. You'll leave me high and dry if you quit."

"Maybe we can trade."

"I already asked. No trades."

"You tried to trade me?" She braced her hands on her hips. "Why?"

Beau sighed. Maybe this was one of those times when honesty was the best policy. "No offense, Nancy, but you're just too damn good-looking. I've promised myself no more women. I need to concentrate on Rachel and getting this dad stuff right."

Nancy's lips twitched. She threw her head back and laughed aloud.

Beau smiled in response.

But she laughed so long it started to scare him.

Had he completely unhinged the woman by being straightforward?

Finally, she wound down to a chuckle, then stopped altogether. "You're afraid of me because you've sworn off women?"

He nodded.

"Oh, that's too funny. I'm the last woman in the world who'd want to get involved with you, Beau Stanton."

That hurt. "What's so bad about me?"

"Come on, Beau, get real. You've been married not once, not twice, but *three* times. You're a slick-talking, woman-loving, son of a gun with a voice that'd melt stone. I've seen your kind before. Shoot, I've *married* your kind before. You're safe with me, buddy."

"The husband you, um, wanted to dance on his grave? I remind you of him?"

"Remind me? You could have given Eric lessons. At least you were smart enough to divorce one wife before you married another. Or am I assuming too much?"

Beau didn't know whether to be fascinated by her disclosure or insulted. "Your husband was a bigamist? Really?"

Nancy sat next to him. "Yes. Really."

He whistled under his breath. No wonder she didn't want another man in her life. It was a damn good thing he had no intention of acting on his attraction to her, because he wouldn't stand a snowball's chance in hell with a woman like Nancy.

Extending his hand, Beau said, "We should be safe as buddies then. Deal?"

She shook his hand. "Deal."

NANCY SQUINTED at the alarm clock by her bed. It was almost midnight. Her heart raced. She picked up the receiver. "Mom?"

"No, it's Beau." He sounded frazzled.

"What's wrong?"

"Rachel was caught shoplifting."

She rose, instantly alert. "Is she okay?"

"It's been a long night. I brought her home about an hour ago. She's to appear before the judge Monday morning. I'm so wired from coffee, I can't sleep. And I can't talk to her because I'm so mad I could wrap my hands around her throat."

"You don't mean that."

"Of course I don't mean that. Oh, I don't know what I mean. I called her mother. Laurie said Rachel had been rebelling, hanging with the wrong crowd. She hoped the move and having her father around would be a 'steadying influence.'"

"You didn't know Rachel was getting into trouble before?"

"Laurie and I don't talk much. I was so stunned when she dropped off Rachel, I didn't think to ask."

"And how about later? After the heat of the moment?"

"I'm, um, not big on long heart-to-heart conversations with my exes."

"Why am I not surprised? It sounds like you could use someone to talk to tonight, though." Nancy paused to gather her thoughts. "Ana's sleeping, so I need to stay home. If you're comfortable leaving Rachel alone right now, you could come over here."

"You're right, I need to talk to a rational adult or I'm going to lose my mind. Rachel's grounded for life, and I'm pretty sure she doesn't want to be around me at all tonight. I'll tell her where I'll be. She's got my cell number if she needs me."

"I'll have some nice, relaxing herbal tea ready when you get here."

"Herbal tea? Don't you have anything stronger?"

"Nope. Take it or leave it."

He sighed heavily. "I'm desperate. I'll take it. Your house is on Evergreen, right?"

"Yes." She gave him the house number and hung up the phone.

Glancing down at her skimpy tank top and flannel boxers, she dashed to the closet and removed a baggy pair of sweatpants and an old sweatshirt of Eric's. Why she'd kept it, she didn't know. Maybe because Eric had been such an important part of her life since high school. It still seemed odd at times, knowing she'd never talk to him again.

Nancy pushed the unsettling thought away and headed to the bathroom. She splashed water on her face and ran a brush through her hair.

The doorbell rang just as she finished.

She took the stairs two at a time and opened the

door. "You must've broken a few speed limits to get here this quick."

Beau shrugged. "Probably."

"You look like hell. Come on in."

"Thanks. That NASCAR sweatshirt of yours is really attractive, too."

Her face warmed. "What were you expecting, a lace teddy?"

There was an evil glint in his eyes. "Now that might just distract me from my problems."

"Dream on, *buddy*. Park your butt at the breakfast bar while I get the kettle going."

"Yes, ma'am."

After she filled the kettle and set it on the stove, she studied him. He had bags under his eyes, a day's worth of stubble on his jaw, and his shoulders slumped in defeat.

"Out with it. The whole story."

"I wish I knew the whole story. That's part of the problem. Rachel won't talk to me. All I know is she went to the mall with her friends and then the police called to say she'd been caught shoplifting."

"In your limited conversations with your ex, did she say Rachel has shoplifted before?"

He nodded. "Once. Right before she came to live with me. So what sage advice do you have for me, buddy?"

"Ah, grasshopper, when you can snatch the pebble from my hand, you still won't have a clue about teenage girls."

"That's what I was afraid of. What do I do besides ground her? Send her to a convent?"

"Hmm. If you want grandchildren someday, the convent's out."

Beau groaned, placing his hand over his eyes. He peered out at her between his fingers. "Don't remind me. She could end up pregnant if I don't get her back on the right path."

"Um, I think you took a gigantic leap there, Beau. A lot of girls shoplift. I'm not saying it's okay, I'm just saying sometimes it's a rite of passage."

"Did you ever shoplift?"

Nancy nodded. "Yep. Makeup. I ended up grounded for a week. What did Rachel steal?"

"Earrings. The stupid part is that she doesn't even have pierced ears. I won't let her mutilate her body like that."

"Hmm. Do you think she was making a statement of sorts?"

He raised an eyebrow. "Let me get my ears pierced or I'll turn to a life of crime?"

"Something like that. Kids can be pretty manipulative."

"How come you're so smart about this stuff with Rachel? But then with Ana, you don't seem to have a clue?"

"I remember being a teen, what I did, how I felt. I can't remember being a toddler. They're completely foreign creatures."

"Exactly how I feel about Rachel. Do you think maybe it's just our own kids we don't understand?"

The kettle sputtered. Nancy removed a couple of mugs from the cupboard and placed them on the counter. She poured chamomile tea, added a dollop of honey and handed a cup to Beau.

Sipping her tea, she pondered his theory. "Maybe you're right. Maybe all parents are baffled by their children. And some are just better at hiding it than others."

"I figured it was because I was so new at it."

"You and me both. Didn't you have visitation while Rachel was growing up?"

Beau flushed and avoided her eyes. "Yeah, um, I did. But I was on the road a lot. I never forgot a birthday or special occasion." His expression brightened. "And I took her on some scouting father/daughter camping trip."

"You were the fun parent. Now you're the mean parent. I imagine that's a hard transition."

"I'm not mean."

"No, you're just a concerned father, trying to do the right thing. But to Rachel, it probably seems mean. And maybe a little confusing. She'd lived with her mom all that time and then bam, she's living with a father she barely knows."

"I guess you've got a point." His voice was glum. "I'd rather be the fun parent."

"Rachel's been with you how long?"

"Three months."

"If she weren't there every day, for some reason, would you miss her?"

"Hell, yes."

"Now that you've been the mean parent, do you think it would be worth it not to see her every day, even if you got to be the fun parent again? Would it be hard to stay away?"

"Yeah. I've gotten used to having her around. At least when the police aren't calling to say she's gotten into trouble."

"Mama?" Ana stood in the doorway to the kitchen, her feet poking out from beneath her little flannel nightgown.

Nancy scooped her up. "I'm here, baby. What's wrong."

Ana pointed at Beau, her eyes wide. She wasn't accustomed to seeing men at the house in the middle of the night and Nancy wanted to keep it that way.

"This is Beau. He's Mommy's friend. He came over for tea because he was sad."

Ana nodded.

"Now, let me take you back up to bed."

Beau watched Nancy's expression soften when she looked at her daughter. The love shining in her eyes was enough to make a man want to lay down his life for her. He resisted the urge to follow her up the stairs and watch her tuck in her daughter.

Raising his mug, he took a big swallow and sputtered. He didn't care what anyone said, chamomile tea sucked, big time.

Restless despite his fatigue, Beau wandered around the room. Nancy's kitchen was large, one wall exposed red brick. Copper pots and pans hung from the ceiling.

The professional-size stove led him to believe she liked to cook. Good, he liked to eat.

Heading into the family room, he admired the feeling of warmth and safety she'd created. The oversize couch and love seat were made of soft, dark-brown fabric. Throw pillows in solid red, purple and blue reminded him of Nancy—bright and fun, yet sensual.

Uh-oh. He looked at family-room furniture and thought sensual. Next he'd be wondering what Nancy's bedroom looked like. No sooner had the suggestion risen than his imagination was off and running. He'd bet his bottom dollar Nancy had an antique four-poster canopy bed with a white eyelet comforter so dense you could get lost in it.

Redirecting his thoughts, he stopped in front of an oak sideboard, where family pictures were lovingly arranged. At least he assumed it was family, because the majority of the photos were of Nancy and Ana. One had been taken in a drab, old-fashioned room, with a stern-looking woman holding Ana. Then there was a photo of Nancy with an older version of herself, probably her mother. The woman's eyes held a lingering sadness.

"There, I think she's asleep again," Nancy said from behind him.

"You've got some great pictures. I'd like to get a studio picture done with Rachel if I can ever catch her in a good mood."

Nancy pointed to the drab photo. "That one's at the orphanage in Pechory, Russia. Ana's house mother was saying goodbye. The staff grows attached to the children and it's hard for them to see the kids go. But they're happy that the children are headed for a better life."

"Ana's adopted?" The realization helped connect a few of the seemingly unrelated dots Beau had found intriguing.

Nancy nodded, moving to the fireplace, as if she needed the additional warmth. "Sometimes I forget it's not common knowledge like in McGuireville."

Beau resisted the urge to follow her, to connect with her. He was afraid she'd quit confiding if he got too close. "I didn't realize Ana came from Russia. She speaks English like any other kid her age. I have to admit, I was curious… You never said how long your husband was dead. But I figured it was none of my business who Ana's father was."

"Eric wasn't in favor of adopting, otherwise I'd probably have two or three children by now. Most people around here probably assume Ana is Eric's daughter." She turned, raising her chin. "I guess I don't go out of my way to correct that assumption until I know someone pretty well."

The rebellious tilt to her chin and the hurt in her eyes touched Beau. Beau started to reach out to her but let his arm drop to his side. He couldn't offer more than friendship.

"What made you decide on adopting after he died?"

Seeing Nancy frown, he realized he'd goofed. "Sorry, that's none of my business, either."

Nancy's features relaxed. "Have a seat." She gestured toward one end of the couch and sat at the other end. "I guess I'm a little defensive. Some of the folks back home in McGuireville were pretty disapproving of a single woman adopting a child. Unfortunately, my mother was one of them. And the fact that I adopted a 'foreign' child didn't help any."

"That's too bad." He sat where she'd indicated. "But you still haven't answered my question. Why?"

"Maybe because I wonder if I've been selfish. I adopted because I've wanted to be a mom for as long as I could remember. And I guess I felt I deserved to have a child after everything I went through with Eric. We never conceived, though he fathered a beautiful little boy with another woman. So, I guess, I figured he owed me in a way."

"That's not selfish. You needed a baby, Ana needed a home. It's a win-win situation. You're a wonderful mother and Ana's obviously a happy, healthy kid."

"Thank you. It's nice to hear someone say that every once in a while. Even though I don't have a clue what I'm doing at times, as you pointed out earlier."

Beau stifled a groan. "Don't listen to me. I'm just a dumb old country boy flapping my gums." He pointed to the coffee table where several child-development books rested. "You're learning all you can and you love Ana like crazy. That's what matters."

Nancy moved to perch on the front of the cushion. "Sometimes…when it's been a really long day and everything has gone wrong and Ana's been like the Energizer Bunny, I wonder if she'd be better off if I hadn't adopted her."

"Aw, darlin', look at the pictures. No matter how much the staff cared about those kids, it's not the same. You're giving Ana a chance to live like a real kid, not in some institution."

Nancy sighed. "That's what I keep telling myself. But some days, there just doesn't seem to be enough of me to go around."

"*Most* days there doesn't seem to be enough of me to go around. Staying one step ahead of Rachel is a full-time job. But I don't know any different—Laurie and I were already separated when Rachel was born. I imagine it's a little easier with two parents because you can tag-team. But I don't seriously think having only one parent hurts as long as there's plenty of love and dedication."

Smiling, she said, "Did you hear yourself, Beau Stanton? You sounded like you could run for the Parent-Teacher Association."

Beau flushed. "Well, as the song says, the times they are a-changin'."

"Folk music, too? What is a good old Texas boy doing listening to anything but hard-core country?"

"I don't want to scare you or anything—" he leaned closer, watching her sea-green eyes widen when their faces were merely inches apart "—but I like to listen to blues and Motown, too."

"Beau Stanton, I do believe you've been holding out on me," she breathed, her accent as thick and warm as sorghum on toast.

Lust nearly knocked him off the couch. It had been so long since he'd bedded a woman. Longer still since he'd spent the whole night with one, talking and laughing in the dark.

Nancy had a terrific laugh. And the thought of her seductive voice coming from the other side of the bed had him instantly aroused.

Nancy's eyes narrowed. "Time for you to go, buddy." Her emphasis on the last word reminded him of his place, which was nowhere near her bed.

This friends stuff was proving to be difficult. Very difficult.

CHAPTER FOUR

NANCY CAUGHT herself gazing out her office window yet again. In the two days since her midnight chat with Beau, she'd found herself doing that a lot.

Her face warmed as she recalled telling him about Ana's adoption and some of the disappointing responses she'd received back home. She shook her head, wondering at her own ability to open up to a man who had originally appeared to be only one step up on the evolutionary ladder from Eric.

But Eric had rarely listened to her like Beau had the other night. And a part of her really wanted to believe Beau's interest had been more than just a ploy to get into her bed. But then she remembered that he'd pretty clearly wanted to seduce her before she sent him on his way.

Sighing, Nancy realized she might never understand the male mind. Worse yet, she wasn't sure she wanted to.

A tap at her open door drew her from her mental maze.

Beau leaned against the doorjamb. "I hope this isn't a bad time."

"I didn't hear you come in. How long have you been there?"

"A couple minutes. You seemed lost in thought so I was enjoying watching you. Nice view." His distracted frown belied his words, telling her he was hitting on her more out of habit than actual interest.

And for some reason, that ticked her off. Her accent deepened, as it always did when she was upset. "Honey, this view is strictly off-limits." Still, she couldn't help but smooth her hair.

His grin told her he knew exactly what she was doing. "Don't worry, I'm here for your business acumen, not to drool over your…attributes. And to thank you for letting me come over the other night. I really did need to talk to someone."

"I think maybe I needed to talk to someone, too. Thanks for listening." Her voice was softer than she intended.

"Anytime." He held her gaze. "And I'll try not to screw it up by letting my hormones get in the way."

Nancy couldn't help but chuckle. "Agreed. Now, you wanted to talk business?"

He took a deep breath, as if he intended to dive into the deep end of a pool—a pool teeming with alligators. "I need a house."

"To rent?"

"No. I want to buy one."

Nancy hesitated. "I would have figured you more for a short-term renter. Have you ever owned a home before?"

"Um, no. This is a first. Emily Patterson said you're the best Realtor in the county."

"Emily's kind of a one-woman PR team. She talks me up way more than I deserve."

"She's very passionate in describing your abilities. Says you found a five-bedroom fixer-upper for her when she was practically broke and if anyone can find a perfect house for me, it's you."

"If she keeps that up, I'll have to put her on the payroll. Have a seat." She nodded toward a chair on the other side of her desk. "How's Rachel? Didn't she have a court appearance yesterday?"

"Yeah. Fortunately, the whole process scared the living daylights out of her, so she didn't mouth off at the judge. He gave her a stern lecture and a few hours' community service in the form of peer mediation training at school."

"I'm so glad, Beau. Maybe this is just what she needed."

"I hope so. We had a long, heart-to-heart talk the other night. To make a long story short, she's trying to fit in. You know how it goes, Rachel's the new kid in school. And um, the kids call her names and stuff— about being skinny."

"Poor thing. Kids can be so mean, especially teenage girls. The peer mediation might give her a way to meet some kids at school, too."

"I kinda think that's where the judge was headed. Smart old guy. But I feel there's gotta be more I can do, too."

"How about Rachel's mom? Is she still determined not to be a part of her life?"

"I called Laurie. It's weird 'cause she's always been there for Rach. But now, it's like she's afraid or something."

"Afraid of Rachel?"

"No. More like afraid of herself. Says she's under a lot of pressure at work and financial stuff, so she's just gotta have some time to get her head straight."

"So you can't rely on her to back you up?"

"No. It looks like I can't rely on her being there for Rachel in any way." He rested his arms on her desk. "That's the reason I'm looking for a house."

Nancy tilted her head to the side. "Oh?"

"Rachel seems to think I'm going to up and leave her and she'll have nowhere to go. I figured if I bought a house, Rachel'd feel more secure—know she had a place to call home. Some place she's always welcome, can always count on."

Funny, for a guy she'd pegged as a redneck wanderer, he sure was astute enough to see the importance of a home and roots. She wondered if he had any idea how attractive his sensitive side was.

Shaking her head, Nancy refused to join a long line of women vying for this man's attention. If she were ever ready to give romance another try, it would be with a man who thought she hung the moon and the stars. A man who wouldn't notice if Pamela Anderson walked through the room naked, because he was too fascinated with the color of Nancy's eyes or her witty

50 HOME FOR CHRISTMAS

observations. Maybe a chubby, bald guy so ordinary no
other woman would look twice or, God forbid, pursue
him.

"Hey, this is probably a bad idea." Beau's voice intruded on her romantic philosophizing.

She cleared her throat. "No, not at all. Tell me what
you have in mind, and I'll check the Multiple Listing
Service, see what's available. But before we do that, I
better get you prequalified so we can see how much
house you can afford."

"Not very different from qualifying for a car loan,
I hope?"

"No, just a little more paperwork." She opened her
desk drawer and withdrew a packet of papers. "Here,
why don't you fill these out and I'll see what I can do."

Nancy found herself watching him while he completed the paperwork, as if looking for clues to his real
personality. The strokes of his pen were firm, decisive.
He rarely paused, except to refer to information contained in a small phone book in his wallet. "Is it going to
be a problem that I've only had this job for six months?"

"It depends. We'll go back to your previous employ-
ment, just in case. Let me run some figures and I can
give you a pretty good ballpark idea of what you can
qualify for."

He slid the completed paperwork across the desk, his
movements strangely tentative for a man who seemed
so confident in most other areas.

Smiling, she tried to put him at ease. "It's painless.
Really. I promise I'll be gentle."

Nancy could have kicked herself.

But Beau didn't seem to notice the double entendre. "Um, I'd pretty much rather have a root canal than think about buying a house. I mean, it's so permanent."

"If it makes you feel any better, most people live in their homes an average of five years."

His face paled a little beneath his tan. "Yeah, um, five years."

"I'm telling you so the thought of a thirty-year mortgage won't freak you out."

Beau turned positively green. She wasn't sure whether it was the thirty-year part or the word *mortgage* that made him ill.

"Anyway, I'll get right on this. There's some coffee over on the table."

"Maybe I'll get some air."

"I won't be but a minute." Nancy could sense the sale evaporating. She wasn't normally so tactless. She'd always prided herself on being adept at saying the right thing to close the deal. But with Beau, she was off balance.

While he paced the room, Nancy concentrated on running the figures—something she should have been able to do in her sleep. But today, her fingers and her brain couldn't seem to connect.

When she was done, she gave him a figure that made him blink. "I qualify for that much? I don't need anything huge, just a normal house with a backyard and all that."

"This is what it takes to buy 'a normal house with a back yard and all that.'"

Whistling under his breath, he said, "And to think I got sticker shock when I started selling new cars. This is unreal."

"Oh, it's very real, I assure you." She pulled up a list of possibilities. "There are eight homes in the area I can show you. What time would be best for you?"

"Now."

"Okay. Let's go."

Three hours later, they pulled into the driveway of the eighth house—a roomy ranch-style house purported to be immaculate inside.

God, she hoped so. Because Beau had found something wrong with each house they'd visited. She could feel a tension headache start at her temples and work its way down her neck, contracting her shoulder muscles into tight little knots. She supposed it was their semipersonal relationship that made this so difficult.

"This is like taking Goldilocks house hunting." Nancy smiled to soften her words. "This one is too small. That one is too tall. Too hot, too cold, too old, too new. Is there something specific you have in mind that I should know about?"

"You've been reading way too much Dr. Seuss lately."

"Sorry, I start rhyming when I'm stressed. I promise not to offer green eggs and ham if you tell me exactly what it is you're looking for in a house."

He shrugged. "I'm not sure. I'll know it when I see it, though. It's gotta feel like home."

"What do you go by, if you've never owned a home? Your parents' house?"

Beau hesitated. "No. My parents weren't the warm, fuzzy kind. They wanted everything perfect. Carpets, furniture, kids."

"Carpets and furniture are rarely perfect. And as for kids, well, they're by nature imperfect."

"Don't tell my folks that. Because they're certain they raised one perfect son. And it wasn't me. Now, let's see this house." His voice was grim.

Nancy processed Beau's admission while she retrieved the house key from the lockbox. Maybe he had a good reason for avoiding roots and everything that went with them.

Opening the door wide, she asked, "What means home to you then?"

Beau glanced around the entryway. "This isn't it, either. Home is…the way I feel when I walk into your house."

Nancy wished she hadn't asked. Because the thought of Beau Stanton making himself at home was only slightly scary. And she should have been terrified.

NANCY SLID into a booth at the little Italian restaurant downtown. "Sorry I'm late. I was with a client."

Emily Patterson winked. "I heard. Beau Stanton. You'll have to find him a big house, 'cause each room will need to be christened. And I think you're just the woman for the job."

"Christened?" Nancy frowned. Realization dawned. "No way. Not me. I have no intention of getting horizontal with Beau Stanton, particularly not on a kitchen counter."

"Did I say anything about horizontal?" Emily's eyes widened innocently. "Or a kitchen counter?" She leaned over and whispered, "It's way more fun to get vertical in the shower together, if you know what I mean?"

Nancy choked on a sip of water. "Emily, you're bad."

"As Mae West said, 'When I'm good, I'm very good, but when I'm bad, I'm better.'"

"Okay, friend, I know you have my best interests at heart. And someday I might date again. But not now and not with Beau Stanton. Did the waiter say what today's special is?"

"Veal Parmesan. I'll allow you to change the subject, but only for a while. Then I want all the details."

Opening a menu, Nancy hoped Emily would forget about Beau. "How are the kids?"

"Bickering and fighting nonstop. Ordinary kids. They're anticipating the first snow and Thanksgiving break. I promised them a day trip to do some sledding."

"Is it almost Thanksgiving already? It hardly seems possible," Nancy murmured, disturbed by a trace of wistfulness.

"Probably because you've been working so hard. How're things going at the real-estate office?"

"Not bad, considering it's my first year. And by the way, thank you for referring Beau, even if he is a pain in the rear at times."

Emily beamed. "My pleasure. Are you going to your mother's for Thanksgiving?"

Sighing, Nancy wished the holidays were as simple

as when she'd been a kid. Things got so complex in adulthood. "I'd considered making the trip, but I think we'll stay home this year. My mom's pretty outspoken in her opinions about foreign adoptions." She selected a bread stick from the basket and started tearing it into little pieces. "I'd love for her to be a grandmother to Ana, but she just can't seem to accept her. This is Ana's first holiday with me and I don't want her to feel rejected by Mom in any way. Our Thanksgiving can be kind of quiet, but I want to make her first Christmas magical. I intend to research Russian orthodoxy and see if I can incorporate some of their traditions for Ana."

Emily squeezed Nancy's hand. "That sounds terrific. If anyone can do it, you can. How about coming to our house for Thanksgiving?"

"But—"

"No buts. That's an order. We have so many people coming, nobody will notice two more. Besides, I need you to show me how to do some of that fancy presentation stuff with food. You know, where you make radishes look like roses and all the other ways you create a beautiful meal. My great-aunt Beatrice will be there, and it will hack her off no end if I suddenly seem domestic. She's the one who said I'd never amount to anything and calls my children little heathens."

Nancy chuckled. "In the interest of hacking off Great-Aunt Beatrice, I'd be delighted to spend Thanksgiving at your house. And I'm sure Ana would love to tag along with your kids."

"It's settled then. I can hardly wait."

CHAPTER FIVE

BEAU PLACED two packages of dinner rolls in a grocery sack. Emily had said he didn't need to bring anything, but he didn't like to show up empty-handed. "Come on, Rachel," he hollered. "We need to leave in five minutes."

They didn't actually need to go for fifteen minutes, but with Rachel, he'd learned to pad the timing to allow for clothing emergencies. She'd change her clothes two or three times and end up wearing the first outfit. Worse yet, were the hair emergencies. Sometimes he swore she started over from scratch, washing, blow-drying and curling, until she got it perfect.

Eyeing the phone, he sighed. He knew he should call his folks and wish them a happy Thanksgiving, but he didn't want to mar his first holiday with Rachel.

A sense of duty weighed heavily on him. What kind of asshole didn't call his parents on Thanksgiving? Particularly since he'd disappointed them by not going home?

Picking up the receiver, he dialed the familiar number before he had a chance to change his mind.

"Hi, Mom. Happy Thanksgiving."

There was a catch in her voice, when she said, "It's so good to hear your voice, William. Please tell me you've changed your mind and booked a last minute flight home."

Beau cleared his throat. He'd let the William part go, even though he'd been called Beau by just about everyone since seventh grade. "No, Mom. I didn't change my mind."

"I so wanted to see Rachel."

"I know you did. But now's not the right time. She and I both need to get settled into our new life."

"You're family. What kind of settling in do you need?"

"It's complicated, Mom. Let's not get into this again today."

Beau heard voices in the background.

"That's your brother and his family. I'll have to go. I love you."

"Yeah, um, love you too." He slowly replaced the receiver. Some things never changed. The minute his brother, Connor, and his perfect family arrived, Beau was dropped like a hot potato. He could just hear the comparisons if they'd made the trip. Connor is so successful. Connor married such a lovely, hometown girl. Connor's children are so well behaved and talented. And what activities is Rachel involved in? Um, shoplifting. Mouthing off at authority figures, mostly her father. Was he dating? Hell, no. He'd done enough of that for a couple lifetimes. But what about giving Rachel a stepmother? He thought of that every second of every day. But that would only compound their problems, not solve them.

"Dad, I think you've finally cracked. You're talking to yourself again." The aroma of Rachel's assorted cosmetics and hair-care products wafted through the air. She tilted her head to the side, as if studying some sort of prehistoric mystery. "I thought we were leaving."

"Yeah, I just called Grandma Stanton to wish her a happy Thanksgiving."

"The dragon lady?" She shuddered for emphasis.

"You've only met her a couple times. She'll warm up when you spend more time with her." He avoided his daughter's eyes.

"Yeah, that's why you spend so much time with them. You're, what, almost middle-age and they don't seem to have warmed up to you yet."

Rachel's observation hit him like a line drive to short-stop. He didn't need any reminders of his age, or the fact that he was the black sheep of the Stanton family. Shaking his head, he said, "I've never been exactly a good son."

"Says who? The dragon lady?"

"That's enough, Rachel. You're being disrespectful when you talk about your grandmother that way."

"Respect is earned. From what I remember of the drag—I mean grandmother, all she does is treat you like chopped liver. Uncle Connor is the favorite."

Beau's respect for his daughter's perceptiveness increased tenfold. "You don't miss a lot, do you?"

"Nope. And you might as well get used to it."

Sighing, he said, "I don't know if I'll ever get used to it. You were such a sweet little thing that summer I took you to Disneyland."

"I was five. Get over it."

"Rachel," he warned.

"I know, I'm being disrespectful again. It's hereditary."

"What do you mean by that?"

"Meaning you don't deal with authority any better than I do. I simply voice my opinions, whereas you swallow yours. Like that conversation with Grandmother. You really wanted to tell the dragon lady that maybe if she'd been a better mother, you'd be there for Thanksgiving."

Beau rubbed his temples, where a familiar ache had started. "Part of being an adult is learning not to say everything that jumps into your mind. Now, let's get going or we're gonna be late. You can psychoanalyze me later."

"Oh, I don't need to psychoanalyze you. You're an open book." She sauntered past him out the door.

That's when he noticed how low cut her pants were. She'd put a plumber to shame if she so much as bent over.

He opened his mouth to tell her so, but then clamped it shut. He was learning to pick his battles. The realization did nothing to lower his blood pressure, though.

NANCY HUMMED a tune under her breath as she put the finishing touches on the fresh vegetable platter. As a child, she'd always fantasized about large family Thanksgivings with beautiful place settings and a mouth-watering array of food—a far cry from the quiet, sparse holiday meals at home.

When she'd married Eric, her place in the McGuire family had been conditional. She'd been accepted as long as she played her role of adoring, ever-patient wife to the family favorite. And though the place settings had been lovely, the tension at family gatherings pretty much ruined Thanksgiving and Christmas. Shoot, half the time Eric hadn't even been in town and she'd attended the events by herself, pasting on a smile and pretending everything was fine.

But that was all in the past and Nancy refused to allow painful memories to sour her first Thanksgiving with Ana. Tipping her head to the side, she decided the tray was gorgeous. Radish rosettes, curly carrot strips, red and gold bell peppers—all gave a festive touch to the run-of-the-mill appetizers Emily had initially described.

She presented the tray for her friend's inspection. "Let Great-Aunt Beatrice get a load of this. She'll be singing your praises to the high heavens."

A whirlwind of giggling girls and rowdy boys nearly knocked the masterpiece out of her hands. Their joyful noise warmed Nancy's heart.

Emily frowned at the retreating children. "The vegetables are absolutely beautiful. Now, if you could just get my kids to behave…"

"Sorry, I can tame a radish or some carrot sticks, but with children I'm a total pushover."

Emily squeezed Nancy's shoulder. "We love you anyway. Would you please put the veggies on the buffet? And make sure Great-Aunt Beatrice gets a good view."

"Absolutely. Then I'll tackle those mashed potatoes."

"Uh-uh. That's where I draw the line. Mashed potatoes are my specialty. I want you to grab a glass of wine and relax."

Nancy didn't have the heart to tell Emily her mashed potatoes were lumpy. "But my favorite cooking show suggests using a ricer, then pressing the mashed potatoes through a pastry tube with a large tip. And maybe a little paprika on top for color?"

"Okay, Martha Stewart, you're going a little overboard now. Shoo."

"Was I doing it again?" Nancy's face grew warm. "I didn't mean to be pushy. It's just so much fun—"

"Out of the kitchen. Now." Emily propelled her through the kitchen doorway.

Nancy faced the crowded dining room and, beyond, the equally crowded living room. With the exception of Emily and her children, Nancy didn't know a soul. Suddenly she felt a little lost in the midst of all the controlled chaos.

So she busied herself with placing the tray on the buffet table and fussing with a few rogue celery sticks.

"Darlin', I haven't seen rosebud radishes in decades. Let me have one of those bad boys." The masculine voice came from directly behind her. The hair on the nape of her neck rose, caressed by Beau's warm breath. At least she assumed it was Beau—there wasn't another Texan in the county, she'd bet.

"Why didn't you tell me you were coming to Emily's for Thanksgiving dinner?" Nancy swatted his hand as he reached over her shoulder for a radish.

Instead of retreating, he nuzzled her ear. "Because you didn't ask. Mmm, you smell like pumpkin pie. Good enough to eat."

Nancy resisted the urge to grab a paper napkin and fan her face. Quickly assessing her options, she saw he'd trapped her against the buffet. Short of elbowing him in the ribs and making a very unladylike scene, she couldn't escape. And if she were being truthful with herself, she'd admit it was nice to have another person she knew there.

He popped a radish into his mouth, crunching enthusiastically. The noise was only amplified by his nearness.

"You find any more houses for me to look at?"

"Not a single one. You'll have to wait for something new to come on the market." She peeked over her shoulder. "Unless you want to reconsider one of the places you previously vetoed?"

"Nope. I'll wait."

"Somehow I knew you'd say that. Would you please move so I can go check on Ana?"

"She was out front playing with the other kids. Rachel teamed up with her for hide-and-seek 'cause she's so little and the other kids found her right away."

The warmth of his presence coaxed her to relax against him for just a second. Then she realized how intimate the small gesture seemed. "Oh. Then I'll go get a glass of wine and sit on the porch to watch."

"Sounds like a good idea. Make mine a beer, would you?"

Nancy froze, then turned around. Anger was her shield against his closeness. "I beg your pardon?"

His eyes glinted with amusement. "There, I knew you'd turn around if I pissed you off. I really hate talking to someone's back." His gaze roamed down her figure. "Lovely though it is."

She pushed by him, plucking a napkin off the dining table as she went, fanning her face furiously. Beau's chuckle only made it worse. Surely, she couldn't be having hot flashes at the tender age of thirty-two, could she?

Glancing back, she almost wished her elevated temperature was due to midlife changes. Beau's crooked grin cranked up her internal thermostat another degree or two.

Nancy hurried to the beverage bar in the corner of the living room. Pouring herself a glass of zinfandel, she quelched the thought of pressing the glass to her forehead. Instead, she made a beeline for the front door, hoping the air outside would chill her into sanity.

"Here, let me get that for you." Beau opened the door. He held a longneck beer in his other hand.

"Where?"

"A Texan is always resourceful. There's an ice chest in the dining room."

The crisp air stung her lungs. It also cooled her cheeks.

She chose a weathered Adirondack chair on the porch and sat, scanning the yard for Ana. The recent snow had partially melted, revealing patches of dead grass. There wasn't a child to be seen, except Emily's youngest son, Ryan, who counted slowly, his face pressed to the trunk of an elm tree.

"I wonder where Ana is?"

A giggle sounded fairly close by, only to be shushed by another child.

Beau sat in the chair next to Nancy and leaned close, pointing. "Behind the woodpile," he whispered.

Nancy sipped her wine and frowned. "I don't see her."

"Relax. She's in good hands."

"I suppose you're right. Still, I like knowing where she is."

"Ready or not, here I come." Ryan opened his eyes and began searching. When he got close to the woodpile, the giggling started again. "You're it, Ana." He tagged her.

Ana appeared from behind the stack of seasoned cedar, pulling Rachel by the hand.

"You gave us away again." The teen swung the girl up in the air. Both laughed as if it were a great joke. "Okay, Ana Banana, you help me count. We have to hide our faces." She settled Ana on her hip.

Ana nodded solemnly, then pressed her face into the crook of Rachel's neck while she counted.

A lump formed in Nancy's throat. It was a beautiful sight, her daughter playing with the other children. "Rachel's really good with her," she whispered to Beau.

"That surprises you?"

Nancy leaned closer. The last thing she wanted was for Rachel to overhear their discussion. "Well, sometimes you make her sound like a demon child."

"I guess it's the nature of the buddy thing. I vent to you, so all you hear is the bad stuff. She's a good kid."

"I didn't doubt that for a minute. Ana doesn't take to other people very quickly. To me, that says Rachel is a very special young lady."

They lapsed into silence—Beau watching their daughters interact, Nancy watching his face go tender. For a second, she could have sworn his eyes misted. Then he blinked and stretched, the moment over.

Rachel still carried Ana on her hip. She pointed toward a row of shrubs and whispered something to the little girl. Then she set her on her feet.

Ana raced behind the shrubs. "Tag. Ew." She turned, puckered and made kissing noises.

Two figures slowly rose from behind the shrubbery. Judging by their sheepish expressions and the traces of snow glistening in the girl's hair, it looked like Ana was correct. They'd been kissing.

Rachel laughed. In that instant, she resembled her father so much Nancy almost did a double take. On Beau, the laugh was almost gleefully wicked. On Rachel, it transformed an ordinary teen into a real beauty.

"You're gonna have your hands full, buddy. The boys are going to be lining up to date your daughter."

"I'm afraid you're right. But she hasn't asked about

dating yet, so I'm hoping for a reprieve, like maybe until she's thirty."

"Good luck." Nancy rubbed her arms, wishing she'd grabbed a jacket on her way out the door. "I take it you don't have family nearby?"

"Nope. They're all in Texas."

"A big family?"

"By Texas standards? No. Just Mom and Dad, my brother and his family."

"I bet they miss you."

"I bet you're going to take forever to get around to what you *really* want to know."

Nancy couldn't help but chuckle. "Hey, I was raised to be a genteel Southern lady. I wouldn't be so rude as to ask you directly why you're here with Emily and her assortment of holiday strays, when you could easily fly to Texas in several hours."

"Do you consider yourself a stray?"

"Aha, answering a question with a question. Did I hit a nerve?" Nancy asked.

"Aha, answering a question with a question with a question. An advanced avoidance technique. Let's just say my family will get along fine without me."

"And Rachel?"

"Believe me, Rachel's better off not having to listen to them compare her to her perfect cousins."

"They'd do that?"

Beau nodded. "In a heartbeat. It would be the same crap they pulled with me and my brother, only extended down to the next generation."

"I'm sorry." She grasped his hand and squeezed. "Nobody deserves that kind of competition." She cleared her throat. "In my case, I'm an only child, so there's no competition. Except maybe with all the *normal* families. The ones with a dad and a mom, the whole ball of wax. It was that way when I was a kid and it hasn't changed much. But I swore Ana wouldn't have the same empty holidays I did."

Nancy thought of the special occasions when she'd wanted her dad home so bad it hurt physically. Her stomach tightened at the thought.

"You've mentioned your mother before, but not your dad."

"He wasn't in the picture." She hadn't seen him since she was ten, but she intended to soon. When the time was right.

"And your mom, what about holidays with her?"

"I want Ana to experience the magic, the joy of the holidays. That leaves my mom out. I told you she's found it hard to accept Ana."

"I figured that was just at first. How about once she got to know Ana?"

"Ana is an extension of my failure. In my mother's eyes, I never could get the marriage-children thing timed right. So I had to travel halfway around the world to adopt a *foreign* child and do the unthinkable—raise her by myself, thus depriving her of the quintessential American family experience. Maybe Ana and I remind her of what she missed by being a single parent."

"You'd think people would be more enlightened by now."

Nancy nodded. "Yes, you'd think. It was just easier for me to accept Emily's invitation."

Beau pointed toward the knot of laughing children. "Looks like the kids are enjoying themselves. You want to go back inside and see if we can help our hostess? You look cold."

"You read my mind. I'm about to turn into a Popsicle." She stood.

Beau put his arm around her shoulder as they headed for the door.

Nancy refused to let herself rest her head on his shoulder. Nor would she allow herself to slide her arm around his waist. She was becoming way too comfortable with this man.

Once inside, Nancy asked Emily if she could put the finishing touches on a few dishes, while Beau was bestowed the honor of carving the turkey.

Watching him, she noted his strong hands, his surgeonlike precision with the carving knife.

Nancy smiled as the children tumbled into the house, complaining of severe starvation.

Ana ran up and wrapped her arms around Nancy's legs. "Me Ana Banana."

Nancy glanced up to where Rachel stood off to the side, pretending indifference.

"That's a wonderful nickname, sweetie, but your real name is Ana—*Ahna*—short for Tatiana."

"Ana Banana. Rachel says."

Sighing, Nancy reminded herself not to sweat the small stuff. "How about if you're Ana Banana on Thanksgiving, and other days you're Ahna?"

Her daughter seemed to think it over. She nodded, satisfied with the arrangement.

Somehow, Emily managed to get every one of her guests to hold hands in a huge circle that stretched through both the living and dining rooms. She said grace, thanking God for the blessing of good friends and good food.

Nancy squeezed Emily's hand as she completed her prayer. When everyone broke apart, Nancy impulsively hugged her friend. "Thanks for everything, Emily. You're the best."

"You might not be thanking me if Great-Aunt Beatrice corners you with one of her long-winded stories."

"It's still worth it to be here. No tension, just lots of love and laughter. You'll never know how much I needed this and how grateful I am to you for providing wonderful memories for Ana. Oops, I almost forgot. Pictures."

She found her purse in the guest bedroom and removed the digital camera she'd bought when she'd gone to Russia for Ana.

Returning to the living room, she took a picture of Ana with Emily. Then Ana insisted on a picture with her new friend, Rachel.

Cheek to cheek, the two girls mugged for the camera. Nancy glanced up to find Beau watching her intently.

It seemed as if the four of them were their own little island.

Beau moved to her side. "Thanks for including her," he whispered in her ear.

"Ana wouldn't have had it any other way. And neither would I. Rachel's a lovely girl, Beau. She'll be fine once she gets past this rocky part of her life. Especially since she has such a caring dad."

Beau didn't answer. He simply dipped his head and kissed her on the lips. A fleeting, *buddy* kind of kiss, she told herself. But her racing pulse said something entirely different.

All she could do was grin at him like an idiot.

His slow smile told her he liked her response just fine. Enough to steal another kiss, this one not nearly as buddylike. Fortunately, the girls and the other guests were too wrapped up in their own celebration to notice.

The rest of the evening was a blur. Rachel helped Ana at the children's table and Beau squeezed in next to Nancy on the couch. Thigh to thigh, Nancy had a hard time thinking. Her heart raced and her mind completely disconnected. She ate as if on autopilot, overwhelmed by Beau's closeness. Or rather, her reaction to his closeness. She wanted to curl up in his lap and make out like a high-school kid.

The way he pushed around the food on his plate, she was pretty sure he felt at least a little of what she felt.

Nancy forced herself to make polite conversation. "Your brother and his family live near your parents?"

"Of course. All the perfect families live in Houston,

or at least that's what my folks think. It's just the black sheep who hide out in Yankee territory."

The candied sweet potatoes suddenly tasted like sawdust. She told herself she was being silly. Just because Beau referred to himself as the black sheep of his family didn't necessarily mean he was anything like Eric, self-described black sheep of the McGuire family.

But that wasn't the end of the similarities. Nancy had gotten so caught up in Beau-the-buddy that she'd forgotten his history as a ladies' man. A history bound to repeat itself.

But that didn't mean Nancy had to repeat her mistakes. She'd learned a lot about herself since Eric's death. And she knew better than to fall for a guy who was incapable of loving her the way she deserved to be loved. So why in the world was she allowing herself to get cozy with Beau?

Resolve propelled her from her seat. Her breathing was shallow. "Excuse me. I need to help Emily in the kitchen."

Beau glanced at her plate and raised an eyebrow, but didn't comment on her abrupt departure.

In her haste, she almost collided with Emily at the swinging door to the kitchen.

"Whoa. That pie was almost a goner." Emily pivoted with surprising dexterity. "Where's the fire?"

"No fire. Just wanted to help." Nancy flushed under Emily's scrutiny.

"I thought I told you to relax."

Nancy shrugged. "Some people are happier busy. I'm one of them."

"Funny, I got the idea you were running from something. Or *someone*."

"What can I help with?"

"You can make some room on the buffet for this pie, while I bring out the others."

"Sure." Nancy was afraid her hands might shake as she accepted the pie, but they remained steady.

"And make sure Beau gets the first piece. I'm sure that Texan's got a soft spot in his heart for pecan pie."

Nancy took the pie to the dining room, admitting only to herself the crust had turned out darn near perfect. She deftly sliced the pie.

Despite Nancy's desire to avoid Beau, she complied with Emily's request and made sure he received the first piece.

As she handed him the plate, he stood. "And here I thought you'd disappeared on me." He lowered his voice. "Are you okay?"

Nancy nodded. "Of course I'm okay. I knew I was needed in the kitchen."

"You're sure that's what it was?"

"I'm sure. Now eat." She waved a hand at his dessert.

He raised the plate and inhaled deeply. "Mmm. Pecan pie, my favorite." It would have seemed an innocent remark, except for the speculation gleaming in his eyes. As if he were the Big, Bad Wolf and she was Little Red Riding Hood on the way to Grandma's house.

Nancy swallowed hard. She glanced toward the children's table, where Ana seemed to be enjoying herself. Her daughter, cheeks puffed out with food, listened raptly to Rachel.

"I, uh, made the pie. It was an old family recipe. I hope you like it."

What a totally lame thing to say. *I hope you like it.* As if his approval really mattered.

"I'm sure I will." He took a bite, closing his eyes with bliss. "Mmm. Delicious. Sweet and decadent, just like you."

Nancy froze. His compliment sounded about as realistic as the laugh tracks used on TV to simulate an audience.

"Fortunately, my pie is a lot fresher than your lines. I'm not a silly teenager, Beau. I've got a child and a life and a past. You can't just flirt without realizing this isn't all fun and games."

Beau frowned. "I thought it was pretty harmless."

"Nothing a man like you does is harmless."

"A man like me?" He stiffened. "What do you know about a man like me?"

Oh, Lord, how had she let this conversation get started? But it was too late to back down. Nancy raised her chin. "I mean a man with your history with women."

Regret flashed in his eyes for a split second, then was gone, replaced by an eerie calm. "I'm sorry. I didn't realize my friendship diminished you in any way. I promise I won't dream of flirting with you again."

"Wait, Beau, I didn't mean—"

"Oh, your meaning was perfectly clear." He turned and walked away, scooting next to Rachel at the children's table—a picnic table with a paper table cloth and a construction paper turkey centerpiece made by one of Emily's boys.

The lump in Nancy's throat grew. She hadn't meant to hurt Beau. Funny, if anyone had asked a couple of days ago, she would have said it was impossible to penetrate Beau's thick hide of self-absorption.

But, now, she wasn't so sure.

CHAPTER SIX

NANCY SIGHED with relief, glad to be back in her own kitchen. Glad for the absence of tension.

It was only seven-thirty, but Ana had fallen asleep as soon as her head hit the pillow. The fresh air and exercise at Emily's house had tuckered her out.

Filling her mug with steaming chamomile tea, Nancy padded into the family room. The room enveloped her like a cocoon as she sat on the couch and tucked her legs beneath her. A fire crackled and popped in the fireplace. She shook out the folds of the chenille throw, tucking it around her legs.

Everything she needed was contained in this house. Her daughter, her refuge and her photos. The rest was window dressing.

Contentment stole over her, until she remembered Beau's attitude during the latter part of the evening at Emily's. He'd been his usual affable, charming self. To everyone but her, that is. He'd entertained the children while she helped Emily in the kitchen so they'd been successful in their attempts to avoid each other.

Nancy sipped her tea, wondering if she owed him an

apology. Shaking her head, she decided not. She'd merely stated a fact. Beau had been married three times previously. Any woman with a brain in her head would consider him a player. And his easy charm only confirmed it. He'd had every female from age two to eighty-two eating out of his hand at the party. Even Emily's Great-Aunt Beatrice had simpered and flirted.

Still, Nancy felt as if she might have been too defensive. But who could blame her? She'd loved Eric with all her young heart and soul, and he'd betrayed her more than once. Finding out he'd fraudulently married another woman and had a son with her had just been the final betrayal. Adding insult to injury was the fact that Nancy had tried for years to conceive and never been blessed with a child.

The phone rang, drawing Nancy out of her thoughts.

She reached across the arm of the couch and picked up the receiver. "Hello."

"Hey, this is Emily. You left your pie tin here and I wanted to drop it off. Great-Aunt Beatrice said she'd watch the kids."

"Tonight? I appreciate the thought, but it's really not necessary."

"Yes, it is. I'll be over in ten minutes. Just wanted to make sure I wasn't interrupting anything."

"No, nothing."

Nancy hung up the phone, smiling. For such an open, loving person, Emily still managed to surprise her.

Several minutes later, the doorbell rang.

Nancy smiled in welcome as she opened the door. The smile died on her lips. "Beau. What are you doing here?"

"I told Emily I'd drop this off." He handed her the pie tin.

"Uh, thank you. She really shouldn't have bothered you. I told her I could pick it up tomorrow." Nancy suspected her friend was up to her old matchmaking tricks again.

Beau shrugged. He wore a lined denim jacket and could have given the Marlboro Man a run for his money in the rugged good looks department. His cheeks and nose were rosy from the evening chill, making him look as if he'd just come from a hockey game.

"Is Rachel in the car?" Nancy couldn't quite keep the hope from her voice. An unchaperoned Beau made her nervous.

"No. She insisted on being dropped off at home before I ran any more boring old errands. That's pretty much verbatim."

Nancy knew what she should do. Any woman with an ounce of manners would invite him in out of the cold. He had returned her pie plate, after all.

But she mentally stomped her feet, like Ana did when she didn't want to do something but knew she'd have to anyway.

"You don't want to come in, do you?"

"How could I resist such an enthusiastic offer?" His humor was generally good-natured and fun, but tonight there was an edge to it.

"Look, Beau, I'm sorry about what I said at Emily's. I was merely stating a fact, not intentionally insulting you."

"Oh, sure. No problem. That makes it better."

Nancy huffed in frustration. She opened the door wide. "*Please* come in. We need to talk."

Beau's gut tightened at Nancy's use of the deadly female weapon—the we-need-to-talk ultimatum. Usually he knew exactly what that phrase implied. It meant a woman wanted to move a relationship to the next level, whatever that level was. To him, it spelled disaster.

He regretted his impulse to return the pie plate. As a matter of fact, he wasn't quite sure why he'd made the offer in the first place. Maybe to show Nancy she was wrong about him. Or maybe in hopes that, given her low opinion of him, she'd consider him an easy, uncomplicated lay.

Nancy tapped her foot, her eyes narrowed. "Well?"

Beau had never dreaded a conversation quite as much as he dreaded this one—and with three ex-wives that was saying a lot.

What had he been thinking?

"Maybe this wasn't such a good idea." He turned, ready to make his escape.

"No, it probably wasn't a good idea. But since you're here, we probably ought to get a few things straight. I'll ask you one more time to come inside."

Beau gave in to the inevitable. He stepped over the threshold and followed her into the family room.

He noted the cozy fire and the soft afghan tossed haphazardly on the couch. His fingers itched to see if the fabric was still warm with Nancy's body heat.

Nancy walked past him. The sight of her in sweat-pants and men's athletic socks sent a message straight to his groin. He could envision a companionable evening where they snuggled on the couch, maybe played cards or a board game. Then, later, he would arrange the afghan on the floor in front of the fireplace, gently lead Nancy by the hand. Once she reclined on the floor, her eyes warm with anticipation, he'd slowly remove every piece of men's clothing from her lush body and make love to her.

"Beau." The sharp tone of her voice was at odds with his fantasy. "I asked if you wanted chamomile tea."

"God, no." The answer exploded from his lips before he had the chance to phrase it in a more tactful way. "I mean, no thank you."

"Have a seat. I'll warm up my tea and then I have something to show you."

Beau noted the absence of a wink, a throaty chuckle or any other indication of flirting. Sighing, he guessed her show-and-tell would not involve naked flesh and edible body lotion. But somehow, he wasn't as disappointed as he would have thought. There was no doubt about it, Nancy McGuire confused him so much he wasn't able to fall back on his old tricks.

She set her steaming mug on the end table, then went over to a large wicker chest placed under the window. She rummaged around for a few seconds, then returned with a large, leather-bound photo album.

Nancy sat on the couch, adjusting the lamp to shine on the album. "Sit here." She patted the cushion next to her.

It was a trap. Beau could practically smell it.

But he did as she requested. He sat next to her, waiting for the show to begin.

She opened the album and quickly flipped through the pages.

Beau caught glimpses of a smiling baby with soft, platinum-blond hair and big green eyes. He stilled her hand. "Wait, I want to see those."

"Those aren't what I want to show you."

"Humor me. I'm interested." That was the problem. He was too damn interested in everything about her. And the photos of her as a kid intrigued him. Maybe he could figure out what made her tick.

Sighing heavily, Nancy deposited the album in his lap.

He got the feeling the lady teaching his Reading-Body-Language-to-Increase-Sales class would have found this somehow significant. As if Nancy had entrusted him with her past.

Shaking off the uncomfortable thought, he flipped back a couple pages to a particularly cute photo of Nancy. She was just a toddler, hanging on to the leg of a man he assumed was her father. The man looked directly into the camera, but the girl's attention was fixed on her father, her eyes shining with hero worship.

Beau cleared his throat. Were there any photos of him and Rachel like this? He didn't think so. The photos of them together were few and far between, mostly taken by bored strangers trying to make a few bucks. And he knew for a fact none of them showed Rachel with anything more than a tentative half smile.

"Keep going," Nancy instructed.

The next page showed more photos of father and daughter. A few included a stunning blonde. "Your mother?"

"Yes. See how happy she was?"

He nodded. Who could miss it? Even a Neanderthal like him could tell she radiated love, most of it centered on the handsome dark-haired man who never seemed to crack a smile.

There were kindergarten pictures, awkward gap-toothed pictures, and it was fascinating to watch Nancy grow before his eyes. He almost wanted to reach out and stroke the sweet face before it lost its babyish roundness.

Then, there was a shift in the pictures. Instead of a family of three, there were only two. The woman and the girl looked confused, as if they'd lost their focus without the man. The girl's eyes no longer shone with adoration and there were deep lines bracketing the woman's mouth, giving the impression she'd turned into a bitter woman.

Beau flipped ahead a few pages. "Did he die?"

"He left." Nancy's voice was flat. "I don't think she ever got over it. I know I didn't."

Wrapping his arm around her shoulder, he hugged her close to his side, thoughts of seduction gone. "Aw, darlin', I'm so sorry."

She tensed. "I don't want your pity. I want you to understand."

Beau eased his arm from her shoulders. This was way more than he'd bargained for. "I do understand."

"No, you don't. Maybe you never will. But I thought I'd try. Turn the page."

He continued looking through the book, watching Nancy grow into a beauty. Her smile was gorgeous, so bright that all the guys had probably fallen in love with her. Some of the girls had no doubt been her friend, others would have hated her guts for being so beautiful.

One photo showed her doing the splits, her cute little cheerleader skirt spread artfully around her long, golden legs. Her hands, clutching pom-poms, rested on her hips. Her smile bothered him.

"Did you like being a cheerleader?"

She shrugged. "I guess. It was a way to get noticed."

"Darlin', you would have been noticed even in the science club."

"Go on." She pointed to the book.

Next were photos of Nancy at the prom, Nancy under the mistletoe, Nancy at a charity car wash. And in all of them, a handsome blond guy was always near, always touching her.

Beau suppressed a pang of jealousy. "Who's this?"

"Eric McGuire. My first love. Maybe my only love."

Swallowing hard, Beau studied the photos of Nancy. She was fooling herself. Or maybe just trying to fool him. But in the photos with Eric, her childish smile of adoration was back, amped up by hormones. This guy wasn't her only love. And he certainly wasn't her first love. Her father had that title. Somehow he suspected Nancy had buried that love once her dad had left, only to lavish it upon Eric McGuire later. The really disturbing part was her facial expression in between the daddy years and the Eric years—all emotion seemed to have disappeared.

There was a photo of her in a graduation cap and gown. Her mother stood next to her, her posture stiff, her smile tight. She didn't much like her daughter, or so it appeared to Beau.

"Maybe I'm just a dense old country boy, but I'm not sure why you wanted me to look at this."

"You really can't see it?"

Beau shifted uncomfortably. "See what?"

"My daddy meant the world to me and he left. Never sent a birthday card, never called. His accountant sent a check to Mom every month, though." She chuckled dryly. "So I guess he did his fatherly duty."

He searched for words, trying in the worst way to be able to communicate with her. He hesitated. "I understand it was rough for you."

"Damn right it was rough. I thought I'd done something wrong to make my daddy leave. My mom certainly thought it was my fault."

"She looks pretty unhappy. It wasn't your fault

though, whatever happened between your mom and dad. Do you ever see him?"

"My dad's in the Elmwood area. It's one of the reasons I came north. But he doesn't know I'm here." She picked a piece of lint off her sweatshirt. "I'm not even sure I'll contact him."

Beau processed the information. He didn't know if Nancy believed the stuff she told him, but he suspected she wouldn't rest until she'd contacted her father.

"Okay…so I guess you see a little of your dad and you in my relationship with Rachel?" It pained him to think so, but the parallel was pretty obvious.

"It's more than that. I felt like my world pretty much ended when my dad left. Nothing was the same. And then one day I noticed this guy. He'd been my friend forever. But all of the sudden I really noticed him. And it was like I was hit by a bolt of lightning."

"It's called hormones."

"Call it whatever you like. That won't change the fact that the world seemed to make sense again. As long as Eric was happy, I was happy. Or at least that's what I thought. And probably the first couple years of our marriage that was true."

"What changed?" Beau prodded.

Nancy shrugged. "It wasn't obvious at first. He started amateur stockcar racing and traveled around the country and I tried going with him. It didn't work. I'm a homebody at heart, and living out of a suitcase made me miserable. Besides, Eric seemed jumpy and picked fights with me."

He snorted, thinking of the stories he'd read about racetrack groupies. "I bet."

"So I stayed home. Every time he left, it seemed like a little piece of me died. But I tried so darn hard to make him happy when he was home. Be the perfect wife. Make his life easy during the day and love him like crazy at night." She glanced at him sideways as if to assess his reaction.

"Okay, I get the picture."

"By the time he died, I'd given away so many pieces of myself, there wasn't much of anything left. I don't ever intend to lose myself like that again."

"I'm not asking you to."

"No, but it's there. Your history with women. It predicts how you will act in the future. Over and over again, you take, but you don't give. Then you end up leaving. I can't do that again."

The abridged version of his life sounded bad, even to him. Beau cleared his throat. "I don't know what to say."

"There's nothing to say. I don't want to hurt your feelings, but if I speak a little bluntly to you, there's a very good reason. We need to be friends for this buddy thing to work. And you need to know why I won't ever allow myself to feel anything for you beyond that."

"Fair enough. But, as you've so kindly reminded me, my behavior with women has developed into a knee-jerk reaction—a bad habit. So if I hit on you by accident, ignore it. It doesn't mean a thing."

"I guess that's a compromise."

Yeah. The compromise from hell.

NANCY STARED into the crackling fire long after she'd walked Beau to the door.

She felt better now that she'd brought everything into the open with him. It made her feel strong and whole to handle the problem in such a mature, rational manner, instead of diving into another disastrous relationship.

Nancy wondered if she could handle her father as rationally if she ran into him on the street. When she'd first arrived in Elmwood, she'd searched every tall, dark-haired man's face, looking for familiar features. Not once in over a year had she encountered anyone who was vaguely familiar.

One course, the easy way would be to call her dad. She had his phone number; the Internet was a lovely tool for gathering information. She hadn't been lying to Beau. Up till now she'd never had the courage to call him.

But tonight, despite what she'd told Beau, the urge to hear her father's voice was strong. It was Thanksgiving, darn it. Glancing at her watch, she decided nine o'clock was still early enough.

Nancy retrieved her address book and found the page with his number. Her fingers shook as she punched the buttons.

The phone rang and rang.

She was about to hang up, when a man answered. She could barely hear him over the background noise of laughter and conversation. Her father was apparently celebrating Thanksgiving to the hilt and she'd very nearly spent the holiday alone.

"Hello...hello," the man said.

Nancy replaced the receiver without speaking.

Hugging a throw pillow to her chest, she rocked forward, tears streaming. She'd only been fooling herself. The lost little girl inside her was still waiting for her daddy to come home.

NANCY HAD BEEN staring at the shampoo bottle for longer than was necessary to read the ingredients. Glancing around, she hoped no one had noticed her concentration level, or lack of it. Fortunately, the store was blissfully quiet this Monday afternoon.

The truth was that she'd been distracted since Thanksgiving. Hearing her father's voice had shaken her more than she'd anticipated. Worse yet was the realization that life had gone on for him. He'd moved, presumably found a new job, made new friends, maybe even remarried.

Shaking her head, she tried to forget her father. He certainly seemed to have forgotten her.

As she glanced up, Nancy noticed a teen slide a bottle of nail polish into her coat pocket.

Frowning, she thought the girl looked familiar, but she couldn't see her face.

Then the girl turned, her profile clear. Rachel.

Nancy's heart went out to the girl. She looked so young and defenseless, yet held her chin at a defiant angle. Nancy remembered seeing a similar expression in her own mirror at about the same age.

Nancy could have kicked herself for having been so self-involved on Thanksgiving. Instead of thinking how potentially horrible the holiday could have been for her and Ana, Nancy should have considered what a difficult transition this was for Beau's daughter. The recent changes in her young life had to have been heart wrenching.

Nancy tossed the shampoo into her basket and casually strolled toward the girl.

"Oh, Rachel." Nancy placed her hand on the girl's arm. "I didn't see you. How are you?"

Rachel froze when she heard the familiar voice, felt a restraining hand on her arm. She'd been caught. Or so she thought.

Assessing the woman's expression, Rachel decided she didn't look angry.

"Oh, hi, Ms. McGuire."

"Please, call me Nancy. Ana hasn't stopped talking about you since Thanksgiving. I think she's got a bad case of hero worship."

Rachel's face warmed, and she couldn't meet the woman's gaze. The compliment made her uncomfortable.

"She really looks up to you. Thanks for taking her under your wing."

Her stomach lurched. Her mother would have said it was her conscience speaking, that Rachel didn't think she deserved the kid to look up to her. But Rachel knew better. It was the cafeteria burrito.

"Um, sure."

"Would you consider babysitting sometime?"

The question caught Rachel off guard. It was the last thing she'd expected. "You mean it?"

"Why wouldn't I?"

"Dad says you're kinda overprotective."

Nancy smiled. "There are worse things than being an overprotective parent. You're right, I wouldn't ask just anyone. You seem very responsible and Ana adores you. Give it some thought. See what your dad thinks."

Rachel nodded. For the first time in days, things seemed a little brighter.

"I'll call you next week. I've got an evening real estate class."

"Okay. Tell Ana Banana I said hi. I've gotta go."

Rounding the corner, Rachel figured she was out of view and slid her hand into her pocket. She removed the bottle of nail polish and placed it on a display as she walked by.

What had she been thinking?

She hadn't been thinking, of course. It had been pure impulse. She'd seen a cool color of nail polish and all of a sudden, the bottle had been in her hand and she was sliding it into her coat pocket.

Rachel knew it was wrong, knew she had the money in her purse to pay for it. But couldn't keep herself from stealing.

Some of the kids at school shoplifted as a game. They claimed to get a thrill from succeeding without getting caught.

But stealing didn't give Rachel a rush. It just made her feel there was something in life she could still control.

Especially since she couldn't control which parent she lived with. Or make them love her.

A pang of regret almost doubled her over.

She'd do anything to be back home with Mom. Clean her room without being told, quit shoplifting, hang out with the geeky good kids. Anything. But apparently that wasn't an option.

So she'd pocketed the nail polish. Because it was the only way she knew to prove to herself that she still existed, even if her mom didn't seem to think so.

That seemed pretty trivial when she thought of what would happen if Ms. McGuire told her Dad. Not knowing was the scary part. Her dad had never been around to discipline her, so she had no idea what to expect beyond being grounded.

Would he give her an "I'm very disappointed in you" lecture like her friend Stephanie's dad? Or would he be so PO'd, he'd send her right back to Dallas?

Hope seeped through her as she recalled the small, glass bottle warmed by her body heat and the threat of exposure.

But what if he sent her back to Dallas and her mom wouldn't take her?

Her spirits plummeted and she got that tight, burning sensation in her stomach.

Rachel swore to herself she'd never steal again. And

like before, it would work for a while. Until she remembered how right it felt to be in control, if only for a few minutes.

CHAPTER SEVEN

BEAU CLOSED his cell phone and leaned back in the chrome-and-faux-leather office chair.

Running a hand through his hair, he wondered if there was any way he could possibly deny Laurie the opportunity of seeing her daughter at Christmas. She'd called, saying she missed Rachel and wanted the three of them to spend the holiday together as a family. What the hell kind of game was she playing? For a once levelheaded woman, she was blowing hot and cold and everything in between.

He hadn't realized he'd actually voiced the observation aloud until Laurie had lashed out at him about her job at the PR firm—the change in partners, the demands for increased productivity, the seventy-hour work weeks. *That* was why she'd given him Rachel. She'd been afraid she'd lose it all financially and didn't have the stamina to deal with Rachel's problems on top of it.

His cell rang again, interrupting his train of thought. *Damn.*

He flipped open the phone and spoke without bothering to greet her. "Look, Laurie, I said I'd think about it. Don't rush me."

"Uh, this isn't Laurie. It's Nancy."

Beau swore under his breath. "Sorry. I thought you were someone else."

"Obviously."

Heart hammering, he hoped she didn't think he had something going with his ex. But after her phone call, he half wondered if Laurie had something up her sleeve.

"It's not like that." He said it as much to convince himself as to convince Nancy.

"Like what?"

"Romantic."

Her throaty chuckle prompted him to exhale in relief.

"Sounded more like a business deal than romance."

"My ex wants to spend Christmas here with Rachel. I told her I'd think about it."

"You don't like the idea, huh?"

"I don't know how I feel." He stood and paced restlessly. "Only a couple of months ago, she dumped Rachel on me. Said I've got her for the next four years. Now, suddenly, the business she works for decides to close over the holidays, so she wants back in the kid's life. It's not fair to Rachel. And it's not fair to me."

"I'm not surprised she wants to see her daughter. I know it would kill me to be separated from Ana for any length of time. But you're right, it's not fair to Rachel."

"I'm not bothered that she wants to see her own daughter. It's the timing. Rachel's just started settling in. I'm still feeling my way blindly through this father thing."

He couldn't begin to talk of the fear uppermost in his mind.

What if Laurie wanted Rachel back?

Beau became aware that Nancy hadn't spoken for several ominous moments.

"You still there?" he asked.

"Yes, I'm here. Are you free to meet me for coffee? I'd like to talk to you. Buddy to buddy."

Her concern touched him. He tried to remember the last time a woman had wanted to talk to him about personal stuff, but he couldn't. Mostly, they'd taken his no-commitment speech as a ban on meaningful conversation. Funny, he hadn't even noticed the lack. And if he had, it probably wouldn't have bothered him. Until now.

He took a deep breath to slow the pounding of his heart. This was no big deal. "How about the place on Cedar, in, say, half an hour?"

"Perfect. I'll see you then."

Beau shut his phone. Shaking his head, he collected the sales reports from his desk and delivered them to the general manager's in basket. He stopped by the receptionist's desk on the way out to let her know when he'd be back.

He arrived early at the trendy coffee house. He waited outside, hoping the fresh air would clear his mind. God knows he couldn't get any work done with his mind and gut churning over this development with Laurie.

Nancy arrived a few minutes later, her cheeks and nose pink from the short walk from her van.

He nodded stiffly, suddenly tongue-tied.

She tipped her head to the side, studying his face. "You look shell-shocked."

"I feel shell-shocked."

"Well, let's get inside where it's warm. Maybe the caffeine will revive you."

"I sure hope so." He held the door for her, then followed. The warmth of central heating enveloped him. The light wood paneling and brass accents gave the place a casual, homey feel. He followed Nancy to where a large sign indicated they were to place their orders.

"You don't drink herbal tea here, too, do you?" he asked.

"No way." She turned to the server. "I'll take a double mocha grande."

When his black coffee and her double mocha whatever was ready, they carried their steaming insulated to-go cups and located a somewhat secluded table in the corner.

"What gives? You seem pretty rattled by the thought of Rachel seeing her mom. Surely you didn't think she'd never want to see Rachel again?"

"To be honest, I didn't give it much thought. I just got the ball and ran with it as best I could. But it's too soon." He hoped his voice didn't contain the panic he felt.

Nancy nodded. "Maybe you could tell her that. Rachel and you both need time to settle in to being family. She'll probably understand."

"What if she doesn't? What if she wonders if something's wrong."

She glanced around the room, avoiding his gaze.

"You think she wants Rachel back permanently, don't you?" he prodded. Verbalizing his worst fears did nothing to allay them. If anything, it made them worse.

Nancy hesitated. "No, I don't. It might be exactly what she says it is. She misses her daughter at the holidays."

"There's a but in there somewhere."

"But I might be wrong. I'm not an expert on working with exes. I guess that's why my parenting experience is different from most of the other members."

"I hadn't really thought of that before. You don't have the hassle of visitation and how to get the other parent to be consistent. You decide on your own what's best."

She shrugged. "Yes, it can be an advantage at times."

"The flip side is that you're it. Like me. There's no one to give you a breather. No one to drop Ana off with when you've absolutely had it."

"Sure there is. Emily." Nancy smiled fondly. "I've been very lucky to have her as a friend. I don't know what I would have done otherwise."

"Yeah, I have to admit, I'm finding this whole buddy thing can really help pull my butt out of the fire at times."

"Sometimes Emily has had to tell me something I didn't want to hear. I guess that means she's a true friend."

"Why do I get the feeling you're trying to tell me something?"

Nancy cleared her throat. "I need to talk to you about Rachel and I'm not quite sure how to broach the subject. And now with the ex-wife thing, you've got a lot on your plate to deal with. But I wouldn't be a good buddy if I didn't let you know what's going on."

Beau tried to decipher her statement but failed. "What do you mean?"

She still wouldn't meet his eyes. "I saw Rachel shoplifting. I mean almost shoplifting."

Beau couldn't help but feel a little like Job—the unluckiest bastard to walk the earth. He decided Rachel's misbehavior must be karmic payback of epic proportions for his sins. "Are you sure? Maybe it was just someone who looked a little like Rachel."

"There was no mistake. I talked to her, Beau." Nancy gave his hand a squeeze. "Let me explain."

"I'm listening." He crossed his arms.

She told him about the incident in the drugstore.

"So she put the nail polish back?"

"My point is that the underlying reason for her shoplifting is still there."

"Great. Just great. And what would that underlying reason be?"

Nancy's pretty green eyes clouded with concern. "I'm not the enemy, Beau. I didn't want to tell you. But I figured you deserved to know. Especially now that Rachel's mother wants to visit."

"Oh, man, I didn't even think of that. If Laurie sees

Rachel's behavior has gotten worse instead of better, she might just haul her back to Texas." The thought lacerated his heart. "And if Rachel'd gotten caught, I don't think the judge would let her off with community service this time."

He glanced around, instinctively looking for a way to escape. As if running away had ever helped his problems. He finally understood that bullshit his dad had spouted about facing his problems like a man. Taking responsibility for his actions.

"What are you going to do?" Her voice was low.

Beau smacked the table with the palm of his hand. "I'll tell you what I *won't* do. I won't sit around and let Rachel slip away from me again. I've been a piss-poor father for the first fourteen years of my daughter's life, and I'll be damned if I'll give up the opportunity of sharing the next four years with her."

Nancy smiled. "That's what I was hoping you'd say. So what next?"

"I'm not sure. Maybe I'll talk to her school counselor. Do some research on the Internet?"

"I have to admit I'm a little out of my depth here. Maybe Emily might be able to give us some pointers. Do you mind if I call her later and ask her opinion?"

"I don't mind. I need all the help I can get."

"Oh, and Beau, I offered Rachel a babysitting job. I'm taking an evening class and I thought the responsibility might give her self-esteem a boost. And it would be a big help for me."

"You'd do that for Rachel?"

Nancy nodded.

Beau reached across the table and squeezed her hand. "Thanks. Nobody's ever gone out on a limb for me like that before."

Come to think of it, no one had listened to him quite like Nancy, either. As if his thoughts meant something. As if she saw more to him than the screw-up brother of Connor or the guy who couldn't seem to get the relationship thing right.

"That's what buddies are for."

"No, it's more than that. You're being a real friend, not just giving me some lame advice." Beau smiled as an ironic thought struck him. "I haven't had a female friend in years. Maybe never."

Sipping his coffee, he had to admit, if only to himself, he hadn't had too many male friends, either. Oh, sure, he'd go out for a beer with some of the guys from work. But that ongoing, know-you-like-a-brother kind of thing didn't seem to come naturally to him.

"Beau, may I ask you a personal question?"

"Shoot."

"What's Laurie like?"

Her question surprised him. In a girlfriend, her curiosity would have been understandable and easily deflected. But in a girl—megaspace—friend, he was at a loss for how to proceed. "Um, she's pretty. Dark hair and eyes. She's in public relations."

"I mean, what kind of a person is she?"

Beau hesitated. "I've never given it much thought."

"You were married to the woman and you never

gave her character much thought? She's the mother of your child for goodness' sakes."

Gone was the warm, accepting camaraderie. In its place was something almost accusatory.

He shifted in his seat, wishing he were anywhere else.

"Okay, she's pretty and smart and too damn good for me. Satisfied?"

Nancy's voice was low. "Did she decide that or did you?"

"What's that supposed to mean?"

"I mean did you use it as an excuse to walk away from her? Tell yourself she'd be better off without you? All that noble stuff, when really you just didn't want to be married?"

"Are we talking about me? Or Eric? Because if you ask me, you were definitely too damn good for him, and he should have done the noble thing and let you have a life with someone who would truly love you. Someone who would come home to you every night, not just when he felt like it."

"Did you? Go home to Laurie every night or just when you felt like it?"

Beau resisted the urge to crumple his to-go cup. He resisted the urge to get up and walk away. And he resisted the urge to lie. He forced himself to meet her eyes without flinching.

"You're changing the subject. But I'll answer you anyway. I told you the truth when I said she was better off without me."

Nancy's eyes clouded. Her mouth turned down at the corners. "And here I'd hoped you'd been a noble asshole instead of a total asshole."

"Honey, in my case, you're better off not hoping anything. Because total asshole is the best I can do." Although there was a time when he'd wanted so much more. He just hadn't been able to follow through.

Nodding slowly, Nancy rose. Her voice was husky. "I'll try to remember that."

Beau told himself it was kinder to disappoint her now rather than later. But darn it all, he wanted her to throw it back in his face. Tell him he was a better man than the man he'd described—more than the scared boy he'd been when he'd married Laurie fresh out of high school.

But the sadness in her eyes told him otherwise. She'd believed every last word of self-condemnation. That was what he'd wanted, wasn't it? For her to know what she was getting into? So when he disappointed her, he wouldn't feel as bad about messing up the first real friendship he'd had in years.

LATER IN THE AFTERNOON, Nancy rested her chin on her hand as she surveyed her best friend and absorbed the homey chaos that was Emily's house. "You sure it was just a regular parent/teacher conference? You're pretty spiffed up."

Emily wore a deep burgundy sweater set with matching slacks. No, sweater set wasn't exactly the way to describe it, at least not in the traditional sense. The underlying tank top plunged to a V, displaying some truly mind-boggling cleavage, barely concealed by a scrap of lace that was demure by Emily's standards. This was her friend's version of her Sunday best.

Emily chuckled—a low, throaty, Mae West kind of sound. "Honey, that peckerhead of a substitute teacher wouldn't know what to do with a real woman. Doesn't know how to handle real kids, either, if you ask me. Said Jason needed a 'reality check,' whatever that's supposed to mean. And that if he and I worked together, there should be plenty of 'teachable moments' to help Jason stay 'on task.'"

Nancy detected concern in Emily's eyes, though as usual she was all bluster.

"I just hope I can put up with this guy until Jason's regular science teacher comes back from maternity leave."

"Jason's a good boy, Emily. I'm sure it will work out."

"Damn right. And here I'd thought maybe this substitute would be a good role model for my son. If I'd wanted Jason to learn how to be a peckerhead, I would've sent him to live with his father."

Nancy grinned. "Speaking of Walt, have you seen him lately?"

"Nah, I think he's lying low because of the back child support. Afraid he'll be arrested on the spot if he sets foot in New York State."

"Are you doing okay?" She knew Emily was proud and independent, but she couldn't help worrying about her sometimes. "You said Larry-the-jerk was behind on child support, too. I can loan you some money to help you get through."

Emily straightened, and since she was five feet eleven, it made her look like an avenging Amazon queen. "Thanks, honey, but I'm doing just fine. I'd rather rob Peter to pay Paul than have those low-life ex-husbands of mine polluting the kids' minds with a bunch of macho BS. I want my boys to grow up to be strong, healthy men who treat women right."

Reaching across the table to grasp Emily's hand, Nancy said, "You're doing a wonderful job of raising your boys. They *will* grow up to be extraordinary men because of you."

Emily eyes misted with emotion. "Thanks, hon, I needed to hear that. Now, tell me about Beau."

Sighing, Nancy examined her teacup, as if the dregs would tell her what she should do. "I caught Rachel shoplifting."

"Ouch."

Nodding, Nancy said, "She put the nail polish back before she left the store, so I guess it wasn't technically shoplifting. But still, it seems like a cry for attention to me."

Tilting her head to the side, Emily said, "Normally, I'd say it was just a phase. But from what I can tell, that child's been through a whole lot of upheaval recently. Poor kid probably doesn't know which end is up."

"Exactly."

"So you want my opinion on whether you should tell Beau?"

"No. I've already told him."

Emily raised an eyebrow. "Hmm. Very decisive."

"I know, I know. I agonize over stuff that affects my own daughter. But this seemed so clear-cut to me. As his buddy and his friend, I had to tell him. I'd want to know if the situation was reversed."

Emily nodded. "How'd he take it?"

"He's scared of losing her. His ex is making noises about spending Christmas with Rachel."

Emily snorted. "His ex will really mess things up, if they don't watch out. Beau and his daughter need time to sort through this."

"That's what I told him."

Nancy stood and carried her teacup to the sink, rinsing it far longer than necessary, hoping her friend couldn't see her confusion, though the other part of her wanted Emily to notice and tell her what to do.

When she shut off the water and turned, Emily caught her gaze. "There's something else, isn't there?"

"I asked Rachel if she would babysit Ana and I'm not sure if I did the right thing. I mean, I trust her with my daughter, but I wonder if maybe my judgment is off. What if I want to help Beau so darn much, I put my own child at risk?"

"Hmm. Good question. But I wouldn't stand by and watch you do something I thought would hurt Ana. She's almost like one of my own."

"Am I fooling myself? Can I make a difference with

Beau and Rachel?" Nancy glanced down at her hands. "Or am I just involving myself in another emotional train wreck on the pretense of helping?"

"Whoa. Back up a second. Exactly who are you worried about?"

Nancy rubbed her left ring finger as if twisting the wedding band she'd removed shortly after Eric's funeral. "I'm not sure. I feel that getting involved might be a huge mistake."

"Beau's not Eric, hon. And you're not talking about marrying the man. You're talking about being a friend to him and a friend to his daughter." Emily hesitated. "You wanna know what I first noticed about you? I mean besides the fact that you're so thin and beautiful I could hate your guts?"

Nancy laughed at her friend's audacity. "That's a compliment?"

"I'm getting to the compliment part. I noticed you have a tender heart. Now, I figure if you allow the past to destroy the best in you, you've allowed Eric to win."

"I've never really thought of it that way. I just think of being tenderhearted as being weak and stupid—putting myself out there to get hurt, over and over."

"Oh, no, hon. If caring makes you stupid, then God knows this world needs more idiots running around trying to make things right."

Nancy's eyes misted. "You're such a good friend. And I'm not the only sap running around Elmwood. You can try and cover with the tough talk all you want, but you care about people a whole lot more than you let on."

"But we're not talking about me. We're talking about you. And how you're doing the right thing by helping a man and his daughter through a tough time. And you're not going to be a coward and turn your back on them simply because you're afraid you'll look foolish."

Hearing Emily state it so bluntly, Nancy saw she hadn't been completely truthful. "It's not so much looking foolish that scares me." Her voice was husky. "It's more I'm afraid of being hurt again. After Eric died, I felt I didn't have anything left to give, that my life was pretty much over. But adopting Ana saved me."

"Ana taught you to open up again."

"Yes. And she taught me some things are worth the risk."

CHAPTER EIGHT

BEAU ALLOWED Rachel's chatter to wash over him as he drove to Nancy's house. There was a certain peace to being with his daughter and sharing these everyday moments, even though he knew they had a ways to go before he could consider them a stable family.

After discussing the shoplifting with Rachel's counselor, he'd decided not to confront her about the incident. Yet. He didn't want to put Nancy in the middle of an awkward situation just when she was reaching out to his daughter. Besides, Rachel had made the right decision and returned the nail polish before she left the store.

The school counselor had agreed with Beau's plan to spend more time with Rachel and try to get her involved in extracurricular activities. Other than that, he'd watch her as closely as possible.

Beau squeezed his daughter's hand. It still amazed him that he'd been part of creating this child. Most days, he felt incredibly lucky.

She glanced at him, arched an eyebrow and squeezed back.

"Doesn't seem like you could possibly be old enough to babysit yet," he commented. "It seems like yesterday, you were Ana's age."

"Dad, I aced the child-care portion of my Life Sciences class. I'll be fine." Her words were brave, but her sentence ended with an unspoken question mark.

"I know. It's my job to worry. Humor me."

"Mom used to say the same thing." Her eyes clouded.

"Hey, what's wrong? You miss your mom?"

"No. Yes. I'm not sure."

"She called the other day."

Rachel's eyes lit. "She did?"

"Yeah. She misses you."

"She has a funny way of showing it."

"Your mom hasn't called before now because she didn't want to confuse things for you. It's not because she doesn't care."

"Yeah, right."

"Sweet pea, adults get confused sometimes, too. I know she loves you."

Rachel folded her arms over her chest. For a minute, Beau thought he saw tears in her eyes.

"You don't have to lie, Dad."

Beau wished he had a crystal ball that would tell him how to handle this delicate issue. Since he didn't, he changed the subject. "Hey, for whatever it's worth, I'm only a couple minutes away tonight. If Ana sets the house on fire or pukes all over the place, you can give me a call."

"If there's a fire, first thing I do is get the child out of the house ASAP. Then go to a neighbor's house and dial 911, *then* call you."

Grinning, Beau said, "How'd you get to be so smart?"

"Oh, I don't know," she replied. "Maybe it's because my dad has moments of near braininess."

"Can I have you put that in writing? Admitting I have moments of lucidity?"

"See, you know what lucidity means. That good-old-boy act may work on the ladies, but I see straight through it. You're as smart as anyone, but for some reason you don't want people to know. Maybe because if they know how smart you are, they'll expect more?"

Beau groaned. "Yeah, I'm the classic underachiever."

"You want to know what I think?"

"I'm afraid to ask."

"I think you were compared so much to Uncle Connor that you quit trying. You figured there was no way you could compete. But you're wrong. You're way better than Uncle Connor will ever be."

Beau wasn't sure if the ache in his chest started because Rachel was too astute or because her version was so much better than what he feared was the truth—that he really was a total screwup with shit for brains.

"Uh, Connor's an okay guy…"

"He treats you like dirt, Dad. The whole family does. How come you let them get away with that?"

"Hey, here we are." Beau had never been so relieved

to reach a destination in his life. "I'll walk you to the door."

"That's not necessary."

"Yes, it *is* necessary. And I will expect the same from any boy who wants to date you. A guy who doesn't care about your safety isn't worth your time. Got it?"

Rachel saluted. "Got it, Dad."

"Good."

Nancy appeared in the open doorway as they walked up the drive. Ana ran to them, wrapping her arms around Rachel's knees, practically bowling her over.

"Whoa, that's an enthusiastic welcome," he commented.

Nancy wore brown leather pants, a gauzy orange blouse, a sweater and low-heeled boots. She looked sexy, sophisticated and successful. A lump formed in his throat seeing the love shining in her eyes as she watched Ana.

"She's been excited all afternoon." Nancy chuckled. "You'd think Santa Claus himself was coming to visit."

Beau noticed Rachel flushed with embarrassment, but seemed pleased all the same. Nancy had been right. It would be good for Rachel to earn some money and maybe some self-confidence, too. Although she seemed to be well aware of his piss-poor view of himself, she was apparently unaware how hard she was on herself.

His steps faltered. A horrible thought hit him. What if his beautiful, smart, loving daughter was so hard on herself because she'd inherited it from him? Or worse yet, somehow observed it as a child and internalized his doubts?

The concept was too terrible to contemplate.

"Hi Rachel, Beau." Nancy's gaze was warm on Rachel, but cooled a bit when she turned to him.

It took a minute for him to find his voice. "Hi. What time you want me to pick her up?"

"My class gets out at eight-thirty. How about nine?"

He nodded and turned to Rachel. "Remember, kiddo, I'm only a phone call away if you need me."

Rachel tossed her head as if the idea were ludicrous, but he detected relief in her eyes.

She lifted Ana and settled her on her hip. "Come on, Ana Banana. We're gonna have a good time."

Beau tried not to appear worried as he said goodbye, but he must've failed miserably.

Nancy placed her hand on his arm. "I'll have my cell phone, too, if she needs me. Don't worry, she'll be fine."

The kindness in her eyes made him wish they'd left the coffee shop on a better note. And reassured him in a way he hadn't known in a long, long while.

The need to lead her to a quiet corner and apologize was almost overwhelming. As was the need to suggest they get together Saturday night. Maybe rent a few goofy G-rated movies, pop some popcorn in the fireplace and kick back with the girls for a simple evening.

Shaking his head, he realized he wanted more from Nancy than a quick roll in the hay. Not only did he want her body, he wanted her companionship, too. He didn't understand what was different about Nancy. Was it her warmth, her compassion? Or was it the way her whole face lit up when she laughed. He didn't have a clue. All he knew was that Nancy had shared a part of herself when she'd shown him her photo album. She'd opened up long enough to let him know he had the power to destroy her. And he couldn't bear to see that happen.

NANCY FIDGETED in class until the teacher frowned at her.

He had no way of knowing she was imagining all the horrible situations that could arise from letting a four-teen-year-old girl care for her precious daughter.

She trusted Rachel as much as she trusted any teen to care for her daughter. Probably more than most. But that didn't change the fact that accidents happened.

At break, she removed her cell phone from her purse to check for messages. No news was good news, right?

One call wouldn't hurt. She started to dial her home phone and then recalled the beauty of Rachel's smile as she'd eased Ana onto her lap for a story. No, she couldn't destroy the tenuous thread of trust they were building.

Still, she drove home a little faster than she should have.

Seeing Beau's truck in the driveway, her heart thumped wildly.

Unlocking the door, she rushed into the house. "What happened?"

Beau came out of the kitchen, a dish towel thrown over his shoulder. "Nothing. I just came by a little early."

Rachel tiptoed down the stairs, shushing them as she went. "You'll wake Ana. You don't know how many stories I had to read," she whispered.

Nancy exhaled silently as she followed Rachel and Beau into the kitchen, where their voices wouldn't carry upstairs. "Usually, it takes at least three books before she drops off."

Rachel smiled and ticked them off on her fingers. *"Goodnight Moon, Cat in the Hat* and *Are You My Mother?"*

"Yep, you hit all her favorites."

"Then she needed a drink. Then she needed a kiss good night…"

"And had you check under her bed—"

"For monsters."

Nancy could have hugged the girl for having such a generous heart. "Thank you for being patient. She has her bedtime routine and can't sleep without it. Sometimes I wonder if it's because she slept in a dormitory at the Russian orphanage."

"Really? She's from Russia?"

"Really."

"How cool. I've always wanted to go there."

"You have?" Beau eyed his daughter intently.

"Sure, Dad. I'm going to study languages in college. Maybe be a diplomat or work in the foreign service."

The loss written on his face would have been comical if it hadn't been so genuine.

In that moment, Nancy understood just how powerfully Beau wanted to forge a relationship with his daughter. Did he have what it took to be a real father for the long haul? Only God knew. But if Beau failed, it certainly wouldn't be for a lack of interest.

Seeing this side of him made her uncomfortable, like a tiny nagging pebble in her shoe, demanding attention but evading her search.

Nancy reached into her purse for her wallet. Withdrawing a crisp twenty-dollar bill, she pressed it into Rachel's palm.

The girl's eyes widened. "This is too much. I was only here a couple hours."

"Think of it as a bonus for being so good with Ana. I'm sure you earned it after so many stories."

"Thank you. Oh, and I washed the dishes we used. Dad dried."

Beau met Nancy's eyes and shrugged. "Her idea, not mine."

Turning to Nancy, Rachel said, "Ana's a good kid. Anytime you need me to babysit, just give me a call."

"I'll need you to babysit Tuesday and Thursday evenings for the next six weeks if you're available."

"Sure, that'd be great. And I can help keep an eye on her at the Parents Flying Solo meetings, if that's okay. Free of charge, of course."

"That would be really reassuring. Jason's great with her and everyone pitches in to watch the kids, but I'd feel a lot better if I knew you were watching her, too." And to her surprise, Nancy wasn't just saying that. She was able to relax because Rachel had proved herself capable. Maybe she'd be able to get more out of the meetings if her mommy antenna wasn't always on high alert.

Beau placed the dish towel on the hook. "Then we'll see you tomorrow. Isn't there some sort of speaker coming?"

"Yes, I think she's speaking about single parenting, dating and, uh, intimacy." For some reason, the thought of being in the same room with Beau while contemplating her sex life was a daunting thought. Almost downright scary.

BEAU PAUSED in the doorway to the community center, wondering what in the heck he was getting himself into.

"Bye, Dad." Rachel headed toward the attached kitchen, where the older kids were going to do some sort of snack or craft with the little kids. The activity served a twofold purpose. It kept the younger children from getting restless during the longer meeting and to keep underage ears from hearing some of the challenges of having a sex life as a single parent.

Beau saw Emily and smiled.

Then he zeroed in on Nancy.

His breath caught in his chest.

Wearing snug-fitting jeans and a soft green sweater, her hair was pulled back in a simple ponytail. Her eyes glowed as she carried on an animated discussion with Luke Andrews, owner of the hardware store and a man old enough to be her father.

All thoughts of keeping his friendship with Nancy

low-key fled at the sight of another man putting the moves on her. As a matter of fact, Beau remembered a pressing need to discuss the minivan's maintenance schedule with her. Moving to her side, he nodded to the older man. "Luke, good to see you."

"Beau, how's the car business?"

"Never better."

"Nancy, I might just contact you about that lot next to the store. It sounds like an ideal opportunity to expand the store and add extra parking," Luke said.

"Exactly. And the seller is willing to work out financing, if necessary."

"I'll call you. Now, if you'll excuse me, I volunteered to set up chairs."

Once Andrews was gone, Beau found himself tripping over his tongue. Nancy wore very little makeup, looking like the fresh-faced teen in her cheerleading photos.

Oh, yeah, car maintenance. "I, um, wanted to make sure you were aware of the maintenance schedule on your minivan. Might void the warranty if you overlook the oil changes."

"Yes, you went over it with me at the dealership. But thank you."

Okay, he should turn around and walk away. He wasn't her type, or more accurately, he might have been her type if he didn't have a string of failed marriages behind him.

Tilting her head to the side, Nancy commented, "Rachel did a wonderful job with Ana the other night."

Beau only heard part of what she said, distracted by

the way her ponytail brushed her cheek when she moved her head like that. By shoving his hands in his pants pockets, he avoided the temptation of trying to tuck the soft bundle of spun gold over her shoulder.

What were they talking about? Maintenance?

The freckles sprinkled across her nose gave her a pixie-ish look. And the deep green of her sweater intensified the gold flecks in her eyes. He could almost see his reflection as her pupils dilated.

"Beau? You were about to say something?"

"Yeah, um, you really need to keep the van on a strict maintenance schedule."

She frowned. "We were talking about Rachel and Ana. Are you okay?"

"Sure. Rachel. Ana." His thoughts raced. Oh, yeah, babysitting. "Rachel seemed to think it went well, too. She had fun with Ana, made it sound like one big girly party."

Nancy's smile was warm. "Yeah, it sounded way better than my boring old meeting. I always wished I had a sister to hang out with."

"There were times I would have given my right arm to be an only child."

"I guess I should be grateful I missed out on all that sibling rivalry stuff. Did you and your brother fight a lot?"

Beau had a hard time concentrating on her words. He wanted to trail his fingers over her smooth, fresh skin. Gaze into the depths of her eyes until he felt he knew her inside and out. Forget Beau Stanton was the worst man in the world for her.

He nodded his head toward the rows of folding chairs. "How about if we grab a couple chairs toward the back."

Her eyes sparkling, she said, "What, you don't want to be in the front row when the speaker discusses sex and the single parent?"

"I'd rather not." Beau-the-jokester came to Beau-the-lost's rescue. "But if you want to sit up front, be my guest. Maybe you'll even be chosen for audience participation." He waggled his eyebrows for good measure.

Laughing, Nancy smacked him on the arm. "Bite your tongue."

Several off-color remarks about what he'd like to do with his tongue flashed through his mind, but he didn't voice them. Instead, he grasped her by the hand and pulled her toward the last row of chairs. "Come on. If we're lucky, maybe they'll have Luke Andrews tell us about the fine art of picking up dates in the hardware store."

"You're bad. He's a very nice man."

"Yeah, nice, but definitely hitting on you."

"We were merely discussing a possible business deal. But he is kind of cute."

He glanced sideways to make sure she was joking. But her expression was thoughtful. "I wonder if he's ever asked Emily out. He'd be great with her boys."

Beau exhaled with relief. "Emily, yeah, sure."

CHAPTER NINE

RACHEL LAUGHED at Ana's antics as they decorated cupcakes in the community center kitchen. The kid really was a little ham. And seemed way older than two.

Crossing her eyes, Rachel could just discern the dot of whipped cream Ana had smeared on her nose. Wiping it with her sleeve, Rachel made monster growling noises and used her creepy witch voice, saying, "I'm going to get you, little girl."

Ana's eyes widened. Then she giggled and pointed at Rachel.

Mike Ruiz, junior class president and all-round-whiz-kid, seemed to appear out of nowhere. "You've got some on your chin, too."

Where in the heck had he come from?

If she'd had any idea he was nearby, she wouldn't have been clowning with Ana.

Stunned, she was unable to formulate a reply.

Mike sat down across from her, picked up a scratchy paper napkin and wiped the smudge from her chin. "Here, let me get it for you."

"Thanks." Rachel didn't know whether to crawl under the table or do a victory dance. Mike had never acknowledged her presence in the three months she'd been at Elmwood High, even though they both participated in the lame peer mediation program.

"You here with your mom or dad?" he asked.

"My dad." She tossed her hair. "My mom got tired of me a couple of months ago and handed me off to Dad."

"Yeah, same thing happened to my cousin. Sometimes parents are that way."

"Who're you here with?"

"My mom. She's in between husbands again. I'm betting she's looking for a replacement tonight. We've gotta be out of my stepdad's house in thirty days."

"Where will you go?"

Mike shrugged. "Wherever my mom can find a guy to take us in."

Whoa. Rachel tried to wrap her mind around the fact that perfect Mike Ruiz had a less-than-perfect home life.

"That's rough."

He shrugged again. "Been through it before. Once I get my scholarship to NYU, it won't matter."

Suddenly Rachel saw his overachievement in a new light. "Is that why you're in all those clubs?" And spend every spare minute in the library? But Rachel would rather die than admit she kept tabs on his whereabouts.

"Yep. Have to be a well-rounded student for most scholarships. That, and it sure beats sitting at home playing video games."

His crooked grin sent a zing of awareness through her. He was just about the handsomest guy she'd ever talked to. Who'd have thought Rachel-the-quiet-new-girl would be talking to Mike like they'd known each other forever?

"Hey, you think we oughta listen in on their sex talk?" He nodded his head to the swinging kitchen door.

Rachel's face warmed. "I'm supposed to be watching Ana." Glancing around, her pulse galloped when she didn't see the girl. "Where is she?"

"Probably hiding. My brother and sister do it all the time. Don't worry, we'll find her." He looked under the table.

Rachel checked the closet. No Ana.

"Ana," she called her name softly, looking toward the swinging kitchen door. "Where are you?"

"She—"

"Shh. I need to be able to hear." Rachel slapped her hand over her mouth. She'd shushed possibly the most popular guy in her school. What had she been thinking? She'd been thinking about survival, pure and simple. Mike might never ask her out, but at least she'd live to see another day. If she lost Ana, her dad would ground her forever, or worse.

Her stomach knotted at the thought of what her dad would say if she told him she'd temporarily forgotten her duties while she chatted with a totally hot guy from her school.

Her breath came in short gasps when she thought of Ms. McGuire learning Rachel had lost her precious daughter. Black spots wavered before her eyes.

"Sit down."

She felt a warm palm on the back of her neck as she complied. Through the haze, Rachel was aware that Mike had actually touched her.

"Put your head between your knees."

"But Ana—"

"We'll find Ana. But we can't do it if you faint on me. Just breathe. In. Out. Slowly."

NANCY CHUCKLED at one of Beau's whispered jokes. His presence was making a surprisingly dry presentation bearable.

As the woman droned on about safe sex, Beau leaned closer. "You think she's ever had sex?" His breath was warm on her ear.

"Maybe. But I bet she didn't enjoy it," she murmured.

"Missionary position, lights off, flannel nightie and a hairnet."

Nancy coughed to cover a laugh.

"Or maybe she only pretends to be a repressed prude." Beau nudged her. "Maybe she's a dominatrix in disguise."

She crossed her eyes in response, attempting to avoid a reproving glance from the Parents Flying Solo president. And attempting to avoid the fact that she enjoyed Beau's warped humor a little too much. His nearness wasn't helping her concentration, either. He sure smelled nice. Clean, masculine, one-hundred-percent male.

"Aw, come on. You can't see her in black leather?" he asked.

The president turned and glared at them.

Nancy resisted the temptation to stick out her tongue at him. She wasn't usually one to challenge authority.

Using her hand to shield her mouth, she leaned closer to Beau. "Yes, unfortunately, it's a visual that will probably be burned in my brain forever. And the poor guy cowering at her feet is the PFS president."

Beau's shoulder bumped hers a couple times. It took a minute for her to figure out he was laughing silently.

Glancing sideways, she was surprised to see him pinch the bridge of his nose as if in pain. But in reality, he was shielding his face as tears of mirth seeped out of the corner of his eyes.

Heads turned. The speaker pursed her lips in disapproval.

Nancy grasped Beau's arm. "Excuse us," she whispered to the man in the aisle seat, as she pulled Beau toward the door.

She just managed to get him outside and shut the door when he burst out laughing. Then she joined him.

Nancy laughed until her sides ached. It felt so good.

RACHEL RECOVERED quickly once she thought about how goofy she probably looked with her head between her knees. Straightening, she said, "Let's check outside."

They went to the garden, calling Ana's name softly.

Rachel's panic rose as the minutes ticked by.

Mike touched her shoulder. "Hey, we'll find her."

His concern for her was real and she fell just a little in love with him. As if she needed any encouragement.

Then they rounded the corner and stopped cold.

Her dad and Ms. McGuire seemed to be having some sort of epileptic fit. Or maybe convulsions. They were laughing like crazy. And it looked like Ms. McGuire was crying, too.

"That's my dad." Rachel stepped forward, ready to call to them, but Mike placed his hand on her arm and shook his head.

Then her dad quit laughing and got this really funny expression on his face. All serious and sappy at the same time. He cupped Ms. McGuire's face with his hands and laid a liplock on her. Not the hot, sexy kind Rachel saw in some of the racier PG-13 movies, but kind of sweet.

Rachel's stomach did a somersault.

She didn't want to think about what the kiss might mean. Couldn't begin to imagine life getting more complicated than it already was.

So she scrunched her eyes shut for a moment and wished it all away. When she opened them, all she saw was Mike, his broad shoulders blocking her view of her dad. Mike's eyes were warm with understanding, as if he knew exactly how she felt. As if he'd been through it himself.

"Come on," he whispered. "Let's check the kitchen one more time."

Grasping her hand, he twined his fingers through hers.

It felt so right to be with him, holding hands, feeling like she'd known him forever, when they'd never even spoken before. Her head was spinning with new thoughts and sensations. Some involved her dad. Some involved Mike. But Rachel knew for a fact she'd never look at things the same again. She felt much older than fourteen. And wished she could go back to being a little kid again, where everything was safe and simple, and parents didn't change. *Life* didn't change.

"Hey, Rach, snap out of it. We've got to find the little girl right away. Otherwise, we'll have to tell her mom."

Following his train of thought, Rachel broke into a jog, pulling him by the hand. "Yeah, won't that be great? 'Hey, Ms. McGuire, would you quit kissing my dad so I can tell you I lost your daughter.'"

How had such a great day turned so crummy?

NANCY FELT bereft when Beau released her. She'd never been so affected by a relatively innocent kiss.

"I should say I'm sorry, but I'm not." Beau trailed his hands down her arms before stepping away.

The man had done nothing more than make her feel cherished and he felt he should apologize.

Regret warmed her cheeks.

"No, I should be the one to apologize." She stroked his jaw, loving the texture of his skin beneath her fingers. "I've become so jaded I refused to believe people could change. Maybe I've been wrong."

"Darlin', I haven't always believed much in people, either. But I have to believe a man can change." His voice was husky. "Because my life pretty much depends on it."

The longing in his eyes touched her heart. His honesty touched her soul. She opened her mouth to tell him so, when she was tackled about the knees. *Later,* she mouthed, as Beau stepped back.

Glancing down at her daughter's smiling face, Nancy felt she'd been blessed by so much more than she deserved.

"Hi, honey. You have chocolate all over your face."

Rachel approached slowly, walking with a teenage boy. A cute teenage boy.

Beside her, Beau stiffened.

"We decorated cupcakes," Rachel explained. "Unfortunately, she got more frosting on her than on the cupcake."

"Oh, well, nothing a bath won't cure." Nancy's heart was light as she kissed Ana's sticky cheek.

"She might have a tummy ache later. Somehow she managed to grab the frosting bowl and hide under the sink." Rachel shifted uncomfortably, her eyes dark with concern. "I'm sorry, really I am. I should have been watching her closer."

Beau stepped forward. "Why weren't you?" His jaw pulsed as he glanced at the boy.

To his credit, the boy met Beau's eyes without flinching. He extended his hand. "I'm Mike Ruiz, sir. It's my fault. I was talking to Rachel. Just talking."

Nancy held her breath as Beau eyed the boy's extended hand. Challenge crackled in the air.

She touched Beau's forearm. "They were just talking."

Beau visibly relaxed, then shook the boy's hand.

"Glad to meet you, Mike. For future reference, Rachel isn't allowed to socialize while she's babysitting."

"Daaad," Rachel moaned, her cheeks flushing a pretty shade of pink.

Nancy wondered if the girl knew how lucky she was to have a father who loved her enough to embarrass her. Nancy hadn't been so fortunate and had paid dearly.

"Rachel, you know the rules." Beau's voice was firm. "And I'm sure Mike wouldn't want you to get in trouble."

Mike shook his head. "No, sir. I won't bother her while she's babysitting in the future." Turning to Rachel, he said, "See you in study hall tomorrow. Save me a seat?"

To Nancy's discerning eye, Rachel practically levitated. But the girl's reply was appropriately unaffected, "Sure. See you tomorrow, Mike."

Nancy had the feeling Beau's relationship with his daughter was about to get a whole lot more complicated.

BEAU RESTED his forearms on his desk, staring at the glossy automotive calendar on the wall without really seeing it.

He'd had a pretty good conversation with Rachel after the meeting last night. She'd been a fountain of information about Mike Ruiz. Including the fact that he'd never really had a home to call his own. How he'd been busting his butt in school to ensure his future. And how he couldn't wait till he was able to go to NYU. Because there he would know exactly how long he would be in a given place. And he would know his dorm room was his own for the allotted length of time. That meant he wouldn't have to worry about his mom's latest boyfriend throwing him out on his rear.

Beau's conversation with Rachel had reinforced the school counselor's earlier advice—to give Rachel a stable home, a place where she felt safe and knew she was loved unconditionally. A place where she would always be welcome.

Beau picked up the phone and dialed Nancy's number from memory.

His palms started to sweat on the second ring. She picked up on the third.

"Hey, it's me. Beau."

"Is everything okay? Is something wrong with Rachel?"

"No, everything's fine."

"You sounded so serious, I figured something was wrong."

"Nothing like that. I know I kind of flaked out on you the last time we went looking at houses, but I want to try again. This time I'm sure."

She hesitated. "I'm with a client right now. Can I call you back in about half an hour?"

"Better yet, how about I drop by your office?"

"That will work. I guess I'll see you in half an hour."

"See you then."

Beau leaned back in his chair and sighed. He was too nervous to wait around the office. A man of action, he decided to leave now and wait in his car at Nancy's office if need be.

He grabbed his jacket off the coat tree and headed out the door, his knees shaking only slightly.

It took him all of ten minutes to drive to Nancy's office.

There were a couple cars in the parking lot, one of which was Nancy's new van.

The receptionist was away from her desk when he went inside. Grabbing a news magazine off the coffee table, he pretended to read, all the while bouncing his foot.

Nervous. Hell, yes.

After about ten minutes, Nancy escorted a young couple to the door, promising to let them know immediately if their counteroffer was accepted.

With her hair twisted in some kind of a knot at the nape of her neck and a slim navy pantsuit, she seemed very businesslike. Almost intimidating. Until he focused on the sprinkle of freckles on her nose and realized she was the same woman he'd seen wearing men's athletic clothes and a girlish ponytail.

She smiled in greeting, but her eyes held a question. "Come on back to my office."

He followed her into her office.

She gestured for him to sit in the oversize upholstered chair opposite her desk. "What makes you think you're ready to commit to a house now, when you weren't before?"

His palms started to sweat again. His instincts told

him to make a run for the door. But he didn't. He sat in the chair and explained, "Something Rachel said made me understand how essential it is. We *need* a house. No matter how much stuff scares me, I've got to get past it. For Rachel."

"What stuff?" she asked.

"You know—a mortgage, home-owners' insurance, repairs, pest control. Things stable, responsible people do."

Stable. Responsible. Who'd have thought Beau would want those things?

CHAPTER TEN

NANCY WAS A BIT SURPRISED by the intensity in Beau's voice. Apparently, he'd rededicated himself to the home-buying cause.

"How about Saturday afternoon?" she asked.

"Yeah, I can do that. I'll just work a split shift at the dealership."

"Do you have a better idea of what you're interested in this time? Any particular neighborhood?"

"No. Just something nice. Not fancy, but safe."

"Most of Elmwood is pretty safe. I'd suggest looking in the same areas we saw before, avoiding the neighborhoods where there is a high rate of rentals. That brings down the property value."

"Okay. Sounds good so far."

Reaching into her desk drawer, Nancy thumbed through file folders until she found the literature she was looking for. "Here, why don't you take these brochures home and read them. I probably should have given you this information the first time around. I have a new mortgage person I'm using and she's top-notch at ferreting out special programs. Mary Ellen will leave no stone unturned finding the best possible deal for you."

Beau nodded.

"I'll have her call you ASAP so we can get you pre-qualified through her."

"Good deal." He rose. "I guess I'll see you tonight when I drop off Rachel. I've been very clear she's not allowed to have any friends over while she babysits."

Nancy chuckled. "Yes, I think you hammered that point home last night. Neither Rachel nor Mike will have the excuse they didn't know."

Beau shifted. "What did you think of the kid?"

"He seemed like a nice enough boy."

"I'm not sure what I'll say if Rachel asks to date. She's too damn young."

"You're her father. You're genetically programmed to think your daughter is *always* too young to date."

"There's no way I'm going to let her go out alone with this guy. I don't care how good a student he is. And I don't care if Rachel hates me for the rest of her life."

Nancy sighed. "I agree with you. Fourteen is too young to car-date. But maybe group dates with a bunch of friends? Or watching movies at your house, super-vised, of course."

Beau grunted. Folding his arms over his chest, he said, "It probably won't be an issue. This Mike proba-bly won't even ask her out."

Nancy had seen the way Mike looked at Rachel and thought Beau was in denial. But she didn't think it wise to share her observation.

Instead, she stood. "My next appointment is due any time. I'll have Mary Ellen call you and get all the information. In the meantime, I'll see what I can find in the multiple listings. Properties are turning pretty quickly now."

"Good. I'd like to find a house and close as soon as possible."

She raised an eyebrow. "Are you going to tell me why you're in such a hurry?"

"Pretty much the same reasons as before. But something she told me about Mike's home life clinched it." Beau hesitated in the doorway to her office. "She mentioned this Mike boy moves around a lot and he hates it. Can't wait to leave home. I don't want Rachel to feel that way. I want to show her that I'm in this for the long haul. That I'm not gonna give up like Laurie did, even if I make a few mistakes or Rachel makes a few."

Nodding, Nancy said, "It makes a lot of sense. Was she close with Laurie?"

"I thought so. But now I don't know what to think. The sad part is, Rachel doesn't know what to think, either. Except that her mother quit loving her."

"Wow, that's intense even for an adult. Throw in hormones and the other teenage angst, and you've got a daughter who really needs you. I think you're doing the right thing."

"Thanks." His pace slowed as they neared the waiting area. Clearing his throat, he said, "Your opinion means a lot."

His awkward admission warmed her heart. "I'm glad."

He touched her arm. "You need a friend, all you gotta do is call. I'll see you tonight."

Nancy saw him to the door and returned to her office, but she couldn't concentrate on her work. When was the last time a man had valued her opinion? Or even asked her to listen?

Sadness washed over her as she realized Eric had never needed her on that level. He'd loved her, in his own selfish way, and been glad to come home to her when he was in town. But he'd never felt the need to confide in her about serious things. It was almost as if he'd held himself apart, watching their relationship from a distance.

She'd thought Beau was exactly the same. But now, she wondered if she might be wrong.

THE DRIVE to Nancy's house that night was nearly silent. Rachel seemed lost in thought as she stared out the window. He didn't want to let her push him away, but he wasn't sure how to get her to open up. When she'd been five, it had seemed simple—all he had to do was produce a quarter from her ear, as if by magic, and the chatter would begin.

"You remember that magic trick I used to do? Pull a quarter from your ear?"

Rachel nodded. Her voice was low when she said, "You used to tell me accepting a penny for my thoughts was selling myself short because I was so much smarter than most kids." Her eyes clouded. "I believed you. Even though you didn't always come visit when you said you would, when you were there I believed I was smart, a fairy princess almost. Then you'd leave and I'd be plain old Rachel again."

Beau swallowed the regret that threatened to overwhelm him. He couldn't redo the past, much as he wanted to. His voice was husky when he said, "Sweet pea, there has never been anything plain about you. You've always been a brilliant fairy princess to me. You remind me of your mom when we met in high school."

"I do?"

"You sure do. When I saw her the first time, I thought she was about the most gorgeous woman I had ever seen." He could remember how he'd felt about Laurie in those early days. How he'd thought he was the luckiest guy in the world. He wasn't quite sure when that changed. But Rachel needed something to hold on to right now.

"And your mom is one smart woman. She had to be, she picked me." He grinned and nudged her with his elbow.

Rachel rolled her eyes. "She calls marrying you a moment of insanity."

"She's probably right. That's why I want you to grow up to pick a guy who loves you the way you deserve to be loved. Don't ever settle for less."

"Why all the fatherly advice?"

"I've been, um, looking back at my life, the things I wish I'd done differently."

"It doesn't change anything."

"No, it doesn't." He shifted in his seat. His chest grew tight as he thought about how selfish he'd been for so many years. "I know I wasn't there a lot for you when you were little...."

He hoped she'd jump in and save him, but she didn't.

"But I want you to know I'm here for you now. One hundred percent."

"Thanks, Dad." She gave him a sideways look. "Is something wrong?"

"No, nothing in particular."

"She told you, didn't she?"

"Who told me what?"

"Ms. McGuire told you about the other day in the drugstore."

"That's not what's going on here."

Rachel folded her arms over her chest. "You're spying on me because you don't trust me."

"I'm *not* spying on you." He felt like Laurel to his conscience's Hardy. *This is a fine mess you've gotten us into this time, Stanley.* "I'm trying to be supportive, Rachel. I thought you needed to know that I regret being a crummy father and I intend to do better. I want you to feel secure."

"Have you been talking about me to Ms. McGuire?"

How had this conversation gone from bad to worse? With Rachel's emotions as changeable as the weather, he never knew at which extreme she'd be from one moment to the next.

"Why would I do that?" The best defense is always a good offense. "Is there something you should be telling me?"

"I knew it. She told you."

They pulled into Nancy's driveway. He turned off the engine. "Look, Rachel, none of this is Nancy's fault. She's a friend. And sometimes friends talk."

"Was that before or after you kissed her?"

He turned in his seat so he could see her better.

Her lips trembled as she fought for control.

"Sweet pea, is that what this is all about? You're mad because I kissed Nancy?"

"No, this is about you not trusting me. And the whole while you're not telling me the truth. What else don't I know, Dad? Do you have a private investigator tailing me? Have you picked out an engagement ring for your 'friend'? Is that when you ship me back to Mom's?"

Beau took a deep breath. Should he tell her about the house? No, things were confused enough as it was and qualifying for a mortgage wasn't a slam dunk by any means.

He shook his head. "No, darlin', none of those things are true. Nancy only told me about the drugstore because she was concerned about you. And she was right to tell me, Rach. What's this really about? The shoplifting? Because I'm wondering if you're trying to distract me so I forget you almost committed a crime."

Rachel's eyes narrowed. "And I'm wondering if you're using this whole alleged crime thing so I forget you're spying on me and lying to me."

Beau's head pounded, his heart pounded and he wanted to throw his hands up in defeat. But he couldn't. There was too much at stake. "Enough."

The one word echoed in the cab of the truck. He'd never used that stern a tone with her before.

Her eyes widened. Then she flung open the door and clambered out. The door slammed behind her.

Beau rested his forehead against the cool, hard plastic of the steering wheel. What the hell had happened? How in the world could he handle this woman-child who could outmaneuver him with one hand tied behind her back?

One thing was for sure, without a felony conviction on her record, she'd make a fine lawyer.

But she didn't want to be a lawyer. Did they hire felons for the foreign service? Somehow he didn't think so. Beau mentally added that fact to his puny arsenal of weapons.

NANCY WAS DISAPPOINTED when she pulled into the driveway and Beau's truck wasn't there. Class had been released early, but she'd still hoped he might be there. It had been, well, nice to have another adult to come home to, however innocuous the interaction was. And she'd enjoyed chatting with Rachel the other night.

Tonight, however, the girl had been unusually withdrawn, hostile almost.

Nancy unlocked the front door and tiptoed in. All was quiet except for the low murmur of voices from a TV sitcom.

Stepping into the family room, she saw Rachel asleep on the couch, one hand tucked under her cheek, the other wrapped loosely around Ana, who snuggled in the curve of her body.

Both girls looked so peaceful she didn't have the heart to wake them.

Removing the chenille throw from the back of the couch, she carefully covered the two sleeping forms. Neither stirred.

Poor babies. They were both exhausted.

She heard a vehicle pull into the driveway.

Hurrying to the front door, she opened it before Beau could ring the bell.

"Shh." She pressed her finger to her mouth, then she gestured for him to follow her through the entryway.

When they reached the family room, she stopped and whispered in his ear. "Aren't they sweet?"

Her heart flip-flopped at the love in Beau's eyes as he looked at his daughter. His jaw softened and he appeared to be anything but a playboy. He looked like a man who would give his life for his child.

Nancy wondered if her father had ever gazed at her that way. Or had he simply walked away from an annoying responsibility and never looked back?

Her vision blurred as she watched Beau tuck the blanket under Rachel's chin, only reinforcing what Nancy had missed growing up without her father.

And in her marriage. She'd never seen Eric exhibit that kind of tenderness.

Brushing the moisture from her eyes, Nancy tried to focus on what she did have. A beautiful daughter and wonderful friends who loved them both. Sadly, she wondered if she was too damaged to choose happiness, even when it might be right in front of her.

Beau turned, gesturing for her to follow him to the entryway.

Straightening her shoulders, Nancy was determined not to dwell on her loss and the confusing emotions bubbling to the surface.

She stepped in beside him.

"I wanted to talk to you real quick." His voice was low. "Rachel doesn't know what we discussed earlier today. And I'd rather keep it that way until we know I'm qualified. So I'd appreciate it if you didn't mention it."

"Sure, no problem. She was sort of…distant tonight. Is anything wrong?"

Beau sighed. "We argued on the way over here. She accused me of spying on her and thinks you helped."

"She's mad at me." It was a statement, not a question. As a teen, Nancy had sometimes felt like the whole world was out to get her. "I'll have to regain her trust."

"So will I."

Nancy touched his sleeve. "She loves you, Beau, and needs you. It will all work out."

"I hope you're right. I feel like I'm in over my head. I know I can't turn back time and relive those years I wasn't there for her. But I want to be the kind of dad she deserves."

She wanted to wrap her arms around his waist and rest her head on his shoulder, telling him how much she'd misjudged him. But she couldn't allow herself to be that vulnerable.

Patting his arm, she said, "You're doing everything in your power to make things right with Rachel, to give her the stability she needs. And I think she senses that, underneath the crummy teen stuff."

He smiled a wistful smile. "Why didn't I meet you years ago? Maybe you could have talked some sense into me."

"You don't really believe that, do you?"

"No, but it's nice to think so. And hope like hell I've learned from my mistakes."

Nancy suppressed a pang of envy. Because she wasn't sure she'd learned from her mistakes. And the knowledge left a gaping hole in her life, in her ability to move on.

"Have you learned?" Her voice was husky.

Nodding slowly, he said, "Yes, I think I have. At least enough to know I want to try. I never wanted that before."

The determination in his voice sent a shiver down Nancy's spine, as if she were witnessing some supernatural transformation. But she wasn't. She was simply fortunate enough to be along for the ride while Beau discovered everything he had to offer.

Nancy blinked rapidly and stepped away. Beau Stanton was a much braver person than she would ever be.

"They're worth it, don't you think? Wanting the best for them." Beau gestured toward the living room where the two girls slept.

Nancy swallowed the lump in her throat.

Had her father ever wondered if he was enough? Wondered if he could make a difference in her life?

Sometimes Nancy wished she could talk to her

mother about her dad. Find out what happened to make him leave. But her mother refused to talk about him.

Restlessness prodded Nancy. She paced the entry-way, straightening a picture on the wall, nudging the throw rug with her toe to achieve some semblance of symmetry.

Without looking at Beau, she asked, "Did I tell you I called my father?"

His hands were gentle on her shoulders as he turned her to face him. "No, you didn't tell me." He hesitated. "When?"

"Thanksgiving night… I hung up without saying anything."

"So he still doesn't know you're in town?"

Nancy shook her head. "No."

"What're you going to do if you run into him at the grocery store?"

"I've lived here almost six months and I haven't seen him yet. At least I don't think so. I've only got those old photos. I probably wouldn't recognize him. Besides, I want to talk to him when the time is right. When I'm ready."

Beau's eyes were warm with concern. "Are you sure?"

Nancy said, "Yes, now more than ever. Seeing how much you regret the time you've missed with Rachel has made me wonder what might happen if I get in touch with my dad."

And made her recognize she was damaged goods.

Beau stepped closer. "I'm afraid you might get hurt."

With a hollow chuckle, she raised her face, knowing he probably saw the little-girl-lost reflected in her eyes. "Too late for that."

"Aw, Nance." He wrapped his arms around her.

"I'm prepared to walk away if he doesn't want to have anything to do with me. But I'm hoping he loves me as much as you love Rachel."

Beau cradled her neck with his hands and kissed her forehead. "I hope so, too, darlin'."

CHAPTER ELEVEN

RACHEL AWOKE to the murmur of voices nearby.

Checking around the room, her pulse pounded. Until she realized she was curled up on Nancy's couch. The conversation was apparently between her dad and Nancy—she couldn't see anyone, but their voices came from the foyer.

Ana snuggled closer in her sleep.

Rachel relaxed, pulling the blanket up around her chin. It was cozy here. Peaceful.

Until the voices from the other room grew more distinct. Straining, she heard her dad call Nancy "darlin" in a tone he'd saved for Rachel before tonight. She'd *never* heard him talk that way with her mom. Her parents seemed more like polite acquaintances than ex-lovers. Rachel had a hard time even imagining them having sex to create her.

As it was, she wondered why her dad had a pet name for Nancy anyway. If she weren't so warm and content, Rachel might tiptoe to the arched doorway and peek. Too bad the angle was wrong for her to see them from the couch.

Then she realized the light outlined their shadows against the opposite wall.

Like finger puppets.

Her dad was the taller one, of course. He stepped closer to Nancy. His voice was deep, sleepy almost.

Nancy's shadow raised her face to look at him.

Then his shadow leaned down to kiss her.

Rachel smothered a groan.

She'd convinced herself the kiss at the community center had been a fluke, nothing more. But a second kiss. That made her wonder if the two were dating.

Her breath caught. Just when she'd gotten to know her dad, he might ruin everything by falling for Nancy?

Flinging back the blanket, she disentangled her arm from beneath Ana.

The little girl sat up abruptly, her eyes open and staring.

"Shh. It's okay, Ana Banana," she whispered. "Lie down on the nice warm couch."

Ana rubbed her eyes, yawned and complied with Rachel's request.

Rachel stood quietly and moved toward the arch.

She stopped to listen, but didn't hear a thing.

When the voices started again, they grew clearer, as if her dad and Nancy were headed in her direction.

Jogging back to the couch, Rachel wedged her body into the space between Ana and the back of the couch just before they rounded the corner.

Rubbing her eyes, Rachel sat up and mumbled, "I must've fallen asleep. When did you guys get back?"

"A few minutes ago," Dad said. "Let's get your stuff and hit the road. Tomorrow's a school day."

Turning to Nancy, he reached out and touched her shoulder. "Think about what I said?"

Nancy nodded. "I won't do anything rash."

What constituted rash? Picking out their china pattern?

Rachel rubbed her stomach. The burning, twisting feeling was back.

NANCY SMILED as she watched Ana cavort with the Patterson boys, chasing them around Emily's family room as Saturday-morning cartoons flashed in the background. Saturday-morning brunch at Emily's house was one of the best ways Nancy knew to chase away nagging thoughts of her father.

Ana's squeal reached an earsplitting pitch.

"Think they'd go for quiche instead next time?" Nancy asked.

Emily rolled her eyes, wrapping her hands around a Betty Boop coffee mug. "I wish. Whose idea was it to make Belgian waffles anyway? I would have been just as happy to take them to the drive-through at Mickey Dee's for a breakfast sandwich. Much easier and no sugar buzz to contend with afterward."

"Oh, but that wouldn't have been nearly as fun as the waffle snowmen. The powdered sugar was a stroke of genius."

"You give me too much credit." Emily smiled into her coffee mug.

Despite her tough exterior, she was the most giving person Nancy had ever met. Maybe that's why Emily adopted the brazen exterior—as a shield to protect herself from the users and abusers who seemed drawn to her kindness.

Which reminded Nancy she had a mission. "Have you been to the hardware store lately?"

"No. Why?"

"Oh, no particular reason." She attempted wide-eyed innocence. "I just thought maybe you might have run into Luke Andrews recently."

Emily's eyes narrowed. "No. What gives? Are you trying to fix me up?"

Shrugging, Nancy commented, "He seems like a nice guy. Stable, owns a business, wouldn't hurt a fly."

"And boring."

"Maybe he's just shy."

"Are we talking about the same man? Luke Andrews, the guy who can talk for hours on the merits of using a wood screw versus a nail?"

"Okay, so he's not the most exciting man around. He's still kind, stable and available." She hated to see her best friend struggle to make ends meet as a single mom on an administrative assistant's paycheck. And Emily had once, while watching a romantic comedy, admitted she missed having a man hold her as much as she missed sex. Nancy wanted to see her friend happy.

"Speaking of the most exciting man around, how are things going with Beau?" Emily asked.

"The buddy thing seems to be working out."

"Your eyes don't sparkle like that when you talk about your other friends. Think maybe you might feel something for him?"

Nancy busied herself clearing the breakfast dishes. "Okay, I admit I find him attractive."

"That's a given. He's definitely been blessed in the looks department. Do you ever talk about serious stuff? Laugh about goofy stuff?"

"Yes, we laugh a lot. And I…told him about my father."

"Honey, that *is* serious. You don't even talk about your dad much with me."

Nancy shrugged. "There's nothing new to tell you about my father. You already know the story. The funny thing is, it's not really romantic with Beau. Just friendly. He's easy to talk to."

"So you're taking it slow. That doesn't mean it won't turn into something hot and heavy later. Besides, I've heard taking it slow is a good thing. I might even try it myself the next time I date."

Chuckling, Nancy said. "I wouldn't count on it. You don't do anything halfway, especially falling in love."

"Who said anything about falling in love? I mentioned dating."

"Point taken. You know, I didn't intend to get involved with a man again this soon. If ever. I'm happy with my life the way it is. I have Ana and my friends." Nancy couldn't meet Emily's eyes. Couldn't admit she hoped there was still a chance her father might welcome the opportunity to be a part of her small family.

"Sometimes a woman needs more." Emily's tone was wistful. Then she seemed to redirect her thoughts. "I know Eric hurt you bad, hon. But maybe meeting Beau is a bonus you didn't anticipate. Maybe you have a second chance at the happily-ever-after part."

Sighing, Nancy tried to put her jumble of emotions into words. "When I first met Beau, I would have sworn he was the absolute worst man in the world for me. I saw a guy who'd failed at every commitment he'd attempted. I saw three divorces and probably three devastated women left to pick up the pieces of their lives. I'd look at him and see Eric all over again."

"And now?"

"Now I don't know what I feel. In here—" she pointed to her heart "—I see a man who's made mistakes but is trying like crazy to learn from them and be a father to his daughter. I see a man whose been hurt by the people he loved and trusted. It doesn't excuse his past behavior, just explains it. And then I wonder if I'm up to taking one more chance, or if I'm nuts to even consider it."

"You're not nuts. You're seeing the real man behind his actions." Emily's eyes were bright, her voice husky. "And you're giving him a chance. Just like you gave me a chance to be your friend."

Nancy reached across the counter and grasped her hand. "Em, I'm honored to be your friend. I don't know what I would have done without you." Swallowing hard, she blinked away threatening tears.

Emily returned the pressure of her hand. "We're

friends because you didn't look at me and see a loud, obnoxious woman who's been around the block a few too many times. You looked into my heart and saw something worthwhile there, just as you saw something worthwhile in Beau."

"Oh, Em." Nancy's cheeks were wet. Stepping around the counter, she gave her best friend a hug. "You've always been worthwhile, except in your own eyes. Thanks for reminding me to keep an open mind, even where Beau is concerned." Especially *where Beau was concerned.*

NANCY'S HEART SKIPPED a beat when she saw Beau across the crowded coffee bar later that morning. She couldn't help but see him in a new light after her heart-to-heart with Emily.

When he glanced up and saw her, his smile warmed her. He waved her over.

Making her way through the other patrons, she nodded and smiled to a few acquaintances.

She eyed the two to-go cups on the table. "Is one of those for me?"

"Yep. I hope I got it right."

"Perfect. Thank you." Nancy was touched that he'd remembered her preferred drink. She took the seat opposite him.

"You said on the phone you had several houses for us to look at today?" he asked.

"Yes. Emily offered to watch Ana. My regular sitter had a wedding today. What did you tell Rachel?"

"I hate lying, but I don't want to get her hopes up about this house and have it fall through. I told her I had to catch up on some paperwork at the dealership."

"Let's hope that after today we'll have a contract on a house and you can share the good news with her." She smiled encouragingly. "Mary Ellen was able to pre-qualify you for more than we anticipated. Even though you haven't been at the car dealership long and you moved around a lot, you were with the same sporting-goods manufacturer for eight years. That shows stability. And your income is consistently growing."

He nodded. "I have a good shot at Salesman of the Month for December. That'll make two months in a row. Word of mouth seems to be working."

"Here's what Mary Ellen was able to get for you." She slid the paperwork across the table. "I think we can definitely find what you're looking for in this price range. It'll give you a larger selection than we had before."

Whistling under his breath, Beau said, "That much?"

"Have some caffeine. It'll help the shock."

"No kidding."

"Here is the printout for six houses I think fit your needs. I've made appointments with the owners. I didn't bother to check if the houses we've already seen are still on the market. Unless you wanted a second look?"

"No. None of them worked for me." He hesitated. "I have to admit I'm kind of nervous. We're talking a lot of money here."

"Nothing to it." She smiled to reassure him. His nervousness was kind of cute. "I'll walk you through the whole thing."

"This is a big step for me. I didn't figure I'd ever be a home owner. I was on the road too much."

Reaching across the table, she grasped his hand. "But it's so important. I think it'll make a real difference in the way you and Rachel view home. There's nothing like walking into a house and knowing it belongs to you. There's something solid and enduring about that."

"I'm counting on it."

SEVERAL HOURS LATER, Beau shifted uncomfortably in the passenger seat of Nancy's minivan. As they pulled into the driveway of an immaculate ranch house, he noted the pluses—big trees, large yard, nice location. But he couldn't seem to work up any enthusiasm. It had been the same at the first five houses.

He felt guilty for dragging Nancy out when he didn't seem to be any more committed to buying than last time. No, that wasn't right. He wanted to buy a house; they just couldn't seem to find the right one.

"This listing went up yesterday. It's priced reasonably. If you decide you like it, you'll want to move fast. Properties like this don't stay on the market long."

Move fast. Why did the thought strike terror in his soul? He was the king of moving fast. And he had the two-day marriage with ex-wife number three and a grainy photo from a Las Vegas wedding chapel to prove it.

But no doubt about it, he anticipated being in a house far longer than he'd been married to ex-wife number three.

"Nice curb appeal," Nancy commented.

"Uh-huh."

She threw him a questioning look as she inserted her key card into the lockbox. Removing the house key, she opened the front door and stepped inside. "Very nice."

"Yes, it is." He could honestly say that. But he couldn't envision this place ever being *home*. The word just conjured up a special feel. Warm, cozy, casual.

"It's got three bedrooms. Rachel would have her own room and you could turn the spare into an office or exercise room."

He nodded in agreement, while all he wanted to do was turn tail and run as fast as he could. Reminding himself this was for Rachel, he forced himself to look in each bathroom and make approving noises about the large master bedroom.

When they reached the kitchen and he commented on the nice stove, Nancy stopped and placed her hands on her hips.

"You hate it. There's no need to pretend for me, Beau. I'm on your side."

"I don't hate it. I just don't feel much of anything about it."

"Out of six houses, wasn't there even one you felt a twinge about?"

"Nope. None. I tried, really I did. But none seemed like home."

Nancy persisted. "Are you looking for something specific that I'm not showing you?"

He shook his head. "They're fine. Really."

"Close your eyes," she instructed. "When you envision the perfect home, what do you see?"

"You really want me to close my eyes?"

"Yes. Now. No arguments."

Sighing, he closed his eyes.

"Okay, you're in the perfect home. It feels good there. It feels right. You know you'd love to wake up there every morning."

A blurred image came to him. As it grew clearer, he was suffused with warmth. Yes, there was one place that made him feel the way she had described. He concentrated on the image. It came into sharp focus, so real he almost felt he was there.

"You're smiling. Tell me what you see."

He opened his eyes. "Same thing I saw last time we looked at houses. I see your house."

But this time, you're in it.

CHAPTER TWELVE

BEAU BOLTED upright in bed, his heart pounding as he shoved back the sweat-dampened sheets. How could he have been so stupid?

No wonder he was freaked out about Laurie wanting to see Rachel. He'd never even thought of having the custody arrangements changed with the courts. As far as he knew, Laurie could take back Rachel anytime. Or have him charged with custodial interference. It would be her word against his. And with his track record, his word probably wouldn't look so good.

Why hadn't he thought to have an attorney draw up documents modifying the agreement? Because he'd been burying his head in the sand, as usual, counting on Laurie to do what was right. But then again, Laurie was behaving erratically.

Should he call an attorney? He didn't even know if his divorce attorney was still in business. Or should he leave sleeping exes alone, hoping things worked out okay?

He'd turned the problem over in his mind until he'd fallen back asleep shortly before dawn.

Hours later, after a shower and a cup of coffee, he was no closer to a decision.

Fortunately, Rachel hadn't seemed to notice how distracted he was as he'd stumbled through their Sunday-morning routine. French toast from the freezer, while reading the Sunday paper—Rachel the comics, Beau the sports page.

Then she'd excused herself and gone to her room. That was normal teen stuff, wasn't it?

Running a hand through his hair, he almost picked up the phone to call Nancy. But it was too early.

A short while later, his phone rang and he sighed with relief. It was probably Nancy, sensing on some level that he needed a buddy to talk to.

He picked up the receiver. "Hey, I was about to call you."

There was silence for a few seconds, then, "Hi, it's Laurie."

Shit. "Hi."

"Have you given any thought to my suggestion for Christmas?"

"I've been pretty busy." *Trying to find the right place to raise our daughter and trying to figure out if I can trust you to do the right thing.*

"Did you talk to Rachel?"

"Yeah, we discussed it. She's not wild about much of anything these days."

"I'm sorry to hear that. I'd hoped things would be better for her there."

"Did you? Or was I just a last-ditch option?"

"That's not fair, Beau. I've already explained I was at the end of my rope. You're her father."

"Damn right, I'm her father. And I don't like to see her hurt. So, I can't help but wonder about your motives."

He regretted being so blunt when he heard Laurie's indrawn breath.

"I'm sorry, Laurie, I shouldn't have said that. I know it wasn't easy for you all those years."

"I did the best I could." Her voice was taut, low.

He recalled the preteen years, when Laurie and Rachel had been practically inseparable. And how effortless Laurie had made it seem. "You're a good mother. She's difficult with me, too."

"Not anything serious?"

Beau sighed. There was no way he'd confide about the shoplifting.

So he chose one of the lesser problems. "She thinks I'm spying on her."

"Are you?"

"Not in an active kind of way. Elmwood's not that big. Word gets back to me when something's wrong."

"What *is* wrong?"

Beau ran his hand through his hair. He wished he could be up-front with Laurie, tell her how much he worried about their daughter. "Just the usual teen stuff."

"May I talk to her?" Her tone was hesitant.

"Sure, you can talk to her anytime. I bet she'd like to hear from you… But the Christmas thing, I don't think it's a good idea. Too disruptive at this point."

"You don't have to give me an answer today." There was an uncharacteristic note of pleading in her voice. "Think about it. I'd just be there a couple days. I miss her, Beau, so bad it hurts. But this was something I needed to do. If I didn't, I was afraid I was going to lose it with her."

"She can be a real pistol."

"Is she there? You said I could talk to her."

"Yeah, hold on a sec."

Covering the receiver with his palm, he called Rachel to the phone. "It's your mom. She wants to talk to you."

His chest tightened as he watched the emotions play over her face. Surprise, fear, excitement. Then he left the room, allowing them privacy and space for Laurie to convince Rachel she still mattered to her mother.

And tried not to worry what that might mean in a custody dispute. Because he didn't intend to lose his daughter again.

RACHEL WANDERED aimlessly in the garden of the community center. She could hear the laughter and voices from inside, but didn't want to join in. Didn't feel like she belonged. In order to escape outside, she'd asked Jason Patterson to watch Ana.

Maybe it was talking to her mom that had put her in this weird mood. It was good to hear her mom's voice, maybe too good.

Her mom had tried to explain that dumping her on Dad had nothing to do with the Texas shoplifting incident. Her mom needed to work some things out, needed a break.

Rachel wasn't sure she believed that.

But no matter how many times she replayed the conversation in her mind, things only got more muddled, not less.

She shrugged off her worries; Rachel had other mysteries to ponder. Mike Ruiz, for one. He'd been friendly at school, but hadn't made any attempt to ask her out.

Rachel heard door hinges squeak and looked up to see Nancy headed her way.

She didn't greet the woman, just ignored her.

Nancy stood next to her. "Are you okay?"

"Why wouldn't I be?"

"I don't know, I just thought you looked like you could use some company."

"Actually, I came here to be alone." Should she come out and say she knew Dad had been with Nancy on Saturday when he'd said he was doing paperwork at the dealership? Should she ask if they'd slept together?

God, she hoped the answer was no. The very thought made her want to gag.

Nancy ignored Rachel's cool response. Or she was too dense to figure out she wasn't welcome.

Instead of leaving, she sat on the bench next to Rachel. "My dad left me and my mom when I was young. It felt like I had this huge hole in my life. Only my dad never came back. You're luckier. Your father is trying his best to be a dad to you now—"

"Yeah, I know he's trying." Rachel couldn't keep the sarcasm from her voice.

"I wonder if you know how hard it is for him? But that's not my point. My point is that I'd love to be able to have a second chance with my dad, even as an adult. Just to have him in my life." Nancy's voice was all husky.

Rachel glanced up. The grief she saw in Nancy's eyes drew her in. This was a new side to the confident woman she presented to the world.

Rachel couldn't help asking, "How old were you when he left?"

"Ten."

"So you had ten years with him."

Nancy smiled wistfully. "Yes, so I knew what I was missing the rest of the time. I'm not saying you weren't dealt a crummy hand. All I'm saying is you have a second chance. Don't blow it."

A male voice intruded on their private conversation. "Well, look who we found, Ana Banana. We found your mom and Rachel hiding out here in the garden."

Rachel turned at the sound of her father's voice and couldn't help but return Ana's happy grin.

"Hey, Ana Banana." She held out her arms to the little girl and settled her on her lap.

"You ladies are missing all the fun. Role-playing." Dad shuddered.

Rachel and Nancy groaned in unison, then traded conspiring smiles.

"Thanks for warning us." Nancy winked.

"To be honest, I was trying to escape, too, but found Ana wandering around looking for you guys. Apparently Emily's boy isn't very sympathetic about boo-boos."

"You got a boo-boo, sweetie?" Nancy checked her daughter's elbows, then knees. "Aw, you scraped your knee and Mommy wasn't there to kiss it and make it better."

Ana twisted in Rachel's lap and patted her face. "Ray kiss."

Rachel hadn't been too excited about the nickname at first, but now it made her feel kind of warm and fuzzy inside. Wrapping her arms around Ana, she gave her a big hug. "You bet I'll kiss your boo-boo." And she did.

"Don't suppose I could convince you ladies to go for an ice cream instead of role-playing?" Her dad grinned wickedly.

"Ice cream," three voices chimed in unison.

And before she knew it, Rachel was licking a double-dip cone at the Dairy Barn, sharing a booth with Ana. Her dad sat next to Nancy on the other side.

Although she pretended not to notice, she watched the two adults closely. They didn't touch. They didn't stare deeply into each other's eyes. All they did was laugh and tease. Rachel and Ana were usually butts of the lighthearted jokes.

No, they seemed more like good friends than boyfriend and girlfriend. Maybe she'd misinterpreted the shadow kiss Thursday night.

But Dad's Saturday afternoon was still unaccounted for.

"So, Nancy, how did you and Ana like the park Saturday?"

Nancy frowned. "We didn't go to the park. She hung out with the Pattersons most of the day."

Interesting. "I must have misunderstood Ana."

How to find out if they'd been together? She'd have to work on that one. In the meantime, she'd enjoy her ice cream and the teasing.

After Ana stuck her nose in the cone and wore it like a rhino horn, Dad said, "You girls are like the Three Stooges. Larry, Curly and Moe."

"No, no, no," Nancy argued. "You've got it all wrong. I'd prefer to think we're Mary, Rhoda and Phyllis from the Mary Tyler Moore Show. You know, the one where Mary drives that great classic Mustang and tosses her beret in the air?"

Dad smiled, as if Nancy'd made the best observation ever. "Or Ginger, Mary Ann and Mrs. Howell?"

"You're a *Gilligan's Island* fan, too?" Nancy squealed.

And it was all downhill from there. Before the ice cream even had a chance to melt, Dad had made a date with Nancy for next Saturday night to watch a ton of those corny old shows. Worse yet, Rachel would have a ringside seat. She and Ana were included in the bore fest.

For a woman who looked like she could be a Cowboys' cheerleader, Nancy seemed surprisingly excited about the domestic side of the evening. "I'll make several flavors of popcorn. Everybody like cheddar cheese? How about kettle corn? Maybe we can make homemade ice cream." Her eyes sparkled.

Oh, yippee.

NANCY PUT the finishing touches on the snack tray. Why did she think it had to be perfect? Had her mother burned it into her brain that she had to be a Stepford Wife in order to keep a man? Nancy honestly enjoyed cooking, entertaining and creating a comfortable home. But she wondered if part of being the perfect wife might have been an attempt to hang on to her husband.

She rolled her eyes at the utter lunacy of that thought. As if rosebud radishes could have kept Eric from straying.

Ana sneaked a handful of pretzels, her eyes alight with excitement. "Ray and Beau're comin'."

Her daughter's joy was infectious. "Yes, they're coming anytime now."

Lifting Ana, she settled the girl on her hip. "You did a very nice job putting out the napkins and paper cups."

"Nice." Ana clapped her hands.

"Give Mommy an Eskimo kiss?"

Ana leaned forward and touched her nose to Nancy's, giggling. Nancy's chest grew tight. *This* was what she wanted from life. A family who loved her and good friends like Emily and Beau.

The doorbell interrupted the tender moment. Ana squirmed to get down. She was off and running the second her feet hit the ground. "Come on, Mommy. Ray's here."

Smiling, Nancy followed close on her heels.

When she opened the door, she couldn't help but laugh at Beau's armful of movies. "Come on in. It will take days to watch those."

"I couldn't decide, so I thought I'd rent them all. It's not like they're new releases and cost an arm and a leg."

"True." Not that she'd mind watching movies with him for days on end. He was turning out to be a pretty entertaining guy.

"Here, can I take your coat, Rachel?"

The girl scowled, but handed her the coat. "Why couldn't we watch something halfway modern, like *The Simpsons?*"

"Ah, grasshopper." Beau wrapped an arm around her shoulder and closed the door behind them. "When you have a true appreciation for culture such as *The Three Stooges,* you will no longer require such crass entertainment."

"Yeah, sure, Dad. Whatever you say. Where's Ana Banana?" Rachel made a show of looking everywhere but at her feet, where Ana bounced excitedly.

"Here, Ray."

"I can hear her, but I can't see her."

Ana tugged on the knee of Rachel's jeans. "Right here."

Rachel glanced down and gasped in surprise. "There she is. I found her."

Ana giggled.

Rachel picked her up and settled her on her hip so naturally they could have been sisters.

Nancy followed them into the family room, with Beau bringing up the rear.

"Wow," Beau said when he saw the table loaded with snacks. "I didn't want you to go to so much trouble."

"It's no trouble, really. I enjoy entertaining."

"Whew. I'm afraid I'm underdressed for entertaining." He glanced down at his gray sweatshirt, the faces of Larry, Curly and Moe barely distinguishable after many washings.

"Humor me, okay. I like to make things nice for the people I lo—I mean, for my friends." Nancy's face warmed at her inadvertent slip. She'd almost said the *L* word and wouldn't that have been awkward? The man was merely bringing their two families together for an innocent evening of wholesome fun, and she'd nearly made it sound as if her mission was to blend the families permanently.

"Where food's concerned, I'll eat anything. But thanks for doing this."

She avoided the question in his eyes.

Pointing to the beanbag chairs she'd filched from Ana's room, she said, "Those are your princess thrones, girls. One of you gets to be Belle and the other will be Cinderella." She referred to the characters emblazoned on each seat.

Ana and Rachel both dived for Belle and almost knocked heads.

"Ana has the advantage of speed and being lower to the ground. Looks like you're Cinderella, Rachel," Beau commented.

Rachel grumbled good-naturedly. Once she was ensconced on her throne, pretend pouting, she stated, "That's okay. Belle gets the Beast. *I* marry a handsome prince." Then she stuck out her tongue at Ana.

Ana promptly returned the gesture, then laughed.

Rachel even managed a chuckle.

"Would you mind getting the DVD ready while I put out a bucket of ice for the drinks?" she asked Beau.

"Got it."

Beau had the DVD in the player, ready to go when she returned from the kitchen. He'd chosen a seat at one end of the couch.

Nancy sat near the other end. Neither of them hugged the arm, but there was a few feet between them.

Rachel glanced at the space separating them, a gleam of approval in her eyes.

After that, Nancy sat back and simply enjoyed the movies and the excellent company.

It was around ten when Nancy heard Ana start to snore. She retrieved two soft throws from the chest and gently tucked one around her daughter.

Her eyes met Rachel's as she handed her the second throw. "So you can get comfortable," she murmured.

Rachel accepted the throw, the nearest thing to an olive branch they would probably get.

Around eleven, she noticed Rachel had fallen asleep, the blanket drawn up under her chin.

She nudged Beau and nodded toward the girls.

He smiled. "Do you want to watch another movie, or should we leave?"

"Another movie."

After Beau changed the movie, he came back to the couch and sat next to her. Not crowding her, but close enough that their knees touched. She leaned against him and sighed with contentment. The warmth of his body soothed her, made her feel as if everything was right with the world.

He draped his arm around her shoulders. "You still think your seventies' comedies are better than my Stooges?"

"They both have their good points. If I'm going to be compared to one of the two, I'm still partial to Mary, Rhoda and Phyllis."

Fingering a lock of her hair, his voice was lazy when he said, "You'd have to be Phyllis then, with your pretty blond hair. You're much nicer than her, though."

"I sure hope so."

"I had fun tonight."

"So did I. And I think the girls did, too."

"You don't have to make a big fuss over us. Rach and I are happy with microwave popcorn and a can of soda. Next time I'll bring the soda. I'm pretty sure I could convince Rachel to do this again."

She raised an eyebrow. "And when are you proposing another movie night?"

"Next Saturday?"

"You've got a date. And I'll even let you pop the popcorn."

Tipping her chin, he kissed her.

He tasted of popcorn and root beer and she wanted to melt into him. It had been so long since she'd been held by a man and really kissed, right down to her soul. She murmured his name and threaded her fingers through his hair.

He deepened the kiss, his hands warm on her rib cage, and her breasts tingled in anticipation of his touch. But she knew they couldn't take it beyond kissing. Not with the girls in the room.

Withdrawing a fraction, Nancy kissed the corner of his mouth before abandoning him altogether. "We need to stop."

"I know. But that doesn't mean I want to." He rested his forehead against hers.

"Neither do I."

A rustling noise came from the direction of the Cinderella beanbag. Rachel sat up and yawned, rubbing her eyes. "Dad, can we go home now?"

Beau's eyes were dark with regret as he drew away from Nancy.

"Yeah, sweet pea, I guess it's time to go."

CHAPTER THIRTEEN

BEAU THREW another load of laundry in the washing machine. Things with Nancy were looking up. He didn't know where they might be headed, but if they took it slow enough, maybe it could work out. Saturday night had been slow, sharing only a few kisses. That would be enough for now. It had to be.

Surveying the dismal apartment laundry room, he smiled at the sad, little artificial pine tree someone had placed in the corner. The tree leaned to one side and dropped artificial needles, but it kind of represented the hope of the season. Hope that he could get past whatever was holding him back from buying a house. And hope that things would work out with Nancy—and Rachel.

He still hadn't told Rachel about looking for a house. A part of him knew he should involve her in the process, but he was afraid it would fall through and he'd be responsible for another disappointment in her life. He didn't want to be the cause of another heartbreak, especially so close to Christmas.

Darn. He'd almost forgotten Christmas was in less

than two weeks. He'd have to decide soon if he'd give Laurie his blessing to spend Christmas with Rachel.

"Here you are," Nancy said from the doorway.

Checking his watch, he groaned. "Sorry, Nance. I lost all track of time. You weren't waiting long, were you?"

"No. Fortunately your neighbor, the friendly gray-haired lady, informed me she'd seen you heading out with a basket full of dirty clothes. So being the super-sleuth I am, I tracked you here."

"Mrs. Buchanan. Sometimes having nosy neighbors is a good thing."

"She was very nice. Told me you needed a wife to give your apartment the feminine touch and to be a mother to your poor young daughter."

Beau leaned against the washer and grinned. "It's a good thing Mrs. Buchanan bakes terrific cookies, or I might be tempted to tell her to mind her own business."

"I imagine she feels it's her duty to bake cookies for the poor, struggling father. You know, just until you find a wife."

"Did you inform her that I've already had my quota of wives?" Beau twisted the cap off his liquid detergent and measured out the appropriate amount. "She might not be so eager to marry me off if she knew that."

Nancy nodded toward the washer. "Seems like you'll be a while. Are you sure you want to look at houses again today?"

"Mrs. Buchanan busted the laundry-room clothes thief a couple weeks back, so my stuff's safe here. I definitely want to look at houses. It's *buying* that seems to be the problem."

"Want some armchair psychology?"

He grinned. That was one of the things he liked about Nancy—she didn't pull any punches. But she was such a kind person, if she laid her cards on the table, he had to listen. "Why do I get the feeling I'll get your opinion whether I want it or not?"

"It's been interesting to watch you find something wrong with each house. Your creativity at detecting flaws is impressive."

"So, I have discriminating taste?"

"After you kissed me Saturday night, I've come to the conclusion you definitely have discriminating taste in women, contrary to my initial beliefs. But the house thing is different. I can practically smell your fear when we pull into the driveway of a property. What are you afraid of, I wonder?"

He ticked off on his fingers. "Let's see, a mortgage for one. What if I lose my job and can't make my payments?"

"You get another job. Borrow money from friends. Sell plasma. Call the mortgage company and explain. And, if God forbid, none of those options work, then you lose the house. It happens to thousands and thousands of people a year. I don't mean to sound flip, but you can't let fear paralyze you. Worst case, you end up back in the apartment. If you're really concerned, we'll get you a zero down loan."

"No, I don't want that. I need to feel like I own my house. I want to be invested in it." It was difficult to explain what he didn't understand himself, this compulsion to establish deep roots in Elmwood. It didn't make sense, because he seemed to be sabotaging his chances of actually getting a house.

"What's your next reason?" Nancy asked.

"It would probably devastate Rachel if I moved her into a new home, then lost the house."

She propped her hands on her hips. "She'd live through it, because you'd be right beside her letting her know things are okay. That as long as you two are together, everything will be fine."

His throat got scratchy. She was right.

But would they be together?

Stiffening, Beau realized he was sick and tired of being afraid. He'd always been a man of action and it was time to regain some positive momentum instead of acting like a whiny baby. He would call an attorney first thing in the morning to make sure Rachel stayed with him. And he would find a home for them.

Shoving his laundry basket under a folding table, he grasped Nancy's hand. "You're right. I have discriminating taste. But I'm afraid, as you so kindly pointed out. What you didn't add is that I'm a persistent son of a gun. And you, Nancy McGuire, are one hell of a woman."

Nancy smiled and squeezed his hand.

God, she was beautiful when she smiled.

He checked his back pocket to make sure he'd brought his wallet. "The laundry can wait. Come on, let's go look at some houses."

Nancy placed her hands on both sides of his face and

kissed him. "You, Beau Stanton, are one hell of a man. Let's go. I'm driving."

Beau whistled a tune. He felt lighter than he had in a long time. Who'd have thought taking on responsibility could make him feel free?

NANCY SURVEYED the house. Even to the eye of a seasoned professional, it appeared darn near perfect.

Beau seemed to take stock of each room carefully. They'd been there at least twenty minutes—usually a good sign. And she didn't detect a bit of tension or fear.

Holding her breath, she slid her hand into her pants pocket so Beau couldn't see her cross her fingers.

"The bedrooms are big," he commented.

"Yes."

"It has a nice kitchen."

"Very nice."

"Looks like it's been well cared for."

Nancy nodded.

"Let me walk through it one more time."

"Take as long as you want." *I'll just walk behind you and admire the view. And try really hard not to fall for the whole package that was Beau Stanton.*

"The master bath is nice. I like that whirlpool tub." He glanced over his shoulder, his grin wicked.

Nancy's pulse leaped at the suggestion in his eyes. Oh, yes, she was perilously close to that fall.

"I want to make an offer on the house."

Nancy blinked. It took her a minute to redirect her thoughts from the whirlpool tub. "You're sure?"

"Very sure." He came closer, lightly grasping her arms. "This one feels like home."

AFTER DRAWING UP the contract, Nancy fed the pages through her home fax machine.

Then she stood back and watched Beau watch the last page transmit. There was something so very focused about him. As if somehow he had a new direction.

"How long till we hear?" His voice was taut, low.

"I gave them twenty-four hours to respond. I'm hoping it won't be that long. It's a good offer." Nancy stood. "Would you like some tea?"

"I'd take a soda if you've got one."

"Come on to the kitchen." She turned out the light and led the way. Opening the fridge, Nancy removed a soda and handed it to him. "No cut-glass tumbler, no coordinating coaster. I gave you the can." She was almost proud of herself, as if she'd passed a momentous milestone.

"I told you it's easy for a woman to give me the can." His voice sounded hollow. "Sorry, bad joke. I'm kind of nervous. See, my hands are shaking." He held his hand horizontal, displaying a noticeable tremor.

Nancy removed the can and set it on the table. She wrapped her hands around his, rubbing them as if restoring circulation. "Your hands are cold."

Noting the tension lines bracketing his mouth, her stomach tightened. She knew how hard it had been for him to get past his doubts. "Your world's pretty much been turned upside down the last several months, huh?"

He nodded.

"I mean one minute, you're footloose and fancy-free. The next, you've got a teen daughter and housing to worry about."

He squeezed his eyes shut. "Please, don't remind me. At first, I was just worried I could go the distance with Rachel. But now, she's a part of me. I can't imagine losing her."

"You won't."

"I'm not so sure. I'm not sure what Laurie might do. And I've been really stupid, not getting everything nailed down in writing. I'm going to call an attorney tomorrow to sort out my legal rights…in case Laurie makes things difficult."

"What do you mean?"

"I didn't get the custody terms changed. As far as the courts know, Laurie is still Rachel's custodial parent. I'm afraid that means I'm twisting in the breeze if Laurie changes her mind."

"She hasn't said anything like that, has she? She just wants to come for Christmas?"

"That's what she says, but I'm not so sure that's all it is. I told her I'd think about it."

"Beau, I hate to see you so worried. Maybe talking to an attorney will set your mind at ease. Whatever you decide about Christmas, I'm sure it will be the best for everyone involved."

"I'm a parent now. I have to do what's best for Rachel. My instincts tell me we're at a crucial point and her mother visiting would be a mistake. But I wonder if I'm being selfish because I'm afraid Laurie might decide she wants Rachel back after she sees her again."

"What does your gut tell you?" Nancy asked.

He hesitated. "My gut tells me that Rachel needs some time to get her equilibrium, build a life here in Elmwood, before we can bring her mom back into the equation."

Nodding, she stepped closer, her hands linked with his. "I'm sure it will be all right."

Nancy tried to reassure herself as much as she tried to reassure Beau. She liked things the way they had been Saturday night—just the four of them watching movies. And, at times, just the two of them. Laughing, teasing, kissing. An ex-wife didn't fit in that picture.

"What's wrong?" he asked.

"Nothing."

"There's something. I can tell from your frown."

"I guess maybe I'm worried your ex-wife will complicate things. Our phone calls, Saturday movies and all that…"

"You're jealous?" The wonder in Beau's voice made her smile.

"Maybe a little."

"Darlin', you have nothing to worry about. I don't have any of those feelings for Laurie. Haven't since shortly after we were married."

"What happened?"

"We were young, infatuated. But the passion died quickly, especially once she was pregnant. After that, there wasn't much left for either of us. I think I told you I moved out before Rachel was born."

She leaned back to look at his face. "I'm curious. Did you ever think of staying for Rachel's sake?"

He flinched. "No. I was too much of a selfish SOB."

"I don't believe you were ever as selfish as you'd like me to believe."

"To be honest, I didn't think it would be all that great for Rachel to grow up in a house where her parents were like strangers to each other. Besides, I could see myself starting to argue with Laurie if I stayed."

"I've wondered. Why weren't you more a part of Rachel's life?"

Beau drew away from her, running a hand through his hair. "I've asked myself that a zillion times. I don't know. She seemed so tiny and I was afraid I'd hurt her."

"That explains the first six months or so. Maybe there was more to it than that?"

He gazed out the kitchen window. "When she was born and I held her for the first time, I saw this tiny, perfect little angel. And I was afraid. I mean knees-shaking, teeth-chattering scared."

Nancy went over to him and touched his shoulder. "What were you afraid of?"

"I was afraid I'd screw up her life just like I screwed up my own life. I knew she was better off with Laurie. I showed up when I could, but left before I let Rachel down. Before she saw what a piss-poor guy I was."

Beau's assessment of himself just about broke her heart. "What a shame," she murmured. An understatement, if there ever was one.

"Yeah, I know. I really screwed up trying not to screw up."

"No, I mean what a shame that you thought the people you loved viewed you that way. That you viewed yourself that way."

Shrugging, he said, "I let my mom and dad down and I really tried with them when I was younger. It seemed like I let everyone down after that, too."

"You know, the first time I met you at the Parents Flying Solo meeting, I thought you were pretty full of yourself. I didn't realize you were just covering."

"Hey, I've got my moments of being full of myself. Just not where relationships are concerned."

"What're you proud of?"

"Rachel, for one. She's a survivor. She'll always come up fighting."

"I meant you. Personally."

He raised an eyebrow, his grin cocky. "I produced her, didn't I?"

"Point taken. What else?"

"Two. I'm a damn good salesman. I don't play tricks with people. I give them the best deal I can. And it seems to work. I'm getting a lot of exposure by word of mouth. Three, I'm a pretty good sport. Now, how about you?"

"Hmm. I'm a survivor, too. I'm proud that I picked myself up after Eric was killed. It took courage to start a new life, travel halfway across the world to adopt a child. And moving north took guts. See, that's something we have in common."

Frowning, he shook his head. "Moving isn't hard for me. It's the staying part that's difficult."

"Today you took a step in the right direction. It sure looks like you plan on staying."

"Oh, I intend to stay all right."

Nancy tried not to show her disappointment when Beau's cell phone interrupted their conversation.

Answering, he frowned. "Rachel, is something wrong? Why are you home from school already?"

Nancy's concern for Rachel warred with a childish desire to have Beau all to herself, if only for a few hours.

"I'll be right there."

He clicked his phone shut. "I've gotta go. Rachel came home sick from school. I wasn't there and she knows I have Mondays off. She called work, thinking I must've gone in to finish paperwork and panicked when I wasn't there."

"And she didn't try your cell phone until now?"

"She wasn't thinking, I guess. Promise you'll call me the minute you hear anything about the house?"

"Of course. I hope Rachel's feeling better soon." Although she couldn't help wondering if the girl was simply checking up on her dad.

CHAPTER FOURTEEN

BEAU SPED HOME. Rachel needed him and he hadn't been there.

Damn.

It seemed like it took him forever to park the truck and jog to their apartment. When he opened the door and rushed in, he found Rachel huddled on the couch. Her cheeks were flushed, her eyes glassy.

"It's okay, sweet pea, I'm here." He pressed the back of his hand to her forehead. "I think you've got a fever. I don't have a thermometer."

"A bunch of kids are out with the flu at school." Her voice was weak.

"I'm worried. You feel pretty warm."

She started shivering. Her teeth chattered and she wrapped her arms around her waist, rocking back and forth.

He picked up the phone handset and started dialing.

"Who're you calling?"

"Nancy. I bet she'll know how to bring your fever down. And she probably has a thermometer we can borrow."

He was relieved when Nancy answered immediately. He explained Rachel's symptoms while he retrieved the comforter from her bed, returning to the front room and wrapping it around her shoulders.

"C-cold."

He covered the mouthpiece with his palm. "I know you are, darlin'. We'll get you warmed up."

On the phone, Nancy offered to bring over a thermometer and stop by the store for a few things that might make Rachel more comfortable.

"That would be great."

"No problem. I know how scary it can be to have a sick child and no one to share the worry with. I'll be there in half an hour."

"Thanks, Nance."

He hung up the phone. "She'll be here in about half an hour."

Rachel nodded, the motion jerky.

"Here, I'll bring in your pillow from your room and hunt down the TV remote. Are you thirsty?"

"No."

"Nancy said it was important to keep you hydrated. Once we take your temperature, we'll know if it's something we need to call the doctor about."

After he tucked the pillow under Rachel's head, he pressed the remote into her slack hand. He brushed a lock of hair off her damp forehead.

"I'm here, sweet pea."

She stared up at him with wide, red-rimmed eyes, so vulnerable. Almost like an infant.

He wouldn't screw up. He wouldn't turn tail and run. He would be the parent she deserved, helping her get better in any way he could.

It seemed like hours before there was a knock at the door, but the clock indicated it had been only thirty-five minutes.

Beau sighed with relief when he opened the door and Nancy stood there, holding two plastic grocery sacks. He didn't think a woman had ever looked more beautiful. Of course, he would have welcomed ex-wives numbers one, two and three with open arms if he thought it would help his daughter. But the sight of Nancy reassured him as no other woman could. He felt whole and capable.

"Come in. Did you bring the thermometer?"

"Yes, it's in this bag. Do you know how to operate it? You press it in her ear."

He removed the gizmo from the bag and stared at it helplessly. How could a man who was fairly mechanically adept have no clue how to operate a thermometer? "My mom used the glass ones with mercury inside. She shook them and shook them and then they went in your mouth. I never could see the silver line she claimed to be there."

"Here, I'll show you."

Part of him hoped she would actually perform the operation for Rachel. But she didn't. She demonstrated on herself, then prepared the gadget. "Here, give it a try."

"What if I hurt her?"

"She'll let you know. Ana had an ear infection once and she hollered holy murder."

Beau felt the blood drain from his face.

"It's harmless, just uncomfortable if they have an ear infection. You'll do fine."

He followed her instructions to the letter as she stood by and watched. At the tone, he read the digital read-out. "One hundred two degrees."

"We'll want to keep a close eye on her fever. If it goes up much more, you'll want to call her pediatrician."

"Oh, God, she doesn't have one here. She hasn't been sick."

"I'll give you the name and number of Ana's doctor, just in case."

"Thank you." He was more grateful than she would probably ever know. "And thanks for showing me how to operate the thermometer."

"No problem. I would have done it for you, but I figured we're operating on the 'teach a man to fish and he eats for a lifetime' theory. Because you're in it for the long haul."

She turned to Rachel. "He did pretty good for a rookie, didn't he Rachel?"

He could have sworn she winked at his daughter.

Rachel nodded.

"Do you feel like eating, honey?" Nancy tucked the comforter under Rachel's chin.

Rachel sighed, as if she, too, felt they'd make it through this with Nancy's help. "Not hungry," she croaked.

"How about a Popsicle? That might feel soothing going down."

Rachel nodded listlessly.

"Shoot, I hope the Popsicles aren't melted." Nancy rummaged in one of the bags and withdrew a colorful package of frozen treats. "Fortunately, it's so cold outside, they seem to be fine."

Opening the flap, she glanced at Rachel. "Grape, strawberry or lime?"

"Strawberry," Beau answered for her.

"How'd you know?" Rachel asked.

"I pay attention, sweet pea, more than you realize." He handed her the strawberry Popsicle.

Her lips wobbled as she tried to smile, but tears trickled from her eyes.

Alarm buzzed through him. "Are you okay?"

Nodding, she said, "Sweet."

He didn't know whether his daughter referred to the treat or the fact that he paid attention to what mattered to her.

"I'll go ahead and put these in the freezer," Nancy offered. "I brought a couple different flavors of sports drinks, too. Keep her electrolytes up."

"How about aspirin for her fever?"

"No, definitely no aspirin. There's some sort of syndrome kids can get if they take aspirin while they're sick. Ibuprofen or acetaminophen are fine, though."

"Which do you use for Ana?"

"Neither, as a rule. I feel it only prolongs the illness. Fever is nature's way of burning up the bad germs. As long as it doesn't go much higher than this. But, please, call the doctor's office." She shrugged and grimaced. "I'm only Doctor Mom. No medical degree involved."

"Your theory sounds logical to me. We'll go with it unless her fever rises. If that happens, I call the doctor ASAP."

Beau sucked in a breath. He trusted Nancy's judgment implicitly. Didn't even think twice about soliciting her advice. Not only was she a top-notch buddy, she was an extraordinary woman, too. And he needed her more than he'd ever allowed himself to need another woman.

Nancy checked at her watch. "I have to pick up Ana. Her sitter has a dental appointment and there's no way she can keep her longer today."

"We'll be fine," he said. What's more, he believed it.

"I know you will. But would you mind if I stopped by a little later? I'll bring some home-cooked chicken soup—the best medicine in the world."

"That would be…nice."

After he closed the door behind her, Beau stood for a moment, lost in thought. He had a visual of Nancy cooking chicken soup in his kitchen, humming under her breath. He could almost smell the aroma, taste the broth. And it warmed him to realize he'd found a woman he wanted to be with during the good times and the bad.

"Dad," Rachel croaked. "I asked if I could have another Popsicle. My head hurts."

"Sure, darlin'. I'll get you another one. Maybe you could sleep a little after that? It might help your headache."

"Dad?"

"Hmm."

"Where were you today?"

Beau hesitated. He could lie and say he'd been running errands. But he'd lied to her so many times in her life, well, lied to himself, really, that he had no intention of doing it again. Taking a deep breath, he said, "We can discuss that a little later. I've been working on something that might be great for us. But right now, you need fluids and rest."

And maybe, she'd forget altogether. Or at least forget until he knew whether his offer on the house had been accepted. He figured they'd know for sure within the next twenty-two hours.

NANCY WAS in her element as she added spices to the simmering chicken broth. Ideally, she would have boiled a chicken all day. But desperate times required desperate measures. So she had started with a high-quality broth purchased at the gourmet food store, then added bite-size pieces of cooked chicken breast, spices and packaged noodles. She figured Ana would nap for another half hour—that meant they could get to Beau's apartment before supper time.

Covering the pot of soup, Nancy turned down the temperature to a low simmer.

She thought she'd heard a noise. The fax machine?

Quickly washing her hands, she went to her office and sure enough, the machine was spewing out a counteroffer on Beau's house.

She picked up the phone and dialed his number.

He answered on the first ring.

"It's me, Nancy. I just received a counteroffer from the other Realtor. I can bring the paperwork in about forty-five minutes. But I wondered if we would be able to discuss it with Rachel there."

There was a long silence.

"Beau?"

"I'm thinking. Bring it with you and we can step outside to discuss it, if need be. Um, it's still…"

"You haven't told Rachel yet. Got it. I'll be careful what I say. See you soon."

It was closer to an hour later, when she had Ana all bundled up and the soup in a large, insulated container.

"Ray sick?"

"Yes, honey. Like you were when you had the flu."

Ana nodded, resting her head against Nancy's chest.

Nancy kissed the top of her head. Closing her eyes, she held her daughter close and sighed. It had been a long and twisted road to get to this point, but life was sweet on so many levels these days.

It took two trips to get Ana, her Clifford backpack, the soup and French bread to the car. Finally Ana was buckled in her car seat.

By the time they reached Beau's apartment and knocked, Ana was eager to see Rachel.

Beau answered the door, tension evident in the lines

of his body. "You're here. Good, you can take a look at Rachel. I think she's worse."

"What's her temperature?"

"Almost a hundred and three."

Nancy rushed to the couch where Rachel lay, her cheeks flushed, her forehead damp.

"Ray sick?" Ana tentatively patted Rachel's hand.

Rachel nodded. She didn't seem to have the strength to answer.

"Did you call the pediatrician?"

Beau shook his head. "I was waiting till you got here. You said you'd be right over."

There was no accusation in his voice, but Nancy felt the dull ache of guilt anyway. "I'm sorry."

"It's not your fault. I'm the one who decided to wait. I'll call right now."

Beau paced for what seemed like forever; Nancy assumed he'd been put on hold.

"Ray play?" Ana asked.

Nancy answered for the listless girl. "No, honey, not today. Why don't you sit down on the floor over there. Your coloring book and crayons are in your backpack."

Beau finished on the phone just as Nancy got Ana settled, a chubby crayon grasped in her hand.

"They said take her to the E.R." The color drained from his face. "There's a respiratory illness going around that's really bad."

"Do you want us to come? We'll keep an eye on Rachel in the back seat while you drive."

"That would be great. Why don't you go grab Ana's car seat while I get Rachel ready."

Nodding, Nancy ignored Ana's protest as she shoveled the coloring book and crayons into Clifford's zippered compartment. Ana loved the big, red dog.

She knelt down in front of her daughter. "Honey, we're taking Rachel to the hospital. That's where the doctors help sick kids get better."

Ana nodded solemnly.

"I'll call Aunt Emily and see if maybe she will pick you up there."

Crossing her arms, Ana stuck out her lower lip. "Stay with Ray."

"It's not a good idea. I don't want you getting sick, too."

"Ana stay."

Nancy could see her daughter working herself into a fit.

"We'll see, okay?" She figured Ana would be more than happy to leave once the E.R. got boring. Nancy just hoped no gory injuries came in while they were there. If they did, she'd just have to cover Ana's eyes. "Now, let's go get your seat moved to Beau's truck."

Nancy quickly installed Ana's car seat in the truck and climbed into the back seat between Ana and Rachel.

Beau handed a wet washcloth to Nancy. "I figured a cold compress might help. I remember my mom doing that, too."

"Good idea." Nancy positioned Rachel so she could

lean her head against Nancy's shoulder. She placed the compress on the girl's forehead.

"Daddy, hurry."

A fresh wave of chills racked the girl's body.

Nancy pulled Rachel into her lap and hugged her tight, attempting to warm her with body heat.

"Yes, Beau, hurry," Nancy whispered.

CHAPTER FIFTEEN

NANCY KISSED Ana. "You be a good for Aunt Emily, okay? You'll have lots of fun."

"You bet we'll have fun." Emily settled Ana on her hip. "We might even bake cookies. The slice-and-bake kind, of course."

"Thanks so much, Emily. I'll take the boys for you one of these evenings so you can go out."

Emily chuckled. "That's an offer I can't refuse. Call me after Beau talks to the doctor?"

"I will." Nancy squeezed Ana's hand. "Bye, honey."

"Bye, Mama."

Nancy watched them walk through the E.R. doors, disappearing into the inky darkness.

Shivering, Nancy drew her sweater closer.

It seemed like days before Beau reappeared, his clothes rumpled, his eyes clouded with fatigue. "I'm sorry they made you wait out here."

"I understand. I'm a buddy, not family." A fact that made her feel strangely hollow.

"I wish they'd bent the rules. I...feel better when you're there."

Nancy's eyes misted. Coming from Beau, it was quite an admission. She got the feeling he tried to get by without needing anyone. Maybe because he'd been let down so many times?

"Has the doctor seen her?"

Nodding, Beau said, "They're short on staff and rooms because this stuff is pretty contagious. The doctor's having her admitted as a precaution. I better get back. I just wanted to let you know what's happening."

"I'm glad you did." She touched his arm.

"Once she's settled in a room, I'll see if they'll let you in."

"I hope so. I feel pretty helpless here."

"I feel pretty helpless myself." His voice was husky. He stood. "I'll come get you as soon as I can."

"Okay."

Then he was gone.

And Nancy waited. Her eyes blurred with exhaustion, her throat grew parched.

She bought some crackers from the vending machine. Unfortunately, the machines didn't carry chamomile tea, so diet soda had to suffice.

A little before midnight, Beau came to get her. Nancy rose, her rear end numb from sitting in the hard waiting-room chair for so long.

"Rachel's in a room now. They're giving her some serious antibiotics and something to help her sleep, not that I think she needs it. She'll be out like a light." Glancing at his watch, he said, "I didn't realize it was so late. Why don't you take my truck to your house? I'm gonna spend the night here."

Nodding, Nancy said, "If Rachel's stable, I'll leave in a few minutes. Would it be okay if I peeked in on her real quick, though? I've been so worried. I shouldn't have told you to let the fever burn itself out."

"Darlin', none of this was your fault. The doctor said he probably would have done the same thing if she were one of his kids."

Nancy's vision blurred. "I'm so glad she'll be okay."

"Come here." Beau opened his arms and she walked into them. He kissed the top of her head.

She drew strength from his embrace, soaking in the healing effects of human contact. Loving contact. God, she cared for this man. And his daughter.

"I would have never forgiven myself if something happened to her," she admitted.

"I'm the one who made the decision to wait when I should have brought her in. I'm her father, and dammit, I'm supposed to do what's best for her."

"And you did. You got her here as soon as you realized it was more than an ordinary flu bug. Promise me you won't beat yourself up over this." She leaned back and held his gaze.

His mouth turned down at the corners. "That's a promise I can't keep. Let's go see her so you can go home and get some sleep."

"What will you do?"

"I'll catch a few winks in the chair by her bed."

Nancy ran her palm over his stubbled jaw. Her chest

ached with the knowledge of how badly she'd misjudged him the first night they'd met. And how extraordinarily lucky she was that he didn't seem to hold it against her.

Standing on tiptoe, she kissed his cheek. "For a self-described three-time loser, you sure seem like a winner to me."

He brushed a strand of hair from her eyes, his hand gentle, his voice soft. "I became a winner the day I met you."

RACHEL AWOKE, her throat dry and sore, her head felt as if it were stuffed with cotton.

Even the simplest movements were exhausting. And she didn't recognize this place. Then she remembered.

The hospital.

Her dad, Nancy and Ana had brought her to the hospital. Today? Yesterday? She wasn't even sure whether it was day or night.

Wow. She'd really been out of it.

Something stirred to her left.

Rachel raised herself up and saw her dad sleeping sitting up in a chair. He looked really uncomfortable. And his whiskers showed, so it had been a day or two since he'd shaved. Sometimes when he had two days off in a row, he'd let it grow like that.

There was a tray next to the bed with a cup and a pitcher of water. Good thing the cup was already full, because it took all her effort just to lift it off the tray and bring the straw to her mouth.

But it tasted so good. Cool as it went down her throat. Soothing. Like strawberry Popsicles.

Rachel smiled a little at the thought. There was something nice associated with Popsicles, but the memory was just out of her reach. Eyelids heavy, she decided to rest for a few more minutes before waking her dad up.

The next time she awoke, the sun streamed through the blinds and her dad bent over her, holding her hand.

"Hey, sweet pea."

"Hi, Daddy."

"How're you feeling?"

Like dog poop. But she couldn't say something like that to him. So she just croaked, "Okay."

"You had me pretty worried. Do you remember us bringing you in?"

"I think so. Were Nancy and Ana there?"

"Yes."

She nodded. "I thought so."

"They were worried, too."

"I was really sick, huh?"

"Yeah. Still are, although you're like two hundred percent better than last night."

"I'm sorry for causing so much trouble."

"Sweet pea, you were sick. That's not causing trouble."

Rachel saw it differently, though. Her dad wasn't used to having kids around getting sick and stuff. "I was a real pain though, I bet."

For the first time in years, he stroked her forehead. The gesture made her want to crawl into his lap and cry and tell him how confused things had gotten.

But she didn't. Because if she was too much trouble, he'd send her back to Texas.

There was a tap at the door and Nancy poked her head in. "Is she awake?"

Her dad turned toward Nancy, but before he did, she saw his face light up, as if he'd just received a fabulous gift.

It made Rachel feel kind of funny inside. Not the twisting, burning thing in her stomach. But more like happy and sad at the same time.

"Yes, she's awake. Come on in."

Nancy stepped in and hovered in the doorway. "Are you up to seeing me, Rachel?"

Like, what was she going to say? No, you held me like a little kid last night and chased away the cold, but you smile at my dad too much and sometimes it makes me mad, so just go away?

"Yeah. I'm good."

Then she noticed the basket in Nancy's hand. "I brought some girl stuff I thought you might like to have here at the hospital."

"Wow."

Nancy set it on the tray next to the bed.

The clear cellophane crinkled when Rachel fingered it. There were ribbon curls in every color of the rainbow holding the cellophane closed.

Tears gathered in her eyes. The basket was something Mom would have done, only not so perfectly. Nancy did everything perfect. Sometimes that annoyed Rachel. But today it made her feel special.

"Thanks."

"You're very welcome. Here's the card that goes with it." She handed Rachel a rectangle of construction paper with lots of swirls and chicken scratches.

"Ana made this for me?"

"Yes. I'm afraid she'll never be the kind of child to color within the lines. She has her own distinct view of the world."

"Coloring within the lines is highly overrated," her dad said. "Although, if I remember correctly, Rachel always did very neat coloring. Everything perfect."

Hearing her dad say that made her want to bawl. Not only that he'd noticed, even when she was a little kid, but the notion that she'd been so stuck on perfection. Even though she'd never been perfect enough to make her dad want to stay. Maybe that was the deal with Nancy and all the Martha Stewart stuff. Her way of trying to be perfect so people would like her.

Rachel's head hurt from all the deep thoughts.

So she reached for the basket and looked at the cool stuff inside. She fingered the lotions and lip gloss, hair scrunchies and manicure set.

"You can tear open the cellophane." Nancy smiled, her eyes alight with excitement. Maybe she liked doing things for other people because it felt good.

Tearing off the cellophane, Rachel dived in. The lotion smelled nice. The lip gloss was an okay color.

Some decent shampoo samples. A manicure kit in a cute little pouch. And several bottles of nail polish.

Her breath caught in her throat. One bottle in particular stood out. It was the same shade she'd almost stolen that day in the drugstore.

She was afraid to meet Nancy's eyes.

But what she saw there was kindness and concern.

Then Nancy winked, and Rachel knew it was going to be okay.

BEAU WALKED Nancy out of the room. "That was really nice, what you did for Rachel."

She waved away his compliment. "Just a few things I picked up at the drugstore. Everyone wants to feel pampered once in a while."

Beau pondered her statement for a few moments as they waited for the elevator. He'd never liked being pampered. It had made him nervous when a girlfriend or wife did one of those cutesy things intended to make him feel special. Made him nervous because he knew they expected something similar in return. And how in the hell did a guy learn to do that?

Shaking his head, he said, "It seemed like a lot more than just picking up a few things. When did you do it? It was almost midnight when you left last night."

"This morning, on my way over. Emily took Ana to the sitter in my car, then she's going to pick me up here. Oh, and before I forget, here are your keys." She handed them to him, her hand warm in his.

"Thanks for everything you've done." He cleared

his throat. "I'm not sure if I could have gotten through it otherwise."

"You would have done fine. Besides, I wanted to be there. For you, for Rachel."

"We're not keeping you from clients, are we?"

"My first appointment is after lunch." Nancy smacked her forehead with the palm of her hand. "The counter-offer. I completely forgot. I'll bring it by later today, if that's okay? You'll be here?"

"Yeah, that's fine. I completely forgot, too."

They reached the lobby and Beau paused. A simple goodbye seemed inadequate. He hugged her, then kissed her on the cheek. Her skin was velvety beneath his lips. She smelled good.

Her voice was husky. "I'll see you later." She headed toward the double glass doors.

"Yeah, later." He watched her leave.

"May I help you find something?"

A nurse was touching his arm, and Beau realized he'd stood there staring for much too long. "No, thank you, I think I've found what I needed."

He needed Nancy.

It should have been the kind of thought that terrified him. Instead, it brought a wistful smile to his lips. He'd found someone special when he least expected it. The only question was whether he had the courage to pursue the one woman who could make him *want* to be vulnerable. And that *was* a scary thought.

Shaking his head, he boarded the elevator and pressed the up button. When he'd arrived in Elmwood, he'd certainly had nowhere to go but up. Could he climb far enough to have the life he'd thought wasn't meant for him? A life so far from his reach he hadn't dared to dream until now?

With Laurie, he'd been young and dumb. With ex-wife number two, he'd been looking for someone with enough self-control for both of them, hoping she could change him into a respectable guy. And with ex-wife number three, he'd simply had too much to drink.

But his relationship with Nancy was totally different. It grew and changed every minute of every day. The more he saw her, the more he liked her. So much so that he'd pretty much forgotten his initial panting lust. Oh, he still wanted her, just in a different way. He wanted the entire package, not just her body parts, beautiful though they were.

No, if he went after Nancy, it would be for keeps.

He exited the elevator on the fourth floor. He needed to devote his attention to his daughter for now. But what about later? Could he possibly be a dedicated dad and pursue a woman for keeps?

It was a daunting thought. One he put on the back burner as he entered Rachel's room. She was sound asleep.

He stood there watching her for a long time. Taking in the beauty of such an extraordinary creature. Beau swallowed hard. He'd certainly lucked out to have a second chance with his daughter.

After a few minutes of sappy gazing, he realized he was dead tired. Sitting in the chair from hell, he resumed his post by her bed. She seemed to be breathing easier already.

Scooting his chair closer, he folded his arms and rested his head on the mattress. He'd regroup for a couple minutes....

THE REST OF Nancy's day was crazy.

The phone seemed to ring off the hook, walk-ins waited in the lobby and she was on hold, waiting for a colleague.

Finally, the Realtor answered.

"Hi, Susan, this is Nancy McGuire. You faxed over a counteroffer last night, and I'd like to request an extension to, say, noon tomorrow? My client's daughter was rushed to the emergency room yesterday and he hasn't had the chance to give the offer proper consideration."

Susan murmured something about her clients being in a hurry and having a backup offer.

"I realize the time constraints are very important to your clients. But my client really could use a break right now. If the home owners have children, I'm sure they'll understand a father putting his daughter's health first. If you could fax an extension to my office number, I'd really appreciate it."

Susan said she'd try and hung up.

Nancy's neck knotted, radiating tension all the way up to her scalp. Too little sleep plus too much stress and caffeine added up to a monster headache in the works.

Grabbing her purse, she stopped at the receptionist's

desk on her way out. "I'm running to the deli, you want anything?"

The receptionist wrote down her order and handed Nancy some cash. "Thanks. The phones have been crazy today."

Nancy threw on her coat and stepped out into the clear, crisp day, inhaling deeply. Her headache eased, her mood improved and she decided it was a great day to be her own boss.

The line at the deli was longer than she anticipated and she didn't return to the office until almost half an hour later.

Her fax machine was spewing paper when she entered her office. The home owners had extended the deadline until tomorrow morning at nine.

She called Beau on his cell phone. It took several rings for him to pick up.

"Hi, it's Nancy."

His voice was slow and sleepy when he said, "Hello, darlin'."

Chills ran up her spine. The pleasant kind.

"Things are wild at the office today, and I won't be able to get to the hospital till about five. The home owners gave you an extension for responding to their counteroffer."

"That's good. Will you bring the papers with you?"

"You bet. And I'll make sure to leave them with you this time."

"See you around five."

Nancy resisted the urge to say *I love you* as she hung

up. They were getting entirely too cozy. But for some reason, the thought warmed rather than dismayed her.

Smiling, she started returning phone calls so she could leave at five.

CHAPTER SIXTEEN

NANCY STOPPED when she opened the door. Rachel was asleep, her brown hair spread out on the pillow.

Beau was also asleep. Sitting in a chair, he rested his arms and head on the bed near Rachel's hand.

He breathed evenly, his five-o'clock shadow heading toward a real beard.

Moving to his side, Nancy brushed the hair off his forehead.

He stirred, then glanced up at her. He smiled that slow, sexy smile of his as he straightened his back and stretched.

"I must've dozed off," he murmured. "I'm glad you're here."

Nancy's heart flip-flopped at the intensity of his expression. She kept her voice low so she didn't wake Rachel. "How's she doing?"

"She's awake, so you can stop whispering," Rachel said. "And the doctor says I'm doing much better. I can go home tomorrow."

"I'm so glad to hear that."

"Ahem."

Nancy turned to see the boy Rachel liked standing in the doorway, shifting from foot to foot.

Rachel's attention flew to his face and her eyes got big.

Filling the awkward pause, Nancy said, "Mike, isn't it?"

He nodded.

"Please come in. I'm sure Rachel is glad to see one of her friends. We old people get boring after a while." She winked at Rachel.

Rachel rolled her eyes. "You're not kidding." She glanced at the small, stuffed puppy he held. "Is that for me?"

"Yeah, to keep you company."

"Come on in and have a seat, Mike." Nancy waved him in. "We're glad you're here, aren't we, Beau?"

Beau sat ramrod straight, his eyes narrowed.

"Aren't we, Beau?" She tugged on the hair at the nape of his neck, out of Mike's line of sight. Then she gave him a warning look. *Be nice.*

Shrugging, he said, "Yeah, I guess."

Mike stepped forward and handed Rachel the stuffed toy.

"Thank you. He's so cute." Rachel's smile was reflected in his eyes.

The stuffed puppy was appropriate because it looked like a bad case of puppy love.

And Nancy and Beau were seriously not needed at the moment.

"Beau, I have that paperwork we discussed. Why don't we go grab a bite to eat and we can go over it."

He glanced at Rachel, then at Mike, and finally his gaze came to rest on Nancy.

"I'm not hungry." He folded his arms over his chest.

Nancy grasped the lock of hair at the back of his neck and tweaked a little harder.

"Ow, would you quit doing that?"

"Dad, I think Nancy's right. You need something to eat. Something besides my leftover hospital food. And you need a good night's sleep."

Nancy smiled at the unexpected help from Rachel. "Yes, you do. And I'm sure Mike wouldn't mind keeping Rachel company."

"No, ma'am, I mean yes, ma'am. I mean I'd like that." His expression was earnest. He was a good kid.

"You're in this together, aren't you." Beau raised his hands in defeat. "Okay, we'll go grab a bite to eat, then I'm going home to sleep for about twelve hours. Happy?" He glanced at Rachel, then Nancy.

"Yes," the females said in unison.

"Come on, let's go before you change your mind. I need to pick up Ana at the sitter's house." She grasped Beau by the arm and pulled him toward the door. "Oh, and Rachel, just call if you need anything or you get lonely. We can always come back."

"I'll be fine. Thanks, Nancy."

RACHEL COULDN'T WAIT to get her dad out the door, but then when he was gone, she was struck with a bad case of nerves. "How'd you know I was here?"

"Word got around school today. Jason Patterson said you were in the hospital on the verge of death."

Grinning, Rachel gestured toward her father's recently vacated seat. "I wasn't quite that bad, but it was pretty intense."

"You seem okay now."

She nodded. "Yeah, I get to go home tomorrow."

Tipping her head to the side, she asked, "So what's going on? At school you barely talk to me."

He avoided her eyes. "Uh, I figured you'd be too much of a distraction. For my plans."

She, Rachel Stanton, was too much of a distraction? *Woo-hoo!* Her heart sang. She managed to stay much cooler on the outside. "You've dated other girls. Weren't they a distraction?"

"They're not like you. You understand. I don't have to tiptoe around the truth with you."

"So you're saying you like me too much to talk to me unless I'm at death's door?"

He bit his lip, then chuckled. "Yeah, I guess that's exactly what I said. See, you're the only girl who would call me on that."

Rachel laughed. "That's about the only time my smart mouth has been considered a good thing."

BEAU EYED his hamburger with distaste. It wasn't much better than hospital food, but the fast-food chain had a play area, so at least Ana was happy.

"You sure there's only one way in and one way out of there?" he asked.

"Positive. I triple-checked the first time I brought Ana here. And I always wait for this table. So I can keep Ana in view at all times."

"You ganged up on me with Rachel. That's not nice."

"Give the kid a break, Beau. It was sweet that he came to see her."

He ate a few greasy French fries, liberally dipped in ketchup. "I don't think it's a good idea leaving them alone."

"They were perfectly supervised and you know it. It seems there's a nurse or an orderly in her room every fifteen minutes."

"A lot can happen in fifteen minutes."

"Don't I know it." She grinned.

He wondered if she referred to her teenage trysts with Eric. It was on the tip of his tongue to remind her how well that had worked out. But he knew he was being a real pain in the neck. "Look, I'm not mad at you. I just don't like the idea of Rachel dating. And sex is out of the question. I know it'll happen eventually, but can't she wait till she's thirty?"

"Not if she grows up to have as much self-esteem as I think she will. And she'll handle it fine, then. Because you're doing a terrific job with her."

"Flattery now?"

"Did it work?" There was an impish light in Nancy's eyes.

"Maybe. Try some more and I'll tell you."

"Okay. You love her, you listen to her, you protect

her to the best of your ability. Those are the things she needs from you and you give it in spades."

"But?"

"But she doesn't need a bodyguard. There's a balance between holding on and letting go."

"I'll remind you of that when Ana's fourteen."

Nancy got kind of a funny look on her face.

"What?" he asked.

"You say that so casually, as if you're positive we'll still be…buddies or dating…or whatever, in twelve years."

His hand froze with a French fry halfway to his mouth. Then he carefully put it down on the hamburger wrapper.

She was right. In a short time, she'd become such an integral part of his life, he couldn't imagine her not being there with little baskets of goodies, homemade chicken soup and that warm, loving heart camouflaged inside that incredibly hot body.

He wanted her. Right now, right here. Inside the netted play area, submerged in primary-colored balls. Sans children, of course. Or anyone else for that matter.

It was such a highly charged erotic image, he had a hard time completing his thought.

Nancy. Twelve years.

"Twelve years is a long time. But I'd like to still be in your life then. Is it that hard for you to imagine?" Had he read her wrong? "I thought you were maybe warming up to the idea of seeing where 'whatever' might take us. Very slowly, of course."

She shifted. "Sure. I'd considered it. And I thought movies were a step in the right direction. You're sounding a little more serious than that, though. It would help if we were both at the same point."

"I see myself as your buddy for years to come…and more." This was harder than he'd anticipated. The man who always had a fresh pickup line was grasping for words.

"That's not getting to the point. Rachel will be grown and gone by then. You won't need a buddy. It's the 'and more' part I need to define."

Why in the world had he brought the subject up? Because it was time, that's why. He leaned across the table and lowered his voice. "Do you realize I've been fantasizing about making love to you over in that play area. Both of us stripped naked and playing hide-and-seek. Then I find you and we make the most sensual love. Again. And again. Those bright plastic balls moving beneath us, like a water bed."

Nancy's pupils dilated. She ran her tongue over her lower lip. It was an incredibly sexy movement and he was pretty sure she wasn't conscious of it. Because she glanced at the play area and her eyes widened.

"Not with children here." Her tone was shocked.

"Of course not. We're alone."

She exhaled in relief. "You want to go to bed with me? That's old news."

"You didn't let me finish my story. You wanna know the best part of the whole fantasy?"

"No." She nodded.

"We're celebrating our twenty-fifth anniversary."

Nancy's mouth made a big *O*, and her eyes were wide.

He'd finally left her speechless.

"Are you proposing?"

Now he was speechless.

He wasn't proposing. Was he?

The idea terrified him. But not nearly as much as it would have a couple months ago.

"What would your answer be if I did?"

Nancy pounded on the table with her fist. A few diners at nearby tables turned and stared.

"Beau, stop messing with me." Her eyes were bright with unshed tears.

He reached across the table and cradled her face with his hand. "Aw, darlin', I'm not messing with you. I would never intentionally hurt you. I guess I'm trying the idea on for size. But you know what? We don't have to jump from being buddies straight to marriage."

"No kidding?"

He winced at the sarcasm in her voice.

"So where do we go from here?" she asked.

"I don't know. Maybe I was wrong to bring it up. After all, you've pretty much told me I'm the last guy you'd ever get involved with."

"And I've apologized. I thought maybe we were past that." She stood, gathering used napkins and containers. "We should probably just call it an evening. I'll get Ana."

Turning, she carried her tray to the trash and dumped the half-eaten contents.

Beau started to call out to her, but there was nothing to say that might make it better. And, with his track record, chances were good he'd make it worse.

NANCY BOUNCED Ana on her hip as she walked up her driveway, trying to act cheerful.

Ana patted Nancy's face. "Mommy sad?"

"No, honey, Mommy's not sad."

Ana frowned, her eyes wide.

"Sweetie, I always told myself I'd never lie to you. Yes, Mommy is sad. But it's nothing you did." She kissed Ana's soft little cheek, then made monster-gobbling noises.

Ana laughed.

The sound was enough to lift Nancy's spirits. She managed to stay upbeat through bathing Ana, reading her the requisite bedtime stories, getting her a drink and checking under the bed.

By the time Ana was fast asleep, Nancy was exhausted from the effort of staying cheerful.

She reached for the phone and started dialing Emily's number. But what would she say? The man is driving me crazy? She could almost hear Emily say, "He can only drive you crazy if you let him."

Or maybe it was her own subconscious.

Whichever it was, the voice was very wise.

She replaced the phone on the charger.

Maybe chamomile tea would calm her. She went to the kitchen and poured water in the teakettle. But instead of heating the kettle, she left it there and retrieved a bottle of wine she'd been keeping for a special occasion.

Pouring herself a glass, she admitted she'd lied to herself once again. She hadn't been saving it for a special occasion. She'd been saving it for the certain train wreck that would occur if her life became too intertwined with Beau's.

Although this didn't qualify as a train wreck, the confusion of the evening certainly could count as a derailment. How could she make such a tremendous leap of faith, if Beau didn't give her a more solid reason than he'd still want to make love with her in twenty-five years? She needed more. She needed a man who could guarantee he would always love her, and her alone, for the rest of his days. And despite all the progress he'd made, Beau didn't seem able to do that. So why complicate their growing relationship with allusions to a long-term future?

Sighing, she noticed her address book teetering on the arm of the couch. Inside was her dad's address and phone number. Calling hadn't worked. Maybe she could drive by his house, drop off a plate of Christmas cookies, see if he was interested in being her father again...

Shaking her head, she jumped as the phone sounded.

"Hello?" *Dad, is it you?*

"Hi, um, it's me. Beau."

"Oh."

"I'm sorry for being such an ass tonight. Just because I'm all confused about where this is heading, doesn't mean I should drag you into it before I get my head straight. Does that make sense?"

Nancy chuckled in spite of herself. "Yes, in an odd way, it does."

"So I'm forgiven?"

Sighing, she tucked her legs under her and sat on the couch. She used the remote to turn on the twinkling Christmas tree lights. The magic of color and light, along with the promise of miracles never failed to lift her spirits. Until tonight.

"You hurt me." How many times had she wanted to tell Eric the same thing? Ten, twenty, a hundred? But she hadn't told him. Not even once. Because, deep down, she hadn't thought it would make a difference.

And her father had never given her the opportunity.

Now here was Beau, giving her that opportunity. She held her breath, waiting to see if her pain made a difference to Beau.

"I know I did." His voice was gravelly. "And I wish I could go back and handle it differently."

"What would you do differently?"

The silence was deafening. But Nancy forced herself to wait.

"I'm sorry, darlin', I just can't do it this way."

The dial tone buzzed in her ear.

She brushed away the tears trickling down her jaw. He'd given her his answer loud and clear. Her pain didn't make a difference to him. Just as she'd feared.

Why did she keep getting involved with men who were incapable of giving her the kind of relationship she needed? Or was she simply the type of woman unable to inspire that kind of devotion?

Draining the glass of wine, she clasped a throw pillow to her chest and cried. She had no idea how much of it was old hurt and how much of it was new.

She just knew there seemed to be a deep well of unending grief.

When the doorbell rang, it barely registered. She was in such a dark, primal place, everyday realities seemed far away.

Wiping her eyes with the hem of her sweatshirt, she trudged to the door. Maybe Emily had sensed Nancy's need.

She opened the door and froze.

Beau stood in front of her with no jacket, his hair disheveled, his eyes clouded. And when her gaze encompassed his feet, she realized he had no shoes.

Her first instinct was to drag him into the house, lead him to the fireplace and bring him a cup of hot cocoa, homemade of course. But she'd been taking care of everyone else for years and it had only left her feeling drained and used.

"What are you doing here?" she asked.

"C-can I come in?" His teeth chattered.

"Just turn back around and get in your truck. I'm sure the heater will warm you up before you get down the street."

"You promised to give me the counteroffer."

Nancy swore under her breath. How could she have forgotten?

She almost shut the door in his face while she went to retrieve the papers. Almost.

"Come in." She grabbed his arm and propelled him inside.

"Stay here while I get the paperwork."

She went to the family room to retrieve her satchel. Her fingers shook as she fumbled with the latch.

Beau's arms came around her from behind and he stilled her hands. "Stop," he murmured. Grasping her by the shoulders, he turned her to face him. "I don't give a damn about the papers. Well, I do, but not right now. It was the only way you'd let me in."

Nancy stood still, her back straight, clutching the satchel to her chest. She refused to meet his eyes. The desperation in his voice was almost her undoing. Add a few more seconds in Beau's arms, and not only would she have a nice mug of cocoa for him, but he'd be drinking it in her bed.

"That was a dirty trick."

"I couldn't talk to you about this over the phone. I've got to make you understand." There was a trace of panic in his voice. "I've screwed everything up and I hurt you just because I'm so damn bad at this. Proposing comes easy to me. It's kind of a knee-jerk reaction when I start to feel something for a woman. It's the, um, long-term affection part I can't seem to get right. So when in doubt, I seem to fall back on what I know. Lust and marriage."

"I don't understand."

Sighing, he murmured, "Welcome to the club."

Nancy peeked up at his face. "Why don't you try to explain?"

"Because that's what I was trying to do at the fast-food place and I only made things worse. Things that worked for me in past relationships don't work with you. It's like I'm flying blind."

"You mean to tell me you've been married three times and you've never been in love?"

"Yeah, that's what I'm beginning to think. Because I care about you in a way I never have before, even with my ex-wives."

Nancy held her breath. If she was following his convoluted train of thought, that meant… "You love me?"

CHAPTER SEVENTEEN

No!

The denial was on the tip of Beau's tongue. He couldn't possibly have fallen in love, could he?

Frowning, he was aware of Nancy waiting. Her beautiful green eyes were dark with some emotion. Hope? Condemnation? Probably the latter. And who could blame her?

"Darlin', I'm afraid that's exactly what I mean. I— I think I'm falling in love with you."

"Oh." The syllable fell soft from her lips.

"That's all you can say? For the first time in my life, I tell a woman I love her and mean it, and all you can say is 'oh'?"

Beau's heart ached at her underwhelming response. Kind of like when he was a kid and would run home to tell his mom and dad about an accomplishment, only to receive an underwhelming "oh, that's nice, William." Because of course, Connor had already done something bigger, better, grander. So pretty soon he quit talking about his accomplishments. And decided not to expect love, because he didn't hurt so much when he didn't receive it.

Maybe that was why he'd gone through the motions with his first three wives. Because if he really, truly loved a woman, what would he do if she didn't love him back?

His throat grew thick with unshed tears. He wanted to cry for the little boy who'd felt so alone, but covered up with bravado. And he wanted to cry for the man who had wasted too much time denying the little boy's pain.

"That's all you can say— 'oh'?" He released her and stepped away. "I'm sorry. Apparently I'm the only one who took this buddy thing too far. I won't bother you anymore."

Nancy tried to untangle the confusing jumble of their conversations this evening. She grabbed him by the arm. "Oh, no you don't, buddy. You're not going anywhere. I haven't understood a damn thing you said tonight except that you're falling in love with me and you've never been in love before. All the other stuff is just a smoke screen you hide behind when things get tough, when things get scary."

He glared at her. "You don't know what you're talking about."

"Then enlighten me. What were you trying to say in that bizarre way of yours?"

"It doesn't matter. This isn't going to work."

"How do we know if it will work or not, until we know exactly what it is we're looking at? Out with it, Beau. Plain and simple. No ifs, ands or buts. No previous wives. I've got news for you, they're not here right now. *I'm* here, and if you have something to say, spit it out. And make it clear. No more BS."

"I love you." His words were terse, his expression fierce.

"Okay. Try it again without the hostility."

The fight went out of him. His fists unclenched, and the anger in his eyes was replaced by deep, dark sorrow.

"I mean I love you so much it scares me." He kissed her, a coaxing gesture, as if he were unsure of her response. "And I'm afraid you won't love me back."

Nancy smiled through her tears. "Beau, how could I not love you back? I've loved you almost since the first time I saw you." She slipped her arms around his neck and kissed him with everything she had.

He pulled back for a second. "You sure had a strange way of showing it."

"Because I was afraid, Beau. I didn't want to believe it. Didn't want to go down that road again."

"But you're willing to try?"

"Yes, I really want to try. I—I love you."

His eyes twinkled as he drew her close. "We're getting better at this already. We just need lots of practice. I love you, Nancy McGuire. With everything I've got."

NANCY AWOKE with a start. She reached to the bedside table and turned up the baby monitor. Sure enough, Ana was awake, talking to herself.

Judging by the sunlight streaming around the edges of the curtains, she'd overslept.

"Just five more minutes," Beau mumbled as he wrapped his arm around her and drew her close, covering them with the fluffy down comforter.

His cheek was scratchy beneath her fingertips. She kissed him gently on the lips. "Time to get up, sleepy-head."

"I'm already up, if you haven't noticed." He pulled her on top of him, his grin wicked.

"Believe me, I noticed. Again and again." She moved her hips against him.

His grin faded, and his expression became intense. "I'm never letting you go."

Her heart skipped at the possessive promise in his voice. "Good." She turned down the volume control on the monitor, until Ana's voice was a merely happy background babble. Then she grabbed one of the condom packets scattered on the nightstand and handed it to Beau.

"You're sure we have time?" he asked.

"Very sure." She leaned over to capture his mouth. Her hips mimicked the motion of her tongue.

"Oh, yeah, plenty of time." His voice was raw.

He groaned in frustration as he tried to rip open the condom.

Nancy didn't see any reason to delay her pleasure. She continued to move against him, his erection providing the perfect amount of friction.

Swearing under his breath, Beau tore the package open with his teeth.

She enjoyed his impatience as he tried to apply the condom with clumsy hands while she continued to move against him. Finally, he accomplished his mission.

"Now, where were we?" He grasped her hips. Holding her still, he thrust deep.

"Oh."

He continued to hold her, when she wanted to move. Wanted to find the completion he represented.

"Is 'oh' all you can say?"

His eyelids were lowered, and he looked so damn sexy. Felt so damn good inside her.

She lowered her voice to reflect the passion she felt. "Ohhh."

"No, that's not what I mean."

"I love you," she murmured, before losing herself to the power of the moment.

"I love you." His words flowed over her at the same moment she lost control.

BEAU STOOD on Nancy's front porch, freezing his ass off. Or more accurately, his bare feet.

Stuffing his hands in his pockets, he jogged in place to keep warm. Fortunately, Nancy had found an insulated flannel shirt he could squeeze into for this charade.

A necessary charade, he had to admit. Now that he had a teenage daughter, he had a whole new appreciation for morals. But in his case, it had to be the appearance of morals.

He heard Nancy's voice within the house and Ana's answering chatter.

He jogged in place for another couple minutes, hoping none of Nancy's neighbors would see how ridiculous he looked, before he knocked on her door.

"I wonder who that could be?" he heard from inside.

Nancy opened the door and feigned surprise. "Beau, how nice to see you. Look, Ana, Beau came to see us. Would you like to have breakfast?"

Her stilted words told him she was no actress.

Unfortunately, or fortunately, as the case may be, he was more accustomed to being caught in a compromising position.

"Th-thought I'd drop by on my way to the hospital. Aren't you going to invite me in? It's rather cold out here."

Nancy grinned, a mischievous gleam in her eye. "Why, Beau Stanton, you've left home without your shoes. Didn't your mother tell you you'd catch your death of cold doing that?"

"Yes, she did. But being the rebellious kind of guy I am, I figured I'd test her theory." He looked down at his toes, wondering if the lavender tint was a sign of frost bite. "Guess she was right. Boy, my feet are cold. See, Ana, you always listen to your mother."

Ana stepped outside and crouched by him. She reached out and poked his big toe experimentally. "Cold."

"Since he's learned his lesson, should we let him in for Belgian waffles?"

Ana nodded solemnly, holding out her hand to Beau.

He gratefully accepted and hobbled into the house.

When he passed Nancy, he whispered, "I'll get you for this."

Her responding chuckle warmed him as socks and

shoes would not. A good thing, because she handed him a pair of pink, fuzzy slippers at least two sizes too small.

He shrugged. Heck, it was worth a little frostbite to hear her laugh like that.

Ana's giggle was just as precious.

"The waffles are almost ready. Then I'll need you to look at that counteroffer," Nancy threw over her shoulder, heading to the kitchen. She gestured for him to follow.

Beau had almost forgotten about the house. Now he wasn't so sure he wanted it, unless he knew Nancy and Ana would be living there with them.

He put the brakes on those thoughts. Yes, he loved Nancy. Yes, he wanted to be with her forever. But he wasn't sure about the whole marriage deal.

Maybe she would move in with him?

Then he glanced down at his feet, only partially encased in pink terry-cloth slippers, and he knew living together wouldn't work for either of them because of the girls. It was all or nothing. Marriage or sneaking around in pink, fuzzy slippers. Man, he wished he'd been paying more attention when they'd had the speaker on this very topic at the Parents Flying Solo meeting.

"Go ahead and sit down at the table. The paperwork's in that file folder by your plate."

He sat where she'd indicated, but didn't pick up the folder. "Do you think they'd give me more time to think about it?"

Nancy shook her head. "I had a heck of a time getting this extension. We can talk about it after breakfast."

Changing the subject, he said, "I called the hospital this morning. Rachel sounds good. They plan to release her after the doctor has rounds."

"Ray." Ana clapped her hands, her eyes alight with excitement.

"Ray's your buddy, huh?" he asked.

"Ray nice."

"Yes, she is a pretty good kid." He ruffled the girl's hair. "And so are you, Ana Banana."

Ana nodded, her self-assurance a wonderful thing to see.

Beau thought he'd died and gone to heaven when Nancy placed a plate in front of him with fluffy, steaming waffles afloat in maple syrup and a whipped cream smiley face. The aroma alone was enough to send him into a diabetic coma.

"Mmm. Smells wonderful. I have quite an appetite this morning." He winked at Nancy.

"I know for a fact you do." She returned his wink.

"The whipped cream looks especially good. I like whipped cream on *lots* of things." When he realized Ana was engrossed in her waffle, he added a leer.

Nancy choked on her herbal tea. "I'm sure you do," she murmured.

"Maybe I'll show you one of my recipes one of these days."

"I might just take you up on that offer." She hid her smile behind her teacup.

Sighing, he cut into the waffle and ate several bites before he came down to earth. "I take that back. These waffles might give my recipes a run for their money."

He finished his breakfast in record time. The waffles were tipping the scales in the marriage direction. No wonder they said the way to a man's heart was through his stomach.

It wasn't hard to visualize talking and joking with Nancy during the day, making love all night long in her four-poster bed. Then regaining his strength through waffle therapy.

He smiled at how eerily accurate his vision of Nancy's bed had been—right down to the white eyelet sheets. Shaking his head, he went to the sink and rinsed his plate, putting it in the dishwasher. He took his seat and opened the file folder.

"Let me know if you need anything clarified," Nancy commented.

"Looks pretty straightforward. They'll give me a partial flooring allowance, but won't leave the refrigerator."

"Yes. Were you counting on getting the refrigerator?"

"No. It would have been nice, but I used it mostly for negotiating room."

Nodding, Nancy said, "That's what I thought. I've indicated the places for you to sign for acceptance. I'll fax it over first thing, if you're sure you want to move forward."

"This is still a scary step." And part of him was back

to wondering what they'd do with two houses if they decided to go the marriage route.

Then we'll sell one.

He could hear Nancy's response in his head, as surely as if he'd asked her the question aloud. Wow, that telepathic thing had never happened with any of his ex-wives. But then again, he'd never felt this close to any of his ex-wives.

Beau signed the papers with a flourish. "I'll tell Rachel ASAP."

CHAPTER EIGHTEEN

BEAU CAREFULLY READ the hospital discharge papers. He wanted to make darn sure he did everything right for Rachel's recovery.

"How come you didn't answer the phone this morning?" Rachel tucked a strand of hair behind her ear, glancing sideways at him.

"I went to Nancy's house to have breakfast with her and Ana."

"At five-thirty?"

Beau winced. "Early breakfast?"

"Dad, I'm not a kid anymore. I see the way you and Nancy look at each other. Yeah, it's hard for me to take, but I'll deal with it."

Standing, he went to Rachel and wrapped his arms around her. "Sweet pea, I didn't see this thing coming with Nancy. I am two hundred percent dedicated to being a good dad for you. I figured that meant no, um, outside distractions. But Nancy's special. I'm hoping I can see her and still be there for you two hundred percent."

She rested her head against his shoulder. "I'll only hold you to one hundred ninety-five percent. Since she seems to make you happy, I'll allow Nancy five percent."

Chuckling, Beau gave her a hug. "Deal. Now you want to tell me why you were calling at five-thirty in the morning? Was something wrong?"

She shrugged. "I couldn't sleep and I figured you might be up."

"Hmm. That answer sounds a little fishy, but I won't pursue the point. Especially since you've magnanimously allotted five percent of my attention to Nancy."

"Come on, Dad, let's go home. Mike said he'd call. He's going to bring by the work I've missed." Rachel looped her arm through his. "If that's okay?" she added in a small voice.

"Yeah, it's hard for me to take, but I'll deal with it. I'm willing to give Mike five percent of your attention, as long as you're supervised by an adult."

"Deal." His daughter gave him a brilliant smile that went straight to his heart.

He kissed her on the top of the head. "Love you, sweet pea."

"Love you, too, Dad."

"Oh, and Rach?"

"Yeah?"

"As long as we're being honest, I don't want you to consider having sex until you're thirty."

"Dad, you are so lame."

"Yeah, I am. But in a good way, right?"

Rachel threw her head back and laughed, a gesture so reminiscent of Nancy, his pace faltered for a second.

"Sure, Dad, in a good way."

They walked to the elevator arm in arm.

"One more thing."

She rolled her eyes. "What now? No dating till I'm twenty-nine."

"No, although the idea has merit. I want to get everything out in the open."

Her body tensed.

"I, um, think we might be getting a house."

Rachel squealed. "A real house—with a yard and everything?"

Her joy made Beau regret his second thoughts. Getting a house was right.

The elevator doors opened at ground level and they headed toward the exit.

"Yep." He hesitated. "Has the apartment been that bad?"

"No. But a house is, I don't know, more like a home. Even if it's a rental. That's okay," she rushed to assure him.

"I made an offer to *buy* a house, kiddo."

"Really?" Her eyes sparkled. "How totally cool."

"The owners counteroffered."

Her smile faded. "That doesn't sound good."

"It just means we compromised. I accepted their counteroffer this morning. That's part of the reason I was over at Nancy's. She faxed my acceptance to them."

"So it's ours?"

"As long as the bank gives us a mortgage. And Nancy seems to think that's a pretty sure thing."

Rachel squealed her delight. "When do I get to see it?"

"I'll have to ask Nancy."

"Wow, dad, a couple of days ago and everything seemed crummy and now everything is terrific."

"That wouldn't have anything to do with a boy named Mike, would it?"

"Maybe a little." She smiled shyly. "But a house means we're a real family."

"That's what I thought, sweet pea."

He wrapped his arm around her shoulder as they left the hospital.

Rachel was absolutely right. Life was pretty terrific these days.

NANCY, HOLDING ANA on her hip, unlocked the front door and stepped aside for Beau and Rachel to enter.

"The owners have already moved out, but they gave permission for you to have your own tour."

Rachel nearly danced inside. "How totally cool."

Ana squirmed to get down and follow her idol.

"Not yet, sweetie," she whispered. "Rachel gets to see the house first."

Ana grumbled but allowed Nancy to continue to hold her.

Beau followed Rachel, grinning. His pleasure in his daughter's joy tugged at Nancy's heartstrings. He really was a softie. Just too scared to show it or really let people in. Until now.

"Don't overdo it, sweet pea. You need to build your strength," he said.

"I'm fine. Which room is mine?"

"The master is mine," he said. "You have your choice of the other two."

She danced between the two bedrooms, excited in her indecision.

"You don't have to pick one today, sweet pea."

"But I need to be able to visualize it to come up with a decorating theme." She glanced shyly at Nancy. "Do you think you'd have the time to help me, Nancy?"

"I would be honored." And that was the absolute truth.

Rachel threw her arms wide and twirled in the middle of the large living room. "I wish we could move in before Christmas."

"Me, too, kiddo." Beau leaned against the doorway. "But mortgage companies don't move quite that fast."

"Where are we going to put our Christmas tree next year?"

"I don't know, where do you think it should go?"

While Beau, Rachel and Ana scouted possible tree locations, Nancy took a moment to gather her thoughts.

Where would they all be a year from now? Beau had told her he loved her but hadn't mentioned marriage. And that disappointed her.

They were taking things slowly, she reminded herself. But who was she kidding? There was an old-fashioned part of her that wouldn't consider their relationship complete unless they married.

Shaking her head, Nancy knew other people would wonder how she could contemplate marriage to a man who'd been married three times before. She could consider it because her heart told her Beau wasn't the same man who had married those previous women.

"Come on, Nancy." Rachel tugged on her hand. "Is this the most fabulous spot for a Christmas tree or what?"

Ana jumped up and down. "Mama see. Mama see."

Rachel gestured toward the picture window facing the street. It was easy to visualize how welcoming this home would look with a tall, brightly lit spruce standing sentinel in the front window.

"It's perfect."

Would she be a part of the Stantons' Christmas next year? She certainly hoped so. Because she'd given her heart to Beau.

"Dad, we need to do our Christmas shopping." Rachel's eyes were bright with excitement. "It's only a little over a week away."

"Who says I haven't already done my shopping?" He acted affronted, but he couldn't quite keep a straight face.

"No way. I don't believe it."

He laughed. "A good thing, because I haven't even started."

Rachel nodded sagely and caught Nancy's eye. "He's such a guy."

Laughing, she couldn't help but agree. "He is that. Are you going to buy Mike a present?"

The girl blushed. "I'm not sure."

"Maybe you could get him something small, just to let him know you were thinking of him."

Rachel nodded. "Would you help me pick something out?"

"Sure."

"Hey, I've got an idea." Beau put his arm around Rachel. "We can do our shopping together on Saturday afternoon, the four of us. Have dinner out, then maybe Sunday we can ice-skate at the outdoor rink. How's that sound to you, Nance?"

"Sounds wonderful."

"Good." He kissed her quickly on the lips.

Ana's eyes widened, her mouth made an *O*. "Beau kiss Mama."

Beau picked up Ana and tossed her in the air. Ana, ever the daredevil, giggled in delight.

"Yes, I did kiss your mama. And I intend to do a lot more of that."

Nancy's face grew warm, but she had to admit she found the idea very appealing.

BEAU SHIFTED several large shopping bags. "Are you sure we're not done yet? I feel like a pack mule."

A happy pack mule.

Rachel looked at him, then Nancy. The two females shrugged and erupted in giggles, as if he'd told a wonderful joke. Then they walked on ahead, arm in arm.

"That's a no, I take it?"

They ignored his question, so he brought out the big guns. "Ana Banana, what do you think?" he asked as she trudged next to him.

He smoothed her shiny brown hair. She was being a real trouper, trying so hard to be a big girl and keep up.

"What's pack mule?"

She never ceased to amaze him with her ability to talk and reason.

By rearranging the bags, he was able to take her hand in his. "Back in the old days, they didn't have cars and trucks. So if they needed to take stuff somewhere a big old clunky wagon wouldn't go, they used mules. They tied all the heavy things to the poor mule's back."

Ana clucked her tongue.

"I know. Not very nice, huh?"

"Mean."

"Are you hungry?" He used his stage whisper.

Ana's eyes lit. "Me hungry. Me hungry."

Nancy turned and scooped her daughter up. "You're always hungry. Where do you put all that food? Do you have a hollow leg?" She tickled Ana's knee.

Ana giggled and shrieked. "No."

"Where shall we go for a late snack?" Beau asked.

Several fast-food restaurants were suggested, even the one with the play area Ana loved.

"You know what I want?" he asked.

"What?" Nancy grinned wickedly.

His thoughts strayed to a hunger of a different kind. Where was he? Oh, yeah, food. "I want pancakes."

Ana bounced in Nancy's arms. "Pancakes."

"At three in the afternoon?"

"Sure. Plenty of the breakfast places serve pancakes all day long."

"Yeah, Nancy. And we can get orange juice so it'll be healthy," Rachel added.

Nancy rolled her eyes and nodded toward Ana. "I'm not sure she needs the sugar."

"Please, Mama?" Ana's Kewpie-doll mouth turned down at the corners, giving her the poor-little-waif look.

Beau wondered how Nancy withstood that kind of pressure. As it turned out, she didn't.

"Okay." She sighed. "I'm outnumbered. I know when to admit defeat."

Nancy linked her arm in his as they headed toward his truck. Rachel and Ana were busy trying not to step on cracks in the sidewalk.

When Nancy smiled up at him, his heart flip-flopped in his chest. He'd seen that smile in her photo album. It was the same smile she'd worn during the times when her dad was home. Or in the early days with Eric.

His step faltered. The implied responsibility fell heavily on his shoulders. But he shrugged it off. He was a better man these days. Besides, nothing would ruin this day with the females he loved.

Nancy elbowed him in the ribs. "That was a dirty trick, Beau Stanton."

"Hmm. I don't know what you're talking about." That was the truth. He'd completely lost the thread of their conversation.

"Bribing my child with pancakes to get out of more shopping."

"Ah, you know me too well." He tried to recapture his enjoyment of the day. "But I should get points for not using ice cream. And, as Rachel pointed out, juice will make it a healthy snack."

"I didn't stand a chance with you two in collusion, did I?"

"Nope. Paybacks are a mother, aren't they? But you gave in gracefully."

"And now you've got Ana on your side."

He chuckled. "I better think up some other concessions while I've got you where I want you."

"Need some help? I could think of a few concessions involving whipped cream." She winked, pulling him along toward the truck.

Beau racked his brain for a way to get her alone long enough to test her idea. But glancing at the two girls, he knew they would fulfill their chaperoning duties with gusto.

Sighing, he had to admit it was one of the few drawbacks of having them all together.

He stopped, did what he figured was a pretty hot dance move, and snapped Nancy into his arms.

Her eyes widened.

And there, in the middle of Elmwood's busiest street, he kissed her very thoroughly.

It took a full minute before giggles penetrated his brain.

Raising his head, he turned to the girls. "What, you haven't seen a couple old folks kiss before?"

CHAPTER NINETEEN

NANCY TIPPED her face to the clear night sky. Fresh air nipped at her lungs when she inhaled deeply. She wanted to extend her arms to embrace all humanity, but she stopped short at such a public display of happiness.

Opening her eyes, she was awed by the sheer number of twinkling stars.

"Mama, tie." Ana tucked her gloved hand in Nancy's.

Her daughter looked adorable in her down jacket, knit hat and scarf. All were purple, Ana's favorite color. She'd wanted purple ice skates, too, and had been highly disappointed that rentals didn't come in that color. But once she'd seen Rachel putting on white skates, she'd quickly forgotten her offended fashion sense.

"Sit down on the bench and I'll tie them for you, Ana Banana." Beau lifted Ana and plopped her on the bench. His fingers were nimble on the laces. "The trick is to get the laces tight so your ankles don't wobble."

Ana nodded solemnly. "No wobble."

Beau laughed. "No wobble."

"Hello, Mr. Stanton, Ms. McGuire." Mike skated up to them. "Hi, Rachel."

Rachel's face lit.

"Hello, Mike." Beau's tone was mild, his face neutral. Apparently he was learning to accept the boy.

"Dad, may I go skate with Mike?"

"I'll expect you to stay on the ice." He checked his watch. "Come back at seven."

When Rachel started to protest, he said, "That's way beyond five percent. Take what you can get, kiddo."

Rachel sighed. "Okay, Daddy. But I'll remind you of that."

She nodded her head in Nancy's direction.

Nancy glanced at Mike.

He shrugged. She shrugged. They shared a smile.

Then Rachel was off, holding hands with Mike and gliding across the ice.

"I didn't know Rachel could skate like that," she said.

"Neither did I." Beau's expression was wistful. "There's so much I missed out on."

Tucking her hand in his, she murmured, "But there's so much left to share."

He grinned. "Yeah, you're right. Let's get Ana Banana out on the ice."

His movements were fluid and sure.

Nancy felt like a klutz in comparison. "So how does a Texas redneck get to be such a natural ice skater? You've been holding out on me."

"Hey, we had ice-skating rinks. What better place to go when it was in the triple digits outside?"

Laughing, she said, "You have a point. Maybe you can teach me to skate backward like you were a minute ago."

"Let's get Ana Banana comfortable on her skates and then I'll show you a thing or two." He winked. "Come on."

They skated, Ana supported by Beau on one side and Nancy on the other. Once, Ana fell and took Nancy with her, laughing the whole time.

After that, her daughter took to skating like a natural.

"I wonder if she's got an inherited affinity for the snow and ice?" Nancy asked. "I don't think the children at the orphanage were outside very much."

"She's a natural, that's for sure." Beau watched her.

The next hour flew by. Rachel checked in twice and Mike won a slight nod of approval from Beau.

The second time they came by, Beau handed Ana off to Rachel.

Ana seemed more than happy to go with the teens, and they, in turn, seemed to enjoy her antics.

"Turn around." Beau stood behind Nancy and placed his hands on her hips. "Now, make big three's with your skates. Start out wide, go in, then out wide again." He demonstrated.

Nancy felt ridiculous at first, like an extremely pigeon-toed stork trying to imitate a swan. But, gradually the movements started to feel natural. And soon, she felt almost like a swan, gliding backward across the ice, with her very own Prince Charming guiding her.

As he seamlessly led her through the other skaters, it seemed as if they were the only two people on the ice. She was acutely aware of Beau's voice in her ear giving encouragement, the gentle pressure of his hands on her hips.

Then the music changed from fun family tunes to a haunting, romantic song. Beau led her to the edge of the rink and pulled her close.

His breath was warm on her face. "Having fun?"

"Oh, yes. This weekend has been absolutely perfect." She cupped his face with her bulky, gloved hands. "Thank you."

He kissed her gently on the lips. "My pleasure. I want more weekends like this. You, me and the girls. Then plenty of time for just you and me."

"I want that, too. But I'm afraid."

"Because of Eric?"

"No. Yes." She hesitated. "I'm afraid to want the forever happily-ever-after thing. Even if it's something you're willing to give…"

He pulled her closer, tipping her chin with his finger. "Darlin', everything I am, everything I have, is yours. I love you in the forever and forever way."

Nancy didn't realize how much she'd wanted to hear those words from him until now. Her eyes blurred. She exhaled slowly. "I love you, too. Forever."

Then a voice intruded on their private world, reminding Nancy they were in a very public place.

"I'm checking in, Dad," Rachel said.

Beau nodded, but held Nancy's gaze. "Okay, Rach."

Then something attacked Nancy's knees.

Rachel laughed. "I thought I'd deliver Ana Banana. I'll check back later."

Nancy lifted Ana and rubbed noses with her.

She was a very blessed woman.

"Here, give the munchkin to me." Beau held out his arms.

Ana went to him without hesitation. She tucked her head against his shoulder and sighed.

"I think someone's tired," he commented.

"I think you're right. Maybe we should leave in a few minutes?"

"Yeah, I'll catch up to Rach and give her a fifteen minute warning. Is that soon enough?"

Nancy nodded.

"Come on, Ana, you want to go fast?"

She clapped her hands. "Fast, Beau, fast."

Nancy watched as he skated off with her daughter in his arms.

Moving to the edge of the ice, she sat on a bench to remove her skates. This was going to be a wonderful Christmas. They would spend the day together, the four of them, just like the families she'd envied since she was ten—the ones with a mom *and* a dad.

The thought made her smile. Maybe, just maybe she'd found the family she'd always longed for. Not the idealistic, white-picket-fence kind of family. But two families cobbled together into a beautiful, cohesive whole.

Maybe fate had given her exactly what she needed.

As she gathered their things, Nancy felt as if she were being watched. Glancing up, she expected to see Beau.

Instead, there was a tall, distinguished man staring at her. He had salt-and-pepper hair and looked away the instant she caught his eye.

There was something familiar about him.

She took an involuntary step toward him but he turned, fading into the crowd.

"What's wrong?" Beau touched her arm.

"I thought I saw someone I knew."

"A client?"

"My father." She handed him Ana's shoes. "Wait here with Ana?"

"Sure. But—"

Nancy didn't stay to hear the rest. She jogged in the direction she'd seen the man disappear.

Had it been her father? Or had she simply conjured his image after thinking about normal families at the holidays?

Checking right and left, she didn't see him anywhere.

Then she caught a glimpse of him.

"Dad," she called.

Several men turned, but not the tall gentleman. His pace increased and it looked as if there might be a woman with him.

Nancy tried to hurry, but a family and two strollers slowed her down.

When she arrived at the parking lot, the man got into

an Escalade. The SUV was too far away for her to see clearly as it departed, but again, she got the impression there was a woman with him.

"Hey." Beau touched her arm. "Are you okay? Was it your dad?"

"I don't know." She sighed in frustration. "I couldn't get close enough to find out for sure. I—I think there might have been a woman with him. It was hard to tell in the crowd."

"You said yourself you probably wouldn't recognize him if you ran into him on the street."

"It probably wasn't him." Because this man hadn't seemed to want to see Nancy. And she'd always dreamed that her father wanted her, he just couldn't stay for some reason. Maybe he was protecting her from something? That had always been her hope. And now that she was an adult, he would welcome her with open arms, because she no longer needed his protection.

But this man had seemed almost fearful.

Riding home, Rachel put her arm around Ana and drew the girl close to her side. Smiling, she leaned back and relived the evening. This had been the best night ever.

Mike had been sweet and attentive and had even kissed her when they managed to skate out of her dad's view. Not an intense kiss, but nice just the same.

Rachel even thought it might not be so bad if her dad and Nancy got married. They had fun together and seemed crazy about each other. And then Rachel would have a little sister.

She kissed Ana on the top of her head.

Rachel had always wanted a little sister but had pretty much given up hope.

Which house would they live in? Nancy's? The house Dad was buying?

It didn't matter much. As long as she got to stay in Elmwood and be with Mike and Dad. Nancy wouldn't be an evil stepmonster, she was pretty sure.

"Are we going to the Christmas party Wednesday night? At the Parents Flying Solo meeting?" Rachel asked.

Dad looked at Nancy. "What d'ya think? Want to go together?"

"I'd love to."

Mission accomplished. Now to coordinate with Mike... She'd give him his Christmas present and maybe sneak under the mistletoe.

"Ray happy?" Ana asked, her voice sleepy, her eyelids heavy.

"Yeah. I'm happy."

"Ana happy."

"Happy's good, Ana Banana."

BEAU JUST ABOUT WENT into cardiac arrest when he picked up Nancy and Ana on Wednesday night.

Nancy wore a simple, deep green velvet dress that left her shoulders bare and dipped low, giving a tantalizing view of her cleavage. Her eyes sparkled with excitement.

Something he was relieved to see. Nancy had been

different since Saturday night. Reserved, introspective. He hoped to hell she wasn't having second thoughts about the two of them. But somehow, he got the impression it had nothing to do with that.

Beau had tried to talk to her a couple times about the man at the rink, but she'd shrugged off his concern. He was no expert at relationships, but he figured couples worked through these sorts of things together. And it hurt a little that she wouldn't confide in him. But to do that, she'd have to admit to herself how much she needed to resolve this thing with her dad.

So he'd have to wait until she was ready. And be prepared for the fallout.

He nuzzled her neck, inhaling her scent. "You look gorgeous."

"Thank you. You don't look so bad yourself."

"Luke Andrews better not get any ideas, seeing you in that dress. You're taken."

"Down, boy. Leash the testosterone. I'm very taken."

"Damn right," he grumbled. Then he turned to Ana, swinging her up in the air. "You look like a Christmas princess in that red dress, sweet pea."

"No sweet pea. Banana. Ana Banana."

Beau laughed. "Princess Ana Banana, it is."

His heart just about melted when she patted his face. "Nice."

"I think you're pretty nice, too."

"Okay, we get the picture." Impatience tinged Rachel's voice. "He's nice, you're nice, everyone's nice. Can we leave now?"

He searched Rachel's expression for jealousy. "You'll always be my first princess."

Her smile trembled a bit at the corners. "I know, Daddy."

"So what's the hurry then?"

"I'm excited. I want to see who's there."

"Like Mike?"

Rachel blushed, reminding him she was still only fourteen, despite the fact that she sometimes seemed forty.

"Maybe. You won't embarrass me, will you, Dad?"

"I didn't embarrass you at the rink the other night, did I?"

"No. You were actually almost bearable."

Beau shook his head. "Thanks for the vote of confidence."

"If we leave now, I'll lie and tell you how totally cool you are."

"I'm wounded. You mean I'm *not* totally cool?" He turned to Nancy. "Were you aware of this?"

She grinned. "You seem pretty cool to me. But then again, I'm ancient."

He eyed her from head to toe. "For an old woman, you hold up pretty good." Extending his arm to her, he asked, "Shall we leave?"

Picking up her tiny purse, she slipped her arm through his, and grasped Ana's hand with her free hand. "Definitely. We wouldn't want Rachel to get old and gray before Mike has a chance to see how pretty she looks in that dress."

Beau got a lump in his throat. "Yeah, she looks beautiful. Just like her mom."

He felt Nancy stiffen. There it was again, that cool shift. "And just like my best girls, Nancy and Ana."

Nancy's forced smile told him it was a lame attempt. "Let's get moving, so Rachel doesn't miss Mike. Is his mother still coming to the meetings?"

Rachel nodded. "Yeah. I guess she hasn't found a boyfriend yet."

Beau shook his head, grateful for having found a woman both beautiful *and* independent. "Not everyone's as lucky as I was when Nancy became my buddy."

Nancy squeezed his arm. "Or as lucky as I was to draw you." She looked at him and mouthed *I love you* over Ana's head.

As much as he was enjoying the closeness of family, Beau would have given plasma for a few hours alone with Nancy. To work through whatever was bothering her, then make slow, sweet love.

He pulled Nancy close and kissed her lingeringly, hoping she understood the promise there.

Her eyes widened. She ran her tongue over her bottom lip. Standing on tiptoe, she whispered in his ear, "Later."

She'd received the invitation loud and clear. But did she realize he wanted her to open up to him completely?

NANCY RESTED her head on Beau's shoulder as they danced in the Community Center garden. It probably would have been one of the most romantic moments in her life if they'd been somewhere tropical. As it was, jackets, scarves and gloves made it difficult to meld with the man she loved. So Nancy settled on a bundled-up embrace. At least they were alone. Rachel had volunteered to watch Ana for a few minutes.

"So when are we going to exchange presents? Christmas Eve, Christmas Day?" Beau's oh-so-casual question raised red flags like crazy.

Could he possibly be considering a ring?

The thought was enough to nearly chase away the odd blue feeling she'd had the past couple days. Because with each minute she spent with Beau, the more she was convinced they were meant to spend the rest of their lives together. "Christmas Eve works for me. Or are you a Christmas Day present opener?"

"Depends. I prefer Christmas Eve. What kid wouldn't? But I guess there's something to be said for the added suspense of waiting until Christmas day."

"You're teasing me, aren't you?"

"Of course. That's part of the fun of giving gifts. Now, you need to give me hints about mine."

Nancy's face grew warm. There was no way she would admit to waiting till the last minute. Originally, she'd been waiting to see if they would be a couple. Now, she wanted to determine if he was considering something permanent. If she thought he might get her a ring, then she had some serious shopping to do. But if he was buying a can opener, then the scarf she was crocheting would be fine.

"I don't give hints," she hedged. "It spoils the surprise if you find out ahead of time."

"Come on, just a little hint? Is it bigger than a breadbox?"

Nancy sighed with relief. Both the expensive watch she'd been eyeing and the scarf would fit in a breadbox. "Definitely smaller."

"Cash? Loads of it?"

"Not even close. How about my gift? Is it smaller than a breadbox?

"Definitely."

"Is it animal, vegetable or mineral?"

"Mineral. Now, that's all the hints I'm going to give."

He held her close and kissed her.

Nancy clung to him. So many things in her life seemed out of control. This surprise relationship with Beau, her dad. It left her feeling unsettled, vulnerable. Sliding her arms around his neck, she kissed him as a desperate woman would, because she intended to make this relationship work, come hell or high water. She would not allow this man to walk away.

Beau pulled back and brushed the tears from her face. "What gives? I'll tell you what I got you if it means that much."

"It's not the gift, silly. *You* mean that much to me."

She could have sworn Beau got a little misty-eyed. "You're sure there's not more to it?"

Her chest ached at his question. His insight was disturbing. Why couldn't he just let her pretend for a little while that her father hadn't run away from her for the second time in her life?

She forced a smile. "We've had this magical, whirlwind, buddy-turned-lover surprise and that's not enough to make me a little teary-eyed?"

He held her tightly to him, as if he'd never let her go.

And that was exactly what she needed from him.

Nancy was barely aware of the throat-clearing noise coming from the direction of the Community Center door.

"I'm sorry to interrupt." Emily sounded hesitant.

A part of Nancy wanted to ignore Emily and the rest of the world and simply lose herself in Beau. But, as a mother, she feared one of the children might be hurt.

Reluctantly stepping away from Beau, she asked, "What is it, Em?"

"Someone's looking for you, Beau."

Beau frowned. "If it's Rachel, please tell her I'll be inside in a minute."

"It's not Rachel." Regret flashed in Emily's eyes.

Nancy's stomach knotted.

"Who is it?" Beau's voice was clipped. Considering his drawl, that meant he was highly irritated.

Emily refused to meet Nancy's eyes.

"It's your ex-wife."

CHAPTER TWENTY

IT WAS TOO MUCH.

Nancy trembled at the thought of Laurie, here, ruining everything.

Beau grasped her hand, but she pulled away.

"Nancy?" Beau touched her arm. "This doesn't change things with us."

"I hope not," she murmured. "Go. I'll be there in a minute."

He frowned, but followed Emily into the Community Center.

Nancy imagined the scene inside. The commotion Laurie's arrival had probably started. Laurie, not just a nebulous concept, but the woman who was the mother of Beau's child, and in that respect, would forever trump the bond Nancy had forged with him.

Shaking her head, Nancy suspected her reaction wasn't rational. It was the same panicky feeling she'd had when Maggie McGuire had stood on a dais at the McGuire family reunion and announced her baby had been fathered by Nancy's husband.

She'd deluded herself with Eric, pretending they had

a stable, committed relationship when her heart had told her differently. And now, she'd convinced herself that she and Beau could have a stable, committed future. Where did Laurie fit in all this?

Three years ago, Nancy hadn't faced her fears until she'd had no other choice. But she'd learned since then.

Straightening her shoulders, she entered the Community Center.

The déjà vu intensified. Public place, surrounded by friends and family. But this time, Nancy wasn't the other wife, she was *the other woman.*

A tall, willowy brunette was the center of attention, hugging Rachel and crying tears of joy.

Nancy's breath caught in her chest.

Emily clasped Nancy's hand and squeezed.

An odd peace descended over her. She wasn't alone this time. She had people who would support her, no matter how bad it got.

Taking a deep breath, she returned Emily's squeeze and nodded, letting her friend know she was okay.

Rachel saw her dad and broke away from the brunette. "Dad, look who's here." The girl smiled, but her gaze darted nervously between her dad and mom.

"Laurie. This is a surprise." Beau's voice was steady, dispassionate.

Nancy found that odd because he was one of the most open, passionate men she'd ever met.

Laurie approached him and placed her hand on his arm. "I'm here for Christmas. When you didn't get back to me, I figured I'd just surprise you." Her smile was a little too bright, her voice an octave too high. "Your nice neighbor lady said you were here."

"This should have been a mutual decision." His voice was low. "And not forced on me in public."

Laurie brushed her hair from her face. She had flawless golden skin and a generous mouth. "I thought you, of all people, would appreciate a little holiday spontaneity."

"Maybe I've matured. My mistake was thinking you would be mature and put our daughter first."

"You've got a lot of nerve lecturing me about our daughter. Have you forgotten I was the only parent she had for the first fourteen years of her life?" Her voice was shrill.

Ana, overcome by the tension, hid her face in Nancy's skirt.

Nancy wished she didn't have a ringside view of their argument. But seeing the stricken look on Rachel's face, she wouldn't have been anywhere else. Her future with Beau might be unclear, but Nancy knew one thing for sure—she loved Rachel like a daughter and would be there for the girl. She wouldn't desert her simply because things had gotten complicated.

The Christmas music grew louder and the Parents Flying Solo leader announced the white elephant gift exchange. Laughing, chatting partygoers seemed immune to the argument as they streamed to the far side of the room to participate.

Nancy could have kissed the president for his tact in drawing attention from an uncomfortable public display.

Focusing on Beau, Nancy could feel controlled anger crackle in the air surrounding him. His voice was terse. "That's enough. If you'd like to meet me tomorrow morning, we'll discuss this like two rational adults who want what's best for Rachel. I'll call you around eight on your cell and we can decide where to meet."

"I thought I'd stay at your place. So I could be close to Rachel. And we could talk about this whole custody thing."

Laurie had just played her trump card. Nancy's heart twisted as she waited for him to reply.

She wondered if he'd ever called an attorney.

Beau crossed his arms over his chest. "There's a hotel not far from my apartment building. I imagine they have a room available."

"What if they don't?"

"Then you should have thought of that before you left Texas."

Laurie's eyes widened. "You've changed."

"I'd like to think so." He moved to Nancy's side and put his arm around her.

"So that's how it is."

"Yes, that's how it is."

"I'll expect your call tomorrow morning."

He nodded. "Now, if you'll excuse us, we have a gift exchange to join. Good night, Laurie."

Shrugging, she said, "Have it your way."

Turning to her daughter, Laurie asked, "D'you want to come stay with me at the hotel tonight, Rach? We can make it kind of a slumber party. It'll be fun."

Rachel shook her head. "No, I'm staying here."

It was then that Nancy noticed Mike standing behind Rachel, his hand on her shoulder. Nancy's vision blurred. His devotion to the girl was touching at any age, but especially so in a teen.

THE DRIVE HOME that evening was subdued.

What's more, Beau had no idea how to lighten things up. Didn't care to, for that matter.

When they pulled into Nancy's driveway, he left the truck idling and the window cracked open, so Rachel would be comfortable with the heater humming away.

"I'm gonna walk Nancy to the door," he told her.

"Okay, Dad."

Lifting Ana from her car seat, he handed her to Nancy.

He wanted to take Nancy's hand. He wanted to return to the wholeness and belonging he'd felt when the four of them were together and everything seemed possible.

But then Laurie had ruined that. No, that wasn't right. Things had been off since Nancy had thought she'd seen her dad. Laurie's appearance had simply been the last straw. Problem was, he had no idea how to fix things.

Nancy's steps were listless as she went up the front steps. She unlocked the door but didn't invite him in.

Ana was sound asleep, her head resting against Nancy's shoulder.

A lump formed in his throat. All he'd ever wanted was here. "I'm sorry things got so messed up."

"It was a wonderful evening. Just ended on a rough note."

He swallowed hard. She was lying.

"I saw the look on your face, Nance. There's a lot more at stake here than just a ruined evening. Can we talk about it?"

Nancy sighed. "It's not just Laurie showing up, Beau. I've got some things to sort out."

"I'm always willing to listen." He fiddled with his watch. He was afraid she'd shut him out of whatever was going on. "Are you having Rach babysit for you tomorrow night?"

"I doubt I'll be in the mood to attend class, but I will anyway. So, yes, if Rachel can make it, I'd like to have her sit with Ana."

"I'm sure she'll look forward to it. And I know I'll want to talk with you, if you're ready."

"Beau, don't push."

"That's a lot to ask from a stubborn Texan." He chuckled hollowly.

She smiled sadly and opened the door. "Good night, Beau."

"Nancy?"

"Yes?"

"Just don't make any plans for Christmas Eve, okay?"

Reluctantly, she nodded.

"See you tomorrow night."

"Tomorrow night." She shifted Ana. "And Beau?"

"What?"

"Thanks for letting me have some space to work through this."

AFTER PUTTING ANA TO BED, Nancy poured a glass of wine and curled up on the couch, tucking her stockinged feet beneath her. The lovely green dress she'd thought so perfect for the party now seemed like a joke.

She picked up the cordless phone. It was too damn late to be calling anyone, let alone a man she hadn't talked to in twenty years.

But she dialed his number anyway. It wasn't logical, but she needed to hear her dad's voice tonight.

The phone rang four, five, six times.

Then a woman's sleepy voice said, "Hello."

Nancy clicked off the phone. She sat there, numb, staring at the phone for what seemed like hours.

Logically, she'd known her father had probably re-married. Maybe even had more kids. But the thought still hurt. Were there half brothers and sisters who were worthy enough to hold her father's attention?

It seemed she came in second with any man she'd ever loved, or worse yet, wasn't even a contender.

RACHEL HAD A HARD TIME concentrating in English class Thursday morning. Not such a strange thing, since it was the last day of school before winter break.

The weird part was wishing her mom would go away.

Was it only a matter of months since Mom had dropped her off at Dad's apartment? Now, it seemed like a lifetime ago.

Rachel remembered begging her not to go. She had promised to do anything if her mother wouldn't leave her with a man who was a virtual stranger.

"I have to," Mom had whispered while she pried Rachel's fingers from her arm. Then she'd kissed her on the forehead and walked away.

Rachel's throat closed up, remembering how lost and alone she'd felt. And now, just when things were going perfect, her mom had to ruin everything.

Rachel didn't think she'd make it till lunchtime to see Mike. He would understand how she felt. He'd been through all this divorced-parent stuff before.

Other kids ditched study hall all the time. Maybe they could duck out and grab a latte or something. She really needed to talk to him.

While keeping her eyes glued to the teacher, Rachel removed her cell phone from her backpack. She'd seen a kid text-message with the phone behind his back, but she wasn't that good at it. Instead, she waited until the teacher turned to the whiteboard.

Tapping her pen on the desk, Rachel was impatient for Mike's response.

Her phone vibrated a few minutes later. Mike would meet her after English class.

Rachel rushed out of class the minute the bell sounded.

Mike was waiting by her locker. His eyes were warm with concern. "You okay?"

"Fine." The response was automatic. "No, I'm not fine. Could you ditch study hall? I need to talk to you."

"Can it wait till lunch? I've got a ton of homework. That advanced-track chemistry class is kicking my butt."

Rachel felt bad even asking. She knew how important his grades were to him. It was one of the first things she noticed about him. He wasn't a brainy geek. Mike just knew where he wanted to go and what he needed to do to get there.

"This stuff with my mom is really bugging me. I—I can't concentrate in class. Please?"

He brushed a strand of hair from her forehead. "Okay. I've got my mom's car today. Let's go."

Rachel hesitated for a second. Her dad would totally freak if he found out she'd been alone in a car with Mike. But then again, he'd totally freak if he found out she'd ditched study hall.

Shrugging, she said, "Okay."

When they got to the juice bar close to school, Rachel didn't know how to begin. And she'd wanted to talk to him so bad.

"It's your mom, isn't it?"

"I wish I could figure her out. Believe she's just here for a visit. I mean, what if she's changed her mind about me staying with my dad?"

"You're afraid she'll make you choose?" His voice was low, more a statement than a question. As if he knew exactly how she felt.

"Yeah, I guess I am. Crazy, huh? She just came to spend a couple days for Christmas."

"You are the least crazy girl I know. Your gut tells

you there was something wrong in the way she dumped you on your dad and your gut tells you there was something wrong in the way she came back. The whole surprise thing. She can't expect you to just welcome her with open arms. She needs to earn your trust."

"Did your mom earn your trust?"

"Nah. I gave up on that long ago. Mom's all right in her own way. She loves me. She's just not good at being without a man. Not good at making it on her own."

"What should I do about my mom? Do I pretend I'm all excited to see her? Do I tell my dad I don't want her here, screwing up Christmas?"

"That's a tough one, Rach. Do what your heart tells you."

He hesitated, then leaned across the table and kissed her on the mouth, right there, in the middle of the juice bar. The sweet sensation of being loved melded with the peach nectar she tasted on his lips.

Sighing, Rachel fell a little harder for Mike.

CHAPTER TWENTY-ONE

NANCY STRAIGHTENED her desk and switched off her computer. She'd worked at home today, unable to concentrate well enough to be in the office greeting customers.

Beau had probably met with Laurie by now.

Nancy wondered about the outcome.

She tiptoed to Ana's door and peeked inside. Sure enough, she was awake, sitting on her bed talking to her teddy bear, Pooh.

"Hi, honey, did you have a good nap?"

Ana nodded, jumped out of bed and ran to Nancy.

She scooped her daughter up and showered her with kisses.

Ana reached down to finger Nancy's small gold belly-button ring. "Pretty."

Nancy didn't know what had possessed her to wear the ring today. Maybe her low-rise jeans didn't look right without it? For that matter, she hadn't worn these jeans in months. Maybe even a year? And the discomfort of the slinky thong reminded her it had been a while since she'd switched to bikini panties.

Shrugging, she decided not to analyze why today she felt compelled to wear clothes from her old life. When she'd tried to be perfect so her husband couldn't possibly stray. Kind of like Martha Stewart in a Jessica Simpson body.

The thought seemed ludicrous now, as did the aggravation of wearing a thong. Her sweatpants were looking better by the second.

Shaking her head, she said, "Come on, Ana Banana, let's get you some lunch."

When she had Ana happily ensconced on the couch watching *Dora* on TV, Nancy gathered the ingredients to make macaroni and cheese.

Elbow noodles, cheddar cheese, flour for the roux. Then she stopped and stared at the assorted items.

What was she thinking?

Ana didn't care if she spent an hour making lunch from scratch. As a matter of fact, there were times Nancy suspected her daughter preferred the packaged stuff.

After searching the pantry, she finally found the blue box she'd been looking for. Mac and cheese in fifteen minutes or less. Mrs. Kraft must be a freaking genius.

The doorbell rang as she put the water on to boil.

Nancy fluffed her hair as she passed the mirror. She'd worn it down today, just the way Beau liked it. Or had it been Eric who liked it that way?

Shrugging, she hoped Beau had good news. Hoped he'd come by to say Laurie had decided to return to Texas posthaste. Better yet, Timbuktu.

Opening the door, Nancy was struck numb.

It wasn't Beau.

"Daddy?"

"Uh, would you mind calling me Dave?"

What the hell? *Nobody* in McGuireville, Arkansas, called a parent by his or her first name.

"I'd rather call you Dad." She raised her chin. After twenty-two years, he had no right to show up on her doorstep dictating terms.

Her father glanced around. "May I come in? I won't be but a few minutes."

Nancy's face grew warm. "Of course. Please come in. Would you like to stay for lunch?" Back to homemade. Too bad she couldn't throw together some of those cute little croissant sandwiches, a cold salad or two, a nice red velvet cake for dessert.

"That won't be necessary."

Ana skipped into the entryway and stopped. "Who's that?"

"No pointing, honey, it's rude. This is your grandpa."

Tilting her head to the side, Ana studied the older man.

He studied her. For a moment, his face relaxed. Shrugging her shoulders, Ana said, "Bye, Grandpa," and rushed back to the family room.

"Sorry. Apparently, the commercial's over and Dora's back. Dora outranks everyone."

"Don't I know it." His eyes crinkled for a moment as he smiled. Then his expression grew serious.

Nancy held her breath. He might want her to call him

Dave, but when he'd smiled, she was transported back to the days when she'd called him Daddy and worshipped the ground he walked on.

"Please, come into the family room." She started to lead the way.

"No." He shifted uncomfortably. "That won't be necessary. I didn't intend to stay this long as it is."

"This long? You've only been here a few minutes."

"I'm sorry. I'm totally bungling this conversation. I'm not here to renew our relationship."

"You're not?" Nancy's chest hurt as she imagined her heart breaking into tiny pieces. "Then why are you here?"

"To ask you to stop calling my house."

"How'd you—?"

"Caller ID. Your calls are upsetting my wife."

"Surely she knew about me." Had Nancy mattered so little that he hadn't even told his new wife about his old family?

"Yes, I told her. However, our daughters don't know. Rene feels very strongly they shouldn't be told until they're old enough to understand."

"H-how old are they, my half sisters?"

Dave had the good grace to flush, as if only then admitting Nancy shared a blood bond with the girls. "Six and eight."

"You came here to get rid of an inconvenience." The dawning realization hurt more than she could have imagined. All her dreams of a loving relationship had ended the minute he'd asked her to call him Dave. She just hadn't understood until now.

"I don't want to hurt you. But I built a new life, a new family. I've requested a transfer. We'll be leaving after the first of the year. I'd like to ask you not to contact me in the meantime."

"Or?"

"Or, I'll have no choice but to take out a restraining order. I won't risk losing my family."

"I'm family, too." The words were wrenched from her soul.

"I'm sorry, Nancy. I can't go back and change history. But I can do a better job with this family. I don't expect you to sympathize, I just hope you'll respect my wishes."

"I think you at least owe me an explanation. Why? Why'd you leave? Why didn't you ever contact me?"

He shrugged, grimacing. "You were part of a life better left behind."

"Are your other daughters as disposable? Or was it just me?"

He recoiled as if she'd slapped him. "I don't expect you to forgive me. I don't even expect you to understand. I just want you to leave me alone."

Nancy's emotions froze. It was too much to bear. "Don't worry, I won't bother you again." She escorted him out and shut the door behind him.

A hysterical laugh built in her chest. Her own father had threatened her with a restraining order. How awful. Worse yet was the knowledge she would never hold a place in her father's heart, even during this season of love and miracles.

THE CAMPUS SECURITY GUARD was waiting for them in the parking lot when they returned. A bald, beefy guy with a warped sense of humor, he was a favorite with the students.

But today, Rachel's stomach tightened when she saw him.

He leaned against a decorative planter, his arms crossed, smirking.

"Ya know, Miss Stanton, you really shouldn't ditch school on a day when your mother is meeting you for lunch. That's a no-brainer, even for a freshman."

Mike stepped between Rachel and the security guard. "Leave her alone. She needed someone to talk to. I convinced her to ditch. So if you want to give someone a hard time, it better be me."

"Chill, Ruiz. I'm just supposed to deliver her to the office, where her mother is in hysterics, talking Amber Alert."

"I wasn't kidnapped."

"Don't worry, the vice principal isn't taking her too seriously. Looks like you're in a load of trouble though."

"They haven't called my dad, have they?"

The guard shrugged. "Wouldn't know. Let's go."

He escorted her to the office, where she could hear her mother's voice coming through the vice principal's door. The word *lawsuit* came through loud and clear.

Sighing, Rachel opened the door. "I'm here, Mom. You can quit hollering."

Her mom enfolded her in a smothering hug. "My baby. I was so worried."

"I ditched class, Mom. I didn't join a cult." She pulled away and stretched her arms wide. "See, I'm okay."

"They said you were with an older boy."

"Mike's two years older. He's nice."

"He drives?"

"Yes, he had his mother's car."

Her mother's eyes narrowed. "Did you sneak off to have sex?"

Sighing heavily, Rachel managed to keep from rolling her eyes. "All this interest is a little overdone, Mom. You didn't give a rat's ass what happened to me when you dumped me on Dad. Mike and I went to the juice bar and talked. That's all."

Her mother's eyes widened. "Don't you speak to me like that. I had pressures you could never imagine." She glanced at the vice principal. "We can talk about that later. I want to know why you ditched class."

"In case you haven't noticed, your little surprise visit has everyone in an uproar. I needed someone to talk to."

Her mother's shoulders slumped. "You could always talk to me. I miss that. I miss *you.*"

Rachel snorted. "Sure, Mom."

Her mom turned to the vice principal and said, "My daughter and I have a lot to catch up on. I'll be taking her out of school for the rest of the day."

"Yes ma'am. Just be sure to complete the sign-out sheet first." He looked like he'd be very relieved when they left.

"I can't leave. I have an algebra test."

"I'm sure they'll let you make it up. Get your things and let's go."

They rode in silence for the first few minutes, the tires of the small rental car making humming noises.

Other than that, Rachel didn't pay attention to much of anything.

Then she noticed they were outside town. Way outside of town. "Mom, where are we going?"

"Just for a little drive." Her mother's smile was forced.

When they reached the outskirts of Albany, Rachel knew something was very wrong.

"Mom, what's going on?"

"I'm taking you home."

"My home is with Dad, now. I like Elmwood."

"He hasn't done a very good job as a father. Apparently, you're still shoplifting. You ditch class and hang out with older boys. Lord knows what else goes on that I haven't heard about."

"Let me out, Mom. I'm not leaving."

"Oh, yes, you are. Our flight leaves in an hour."

BEAU ALMOST DIDN'T answer the phone, afraid it might be Laurie alternately hollering and crying, begging for Rachel to move back to Texas with her.

He'd pretty much called every attorney in the yellow pages immediately after meeting with Laurie. He'd left messages with the few who were still holding office hours before the holidays, but he probably had a snowball's chance in hell of getting a return call until after the first of the year.

He was trying to decide whether asking Nancy to marry him on Christmas Eve was still out of the question. He had the ring, he had the plan; he just wasn't sure if she would be receptive.

When the phone kept ringing, he finally picked up.

"Mr. Stanton, this is Mike Ruiz, Rachel's friend."

Beau sighed and pinched the bridge of his nose. "Yes, Mike, I know who you are."

"I wouldn't bother you, but I think this is important. Rachel went out to lunch with her mom today."

"Yeah, Laurie mentioned something about that."

"But she didn't come back."

"Long lunch maybe? It's been a while since they've had a chance to talk. They're probably just catching up."

"That's what I thought. But then I got a text message from Rachel. It says she's at the airport in Albany."

Beau swore under his breath. "How long ago did she send the message?"

"About half an hour. She gave me a flight number, if that will help."

"Give it to me." He grabbed a pencil and wrote down the number. "Thanks, Mike."

He immediately called the airline and found the plane was due to leave in forty-five minutes. They refused to hold the flight or detain Laurie and Rachel.

Panic hit him hard. What would this mean in a custody dispute? Worse yet, what if this flight was connecting somewhere other than Texas? What if Laurie was taking Rachel somewhere he could never find her?

A phone call to the Albany police department was a total waste of time. Since Laurie was still the custodial parent according to court records, he couldn't stop her.

Damn.

He grabbed his wallet and sprinted out the door. He'd have to drive like a bat out of hell, but he might just make it to the airport in time.

NANCY TRIED Beau's cell for the third time, but it went straight to voice mail. She hadn't left messages the first two times.

"Beau, it's me. Do you want to come over early tonight? I need to talk to you. I could throw something together for dinner. Call me, okay?"

There. She'd reached out to him. It made her nervous asking for more than he'd offered. That had been an unwritten rule with Eric. Accept what he offered, but don't ever ask for more.

It had been the same thing with her dad. Except the only thing he'd offered was a restraining order.

Tears gathered in her eyes. She would *not* cry.

Ana came up to where she sat at the kitchen table and gave her a hug. "Mama sad?"

"Yes, honey, Mama's sad."

Ana scrunched up her little brow. "Why?"

"Because your grandpa Dave said something that hurt my feelings."

Ana patted her hand.

"Bad Grandpa."

Nancy had to chuckle at her daughter's assessment. But in her simplicity, she'd hit the nail squarely on the head. Nancy had been feeling ashamed and unworthy. But it had been Dave's problem, not hers. It wasn't unreasonable for her to try to contact her father. He had overreacted, apparently out of fear.

Nancy knew all about being afraid of losing someone's love. She'd lived that way for most of the eleven years of her marriage. And she refused to allow anyone to make her feel that way again.

Bad Grandpa, indeed.

How dare he act like she was some kind of psycho stalker?

And Bad Nancy for letting him shovel all that self-serving bull without calling him on it.

Nancy forced herself to quit mulling over her father's actions.

Holding out her hand to Ana, she said, "Come on, honey. Let's get you bathed and ready for Rachel. I'm hoping she and Beau will come for dinner."

BEAU SKIDDED sideways coming off the interstate, but quickly corrected. Getting himself killed wouldn't help Rachel.

He parked as close to the terminal as he could. But the clock on his dash told him he was fifteen minutes too late.

Pounding on the steering wheel, he swore.

In the past, Beau might have shrugged and walked away, hiding his pain.

But he was gonna be damned if he'd let his daughter go easily this time. If Laurie wanted a custody fight, then she'd sure as hell get one.

Beau locked the truck and sprinted toward the terminal entrance.

It ain't over till it's over.

CHAPTER TWENTY-TWO

NANCY PUSHED her lasagna around on her plate without really eating.

Beau hadn't returned any of her calls. Nor had he shown for dinner. And he hadn't brought Rachel to baby-sit.

Why should it surprise her that he'd gone missing in action when things got messy? Maybe that was simply what men did. Her father certainly had. And Eric.

But Beau was different. The relationship they shared was different. Or was she just kidding herself?

"Here, let's get you cleaned up, Ana." She wiped Ana's hands and face.

"Ray?"

"I don't know, honey."

"Bad Ray?"

"No, I don't think so. Something must've happened."

"Bad Beau?"

Nancy hesitated. She could believe the best or the worst. "No. I'm sure they had a good reason for not being here. I'll have to miss class."

Coming to a decision, she retrieved Ana's jacket,

mittens and hat. "Instead of sitting here feeling sorry for ourselves, why don't we go to Beau's apartment and make sure everything is okay."

Ana clapped. "Ray."

BEAU'S FIRST REACTION when he saw Rachel and Laurie in the waiting area was relief. It was followed quickly by rage.

He strode up to Laurie. "What the hell do you think you're doing?"

Her eyes widened. "Beau."

"I've been worried sick. Imagine how I would have felt if Mike hadn't called to tell me Rachel was here. I'd have been waiting for her to come home from school, worrying when she didn't show up."

"She needs to be home in Texas with me."

"She needs it or you need it?"

"How dare you?"

"Oh, I dare all right. She's not getting on that plane with you. Come on, Rach, let's go home."

Laurie grabbed Rachel's arm. "Come home with me. I—I need you. My job isn't a problem anymore. We can spend plenty of time together."

Now they were getting at the truth.

"What're you talking about?"

"I was…let go. Staff cut."

"I'm sorry to hear that. But it doesn't give you the right to jerk our daughter around."

Laurie propped her hands on her hips. "I'm not leaving without her."

Glancing at Rachel, he noted her pallor. The poor kid looked stressed to the point of exhaustion.

Here they were, two supposed adults, pulling her apart like a Thanksgiving wishbone.

"Look, we shouldn't hash this out in the middle of the airport. Why don't you come back to Elmwood and spend the holidays there, like you'd planned? During that time, we'll see if we can come to some sort of an understanding. We'll work out a visitation schedule we can all live with."

"Come on, Mom. Let's go with Dad, please?" Rachel begged.

Laurie glanced from her daughter to Beau and back again. "All right. But we won't discuss it until Christmas is over."

Beau breathed a sigh of relief. "Agreed. Let's go home."

He wrapped his arm around Rachel's shoulder and hugged her tightly. "I'm so glad I got here in time, sweet pea."

"Me, too," she whispered. Then a little louder, she said, "Our plane was delayed for repairs."

Thank you, God. And Beau meant it from the bottom of his heart.

His throat got all scratchy. He loved this child more than life itself.

NANCY KNOCKED a little louder on Beau's door. She couldn't see a light beneath the door and hadn't been able to detect any sound coming from within.

The elderly lady next door poked her head out. "He left in a terrible hurry, dear. Must've been an emergency."

"Oh. Thank you."

"'Mergency." Ana squirmed to get down.

Nancy called his home phone again and heard it ring inside. Nobody picked up.

Then she tried his cell one more time.

She heard its distinctive ring coming from inside, too.

Wherever he'd gone in such a hurry, he'd forgotten his cell phone.

Nancy felt pretty foolish about imagining he was avoiding her.

Then she heard a jumble of voices and the next thing she knew, Beau and Rachel came around the corner, shoulder to shoulder with Laurie. It looked like she'd interrupted a fun family outing. Boy, did she feel even more foolish. And pathetic.

"Nancy, what're you doing here?" Beau asked.

"I'm sorry if I'm interrupting. I just got kind of worried when Rachel didn't show up to sit."

Smacking his forehead, he said, "I totally forgot. Rachel was supposed to babysit tonight." He unlocked the door. "I'm really sorry. Come in, everyone."

His neighbor opened her door a crack.

Nancy wanted to tell the old busybody to mind her own business. But then she realized it wasn't Beau's neighbor she was angry with. "Beau, I don't know what's going on, but I was worried. And you're acting as if it's normal for you to drop off the face of the earth."

He grasped her hand and pulled her inside.

"Rachel, get Ana," he said.

"Where should I put my overnight bag?" Laurie asked. "And what about my suitcase?"

Nancy felt like she'd been hit by a truck. Her imagination went wild with the implications.

Sighing, Beau said, "You can bunk with Rachel tonight. We'll talk about arrangements tomorrow when everyone's rested."

Nancy pulled her hand from Beau's. The whole tableau was too weird for her to take. "Now that I've reassured myself that you're okay, Ana and I will leave."

"Don't go." He touched her arm. "I thought maybe we could talk for a minute. Go out on the balcony?"

"Really? With your ex-wife nice and cozy in your apartment?"

Beau frowned. "You don't really believe I'd do anything, do you?"

"You promised you'd be there tonight." When she'd needed someone to show her she mattered, she was loved. While her father threatened her with a restraining order.

"Something came up. I'll explain later."

"Why didn't you call?" Her words sounded stilted and angry, even to her. She felt childish, but her whole world seemed to be spinning out of control.

"Rach, you keep an eye on Ana." He grabbed Nancy's hand and led her out on the balcony. "Come on, we'll talk."

The chill wind was a shock after the nice, toasty apartment.

"You want to explain what's going on? It's more than just finding Laurie here, though you have absolutely nothing to worry about between her and me. I've never seen you like this, Nance. You seem, I don't know, jumpy."

"*Me* explain? I wasn't the one who blew off my girlfriend and her daughter. I wasn't the one who was unreachable by phone while I went out and had a wonderful time with my ex-wife." The anguish in her tone embarrassed her, but she couldn't seem to stop. "But why worry? Nancy won't mind. Heck, she's used to staying at home and wondering if someone she loves is hurt, or dead, or worse."

Tears ran down her face. She dashed them away with the back of her hand.

Beau's expression was thoughtful.

"Well? Are you going to say something?"

"I'm sorry I worried you. I'm sorry I didn't call. Laurie took off with Rachel. I had to reach them at the airport before their plane boarded. And later…I guess I got sidetracked wondering how I could keep my daughter if she told me she wanted to live with her mom again. 'Cause Laurie wants her back."

Nancy's anger faded, replaced by an overwhelming fatigue. "Beau, I'm so sorry. And I know I can trust you. I know you'd be there for me if you could. But I needed you so badly today."

"What happened, Nance?"

"My father…came to the house. When I saw him there, standing at my door, I thought my dreams had finally come true, that he wanted to be a family again. I really thought it was a holiday miracle." She laughed hoarsely. "What a joke."

Beau stepped close, wrapping his arms around her.

"You want to know why he was there? He asked me not to contact him again. My phone calls bothered his wife, because she didn't want their daughters to know about me. I have half sisters, and they don't want the girls to know about me. Like I'm something to be ashamed of."

"Aw, darlin', it's not you. It's him."

"The worst part is…he threatened me with a restraining order."

"That's just an idle threat. And you're wrong. The worst part is that he wasn't worth your love, darlin'."

"I asked him why he left me and never came back."

"What'd he say?"

"I was part of a life better left behind. Like I wasn't of any consequence. I asked him if his other daughters were as disposable as I was. He got mad and left."

"I wish I'd been there for you."

"Me, too. But see, that's what's wrong with me." Nancy finally understood what seemed so odd about this day and her anger with Beau. "I've always expected a man to make up for what my father lacked. With Eric, I waited and waited. Tried to pretend I was part of his family. Tried to pretend he loved me more than my dad and that everything was okay. Even when

Eric proved, time after time, everything was far from okay. Proved that I was disposable, no matter how nicely I kept house, or how pretty I dressed, or how much BS I put up with from him and his family."

Beau made a noise low in his throat. "Nance, you're not disposable to me."

"Don't you see? It really has nothing to do with the way you view me. I'll never know if what we have is real as long as I'm expecting you to erase all the bad stuff."

Nodding slowly, he rubbed the back of his hand along her cheek. "You have to erase the bad stuff yourself."

"You do understand," she breathed.

"Probably more than you realize."

She drew away from him. There really wasn't a choice, not unless she wanted to repeat old mistakes. "Then you'll understand why I can't have a relationship with anyone right now."

He stepped forward, but she held up her hand. "Don't."

"You're upset. You've had a big shock. Nothing needs to be decided tonight. Take a couple days to think things—"

Nancy shook her head, her throat thick with emotion. Then she gathered her daughter from inside the apartment and left.

THE NEXT MORNING, Beau grasped his to-go coffee and walked over to the table at the coffee bar. This wasn't going to be a comfortable conversation.

"Hey, Emily, thanks for meeting me on such short notice. You should have waited to order." He nodded toward her cup. "The least I could do is buy you coffee or cappuccino or whatever."

She chuckled. "I got here early to enjoy a few moments all to myself without kids. I'll let you buy me a refill if I need it, though."

"Sorry, I didn't even think how hard it might be to find a sitter so early. I can reimburse you." He reached toward his back pocket.

"Don't be ridiculous. Besides, a friend owed me."

Beau groaned. "Not Nancy?"

Emily nodded. "Yep. Kind of ironic, don't you think?"

"It is that. Does she know you're meeting me?"

"No. I didn't specify. And, bless her heart, she was too distracted to ask. You're safe for now. Sit." She gestured toward the opposite bench. "If I didn't think this was for her own good, I'd have felt horrible even asking her to sit. Poor thing's miserable."

"Did she tell you we had a fight?"

Shaking her finger at him, she said, "Now, Beau Stanton, that's not playing fair. I won't divulge a confidence. But I'll give you advice, if I think it'll help."

"You're right, I shouldn't have asked." He leaned forward. "I'm going to assume she told you about seeing her dad?"

"Yes."

"It's opened up a whole lotta stuff…and, well, I think she's getting ready to break it off with me. Probably would have last night, if I'd let her."

Emily smiled sadly, her warm brown eyes somber. He noticed she didn't contradict him.

"Nancy's pushing me away and I don't know how to stop her. I've always been the one to walk away, so I have no idea how to hang on. I love her so much it hurts."

"What if the only way she can ever be happy is to work through the mess her father made of things? Are you willing to leave her alone to do that?"

Beau stared at his cup. "I'm not sure I'm strong enough to let her go, Em." His voice was husky. "I've heard all that crap about if you love something let it go—"

"Crap is right. Everyone in Nancy's life has let her go too easily. So, I guess what I'm wondering is if you're any different? Are you man enough to go the distance? Is she worth fighting for?"

"Yes." He held her gaze, willing her to believe him. "On both counts."

"I'd think hard on that answer, Beau. And make damn sure you're ready, willing and able to go the distance. Because if you aren't, you'll break her heart."

"Em, I'll do anything. Except walk away."

"Good. That's all I wanted to hear."

"So how do I get through to her?"

"This is where you're going to be real glad you didn't buy me that cup of coffee. *You're* the one who has to figure out how to get through to her."

He blinked. "What?"

"You heard me. I have confidence you'll find a way."

Beau shook his head. "I'm glad you do, 'cause I don't have a clue."

Emily got to her feet, her smile wide. "Oh, you have more of a clue than you realize. Be good to her."

Then she walked out the door, her hips swinging as she passed a computer geek eyeing her over his laptop screen.

CHAPTER TWENTY-THREE

NANCY SET OUT three mugs of cider and a plate of Christmas cookies. "There, honey. We'll have a little celebration and then it's off to bed for you. Santa won't come if you're still awake."

"Carrots for Rudolph."

Ana's reminder made her smile, something that had been nearly impossible over the past two days.

Emily thought she was grieving over the loss of her father. Her friend was probably right, because Nancy felt as if someone had died. The scary thing was, it felt like a part of Nancy had died, too.

Struggling to make Ana's holiday special, she somehow produced a smile and a cheery voice. "Of course. We need carrots for Rudolph. How could I have forgotten?"

She removed a few baby carrots from the fridge and added them to the plate.

Ana nodded with satisfaction, her hand hovering over the plate as she decided which cookie to choose for herself.

Nancy's eyes misted. Her daughter was such a precious creature.

Leaning close, she whispered, "I think the Christmas tree is the biggest."

Ana giggled and chose a generously frosted tree. Biting into the cookie, she mumbled, "Good."

"Yes, they are good." Though she had absolutely no appetite, Nancy selected a sparsely frosted cookie Ana had decorated. "You did such a beautiful job with this one. Picasso himself couldn't have done better."

Ana beamed. "Last candy?"

"Yes, tonight we remove the last candy from the Advent calendar." She'd tried so hard to create traditions that would mean something to her daughter and were consistent with her Russian Orthodox roots. "Do you remember what the last candy means?"

"Baby Jesus's birthday."

"Yes. Exactly right. You are such a smart girl."

Ana enjoyed the praise, but it made Nancy sad. She was reminded of how often Beau told Rachel she was smart.

She ached for him, and she ached for Rachel. The past two days had been hell. But a necessary hell, she reminded herself.

Beau and Rachel deserved better than a potential wife and stepmother struggling with baggage. They deserved someone healthy and joyful, loving and tender.

Up until Thursday night, Nancy would have sworn she was that woman.

So what had changed so much? Her father didn't love her and would never be a part of her life.

He hadn't changed. He'd apparently felt that way for

more than twenty years. The only difference was that now Nancy knew it and couldn't hold any illusions close to her heart.

Shaking her head, she reminded herself things were better this way. She would build a life for Ana without the uncertainty of depending on a man.

But when Nancy thought of Beau, she could only think of the precious things she and Ana would be missing without him. His sense of humor, his warmth and fun. The way he made them feel as if they were special.

"Candy, Mama," Ana reminded her.

"One candy, then off to bed." She'd decided to open their presents on Christmas morning. It was just too painful to do it tonight, when she'd hoped to be sharing a special Christmas Eve with Beau and Rachel. Who was she fooling? She'd hoped Beau would give her an engagement ring.

But that was before her world had turned upside down.

She removed the candy from the calendar for Ana. "Better hurry upstairs if you want me to read a story before Santa gets here."

"Three stories." Ana held up three fingers. Her pink footed sleepers rustled as she hopped up the carpeted stairs.

Nancy laughed, following close behind.

Her heart swelled with emotion as she watched her small daughter go into her room, dragging Pooh by the arm.

They settled into the rocking chair and Nancy started to read. "'Twas the night before Christmas—"

She was interrupted by someone pounding on her front door.

"Santa." Ana's eyes were wide with awe.

Nancy couldn't help but laugh. "No, honey, Santa doesn't knock on the front door. Let's go see who it is."

She hoisted Ana on her hip.

Please have it be Beau.

Why she prayed for that, she didn't know. She'd already said goodbye.

But not in her heart.

Opening the door, her pulse leaped at the sight of Beau and Rachel standing there, smiling from ear to ear.

"Merry Christmas," they shouted.

"I don't know what to say."

"Merry Christmas," Ana squealed, clapping her hands together.

Nancy stood there, speechless.

"Get your coats," Rachel commanded. "We have a surprise for you."

"I was just putting Ana to bed."

"S'prise." Ana bounced up and down on Nancy's hip.

"Yeah, I can tell she's all tuckered out." Beau's voice was full of irony. "You don't want to disappoint her on Christmas Eve."

"That's not fair."

"No, it's not. I may not fight fair, but I fight to win. Now, please get your coats."

Her mouth went dry. "You're making this difficult."

"I know." His voice was soft, his eyes warm with regret. "It's the only way."

He held out his arms. "Come on Ana Banana, you want to see the surprise, don't you?"

Ana leaned forward, and Beau plucked her from Nancy's tenuous grip.

"I'll get our coats." It wasn't a gracious response. But then again, the man was all but kidnapping her child.

Rachel's eyes sparkled with excitement. She seemed oblivious to the undercurrents. "Hurry."

"Okay."

The truck was mostly silent after they got in. Christmas carols played softly on the stereo. The heater created a warm cocoon.

Sighing, Nancy fought to regain some detachment.

Beau placed his hand on her knee. "I missed you." His voice was husky.

Shaking her head, she couldn't trust herself to speak.

They pulled into the driveway at the house Beau was in the process of buying.

Nancy could barely believe her eyes. There, in the front window, stood the most gorgeous Christmas tree she'd ever seen. Ornaments and tinsel shone in the multicolored twinkle of lights.

"It's beautiful," she breathed.

"I helped," Rachel crowed.

"Shh. Remember, this is a solemn occasion." Beau took Ana from Nancy's arms and handed her to Rachel.

"This doesn't change anything, Beau."

He ignored her protest, wrapping his arm around her waist and drawing her into the house.

"It's open? It shouldn't be—"

"Shh. Christmas miracle, courtesy of the other Realtor."

Nancy gaped as they walked through the door.

The tree was just as gorgeous up close as it was from the street. There was no furniture in the room, but there was a red-and-white tablecloth spread over the carpet. A picnic basket, a bottle of champagne and two glasses were carefully placed in the center of the tablecloth, along with what looked like an overnight courier box.

A fire crackled and popped in the fireplace, bathing the room in a warm glow.

Beau had obviously gone to a lot of trouble.

"Presents," Ana squealed.

Nancy turned to the tree and noticed there were, indeed, several wrapped packages under the tree.

"Rach, remember?" Beau's voice was low.

She nodded. "Yeah, Dad, make ourselves scarce. Come on, Ana Banana, I'll show you my room. We open presents later."

Beau shifted. "Um, I know you gave me the heave-ho the other night, but being the stubborn Texan I am, I've chosen to ignore it."

Nancy chuckled in spite of her resolve not to be moved. "In a big way."

"Is there any other way?"

"Not, apparently, in Texas."

He removed her gloves and jacket, gentle as a lamb, leading her to the tablecloth. "Please sit down."

"Beau, I ca—"

"Yes, you can. A while back, you showed me a photo album to explain why you'd never have anything to do with me. Now, I'm asking you to look at a photo album, so I can explain why you can't do without me. And vice versa."

Stunned, she complied, kneeling on the table-cloth/picnic blanket.

Beau sat next to her and handed her the courier box. "I had Mom overnight it. It's from when I was a kid."

Her hands shook as she removed the handsome, leather-bound album. Inside were baby pictures labeled "William."

"That's me. William Beauregard Stanton III."

"You were a beautiful baby."

"So my mom says. I'm the oldest, so of course there are tons of pictures of me."

And he was right. Nancy flipped through the pages, losing more of her heart with each one. Beau, as a sturdy toddler, with mischief in his eye. Beau, a kinder-gartner, with mischief in his eye.

"Beau, these are wonderful. But they don't change a thing."

"Maybe not yet. Keep turning."

The next page showed Beau holding a brand-new baby, his face serious, responsible.

"That's Connor." He leaned over her shoulder, his breath warm on her face.

The pages continued, some showing a laughing, mischievous Beau, others showing him more somber.

"What are you trying to tell me, Beau?"

"Things in my past affected me, too, made me who I am. Rivalry with my brother is a biggie. But so is feeling responsible for him. I tried really hard to be a big brother he could look up to. But everything I tried, I seemed to screw up. After a while, I quit trying."

"It's not the same as my dad leaving."

"No, it's not. And no matter how hard I want to, I'll probably never understand what that did to you."

"What's your point then?"

"My point is that you trusted me enough to share your past with me. I don't think that was just a whim. And I've trusted you with my past. We've both got a pretty good idea what we're getting into."

"I told you, I need time to heal."

"How much time do you need? Two weeks? Two years? Twenty years? Because I'm not willing to give up another minute of my life with you. Yes, you've got stuff to work through. So do I. But I don't intend to let you push me away. It's something we'll just have to do in the middle of a messy life."

For a second, Nancy almost believed it could happen.

"No, I'll never know if I want you simply to slay the dragons from my past."

"Darlin', you know I'm not a knight on a horse. I

don't slay dragons. I'm just a dumb old country boy who loves you with everything I've got and refuses to take no for an answer."

Nancy's vision blurred. "I'd love to believe it could be that easy."

Beau threw his head back and laughed. "Easy? Hell, no. It'll probably be one of the hardest things either of us will ever do." He cupped her face with his hand. "But I believe it will be one of the most rewarding things we could ever dream of. It just takes a little faith. And I know there's a part of you that still believes in Christmas miracles."

She nodded slowly, a tear trickling down her cheek.

He rubbed it away with his thumb. Leaning down, he kissed her, slowly, sweetly.

Then he pulled away. "Faith, darlin'. Have faith."

She opened her mouth to protest, but he held up his hand.

He stood and went to the Christmas tree. "I think there's a present here for you."

Nancy swallowed hard.

Please, God, no.

He returned to her side, clasping a small square box. Pressing it into her palm, he held her gaze. She saw the warm, steady promise in his eyes.

Please, God, yes.

Nancy dashed away the moisture from her eyes.

Beau braced himself on one knee. "You'd think I'd be better at this part. But, um, this is the first time I've gone all out."

"Beau, it's a lovely gesture, but—"

"Nancy, will you marry me?"

She couldn't hold back the tears any longer. "No. I can't."

"Yes, you can. Just have faith."

"It's not enough."

"Yes, it *is* enough. We're put on this earth to learn and grow. None of us is perfect." He gestured toward the nativity set under the tree. "That's the reason He was sent here."

The beauty of his statement washed over her. "For a dumb old country boy, you sure are pretty smart."

"Tell me that's a yes."

She kissed him, gently, reverently. "Yes, Beau Stanton, I will marry you. I promise to love and trust you for the rest of my life. And I promise to love your daughter as my own."

Beau made a noise low in his throat and wrapped his arms around her, holding her tight. "I was so afraid you'd say no."

"How could I say no to a proposal like that?" She kissed him on the lips, then pressed tiny kisses on his jaw and throat, claiming him as her one and only.

"Tell us what she said. Are we gonna be a family or what?" Rachel stood in the doorway, holding Ana.

Nancy laughed, feeling freer than she had in days, maybe even years. "I said yes and we're going to be one terrific family."

EPILOGUE

EYEING THE SPACIOUS counters brimming with food, Nancy was glad Beau had chosen a house with a large kitchen. Perfect for entertaining.

Just as her home was perfect for the young couple now renting it.

Nancy put the finishing touches on the refreshment tray. "Are you sure you've got it? It's kind of heavy."

Nodding, Rachel said, "I'm sure. Pretty cool Christmas, huh?"

"Yes. But my favorite Christmas will always be last year's. Your dad really does know how to propose."

"Only to you. I think the other times were just practice. Even my mom."

"She looks happy."

"Yeah, she likes her new job. And Joe seems like an okay guy."

"Did you notice her ring?" Nancy figured it would come out sooner than later. She'd never tried to hide things from Rachel and thought they had a pretty good relationship because of it.

"How could I miss that rock?" Rachel laughed. "She

says I don't have to stay with her the whole summer, either, 'cause they'll be away on their honeymoon."

"It'll be nice to have you around. We missed you last year. But I'm glad your dad and mom came to an agreement that seems to work for all of you."

"Yeah, I guess I can handle Texas in small doses. Especially if I don't have to spend much time with the dragon lady."

"Rachel," Nancy warned.

Sighing, the girl said, "Okay, she's not as much of a dragon lady these days. Maybe because Dad doesn't take much crap off her anymore. Or maybe because of Uncle Connor's midlife crisis."

"Rachel!"

Rachel gave her a saucy wink. "Grandma says it's disgraceful."

Nancy suppressed a chuckle. "*You're* disgraceful."

"Yep. Isn't it great?"

Nancy gave her a quick hug. "You're a great kid and I love having you around. Maybe we can plan a vacation for this summer. Disneyland or something?"

Beau entered the kitchen. He kissed Nancy lingeringly on the lips. "What's taking so long? I've made nice with my side of the family for about as long as I can, and it looks like your mom is chomping at the bit to leave for her Red Hat Society cruise."

Nancy shrugged. "She's broadening her horizons. That's a good thing."

Her mother continued to avoid any discussion of Nancy's father and his refusal to be a part of his daughter's life. Still, she'd been surprisingly supportive of Nancy's new family, even overlooking her original misgivings about Ana's adoption. She treated Ana and Rachel as if they were her flesh and blood granddaughters. For that reason alone, Nancy felt closer to her mom than she had in years.

He nuzzled her neck. "A very good thing. But I want to get all these relatives, in-laws and outlaws on the road, so I can open my present."

He flicked the big green bow in Nancy's hair.

She blushed and smacked him on the arm. "That's not why I wore it."

Beau studied her for a few seconds, then winked.

The man could read her mind. Okay, so that *was* what she'd intended, but there were a few harmless secrets she intended to keep from Rachel. There was no need to broadcast that Nancy was more passionately in love with Beau now than she'd been on their wedding night six months ago.

Beau took the tray from Rachel. "Here, sweet pea, let me get that. You're not moving nearly fast enough. Besides, I think Mike is looking for you."

Rachel huffed, but at the mention of Mike, she apparently forgot all about hostess duties. The kitchen door swung shut before Nancy could even catch a breath.

"Hey, you're good."

"I know. I'll show you exactly how good a little later." His eyes were full of promise.

"Here, let me take that." Nancy pried the tray from

his hands and sashayed into the family room. "You take too long," she threw over her shoulder.

The sound of his laughter warmed her heart.

And the sight of so many of their friends applauding Ana's rendition of *The Night Before Christmas* brought tears to her eyes.

She ached for her father at times like these, but she was learning to focus on the people who truly loved her—the family of her heart.

Emily stood and held her glass of cider aloft. "A toast to our host and hostess, the ultimate Parents Flying Solo success story. To Beau and Nancy. Thank you for including us in your Christmas."

Nancy wrapped her arm around Beau's waist as she raised her glass. "And to our friends and family. We feel incredibly blessed to have you here."

Beau leaned close and whispered, "All it took was a little faith."

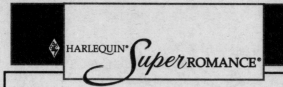

An Unlikely Match
by Cynthia Thomason

Harlequin Superromance #1312
On sale June 2005

She's the mayor of Heron Point. He's an
uptight security expert. When Jack Hogan
tells Claire Betancourt that her little town
of artisans and free spirits has a security
problem, sparks fly! Then her daughter goes
missing, and Claire knows that Jack is the
man to bring her safely home.

Available wherever
Harlequin books are sold.

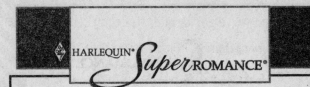
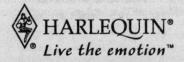

If you enjoyed what you just read,
then we've got an offer you can't resist!

Take 2 bestselling love stories FREE!

Plus get a FREE surprise gift!

Kate Austin makes
a captivating debut
in this luminous tale
of an unconventional
road trip…and one
woman's metamorphosis.

dragonflies AND dinosaurs
KATE AUSTIN

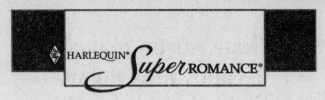

COMING NEXT MONTH